W9-DJM-951

WITHDRAWN

Born to the Brand

*Also by D. B. Newton
in Large Print:*

Ambush Reckoning
Bullet Lease
Crooked River Canyon
Hangman's Knot
The Lurking Gun
The Oxbow Deed
Shotgun Freighter

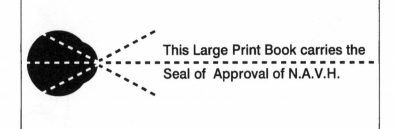

This Large Print Book carries the
Seal of Approval of N.A.V.H.

Bremen Public Library
Bremen, Indiana

WITHDRAWN

Born to the Brand

Western Stories

D. B. Newton

Thorndike Press • Waterville, Maine

Copyright © 2001 by D. B. Newton

Additional copyright information on page 351.

All rights reserved.

This collection is a work of fiction. Names, characters, places, and incidents are either products of the author's imagination, or, if real, used fictitiously.

Published in 2002 by arrangement with Golden West Literary Agency.

Thorndike Press Large Print Western Series.

The tree indicium is a trademark of Thorndike Press.

The text of this Large Print edition is unabridged.
Other aspects of the book may vary from the original edition.

Cover design by Thorndike Press Staff.

Set in 16 pt. Plantin by Minnie B. Raven.

Printed in the United States on permanent paper.

Library of Congress Cataloging-in-Publication Data

Newton, D. B. (Dwight Bennett), 1916–
    Born to the brand : western stories / D.B. Newton.
       p. cm.
    Contents: Reach high, top hand! — The taming of Johnny Peters — Tinhorn trouble — Breakheart Valley — Black Dunstan's skull — Born to the brand.
    ISBN 0-7838-9116-4 (lg. print : hc : alk. paper)
    1. Large type books. 2. Western stories. I. Title.
PS3527.E9178 B67 2002
  813′52—dc21   2001039384

For
Mary Jane

Table of Contents

Foreword   7

Reach High, Top Hand!   35

The Taming of Johnny Peters   103

Tinhorn Trouble   141

Breakheart Valley   181

Black Dunstan's Skull   261

Born to the Brand   271

Foreword — Up from the Pulps

I

It would have been April of 1928 when my mother learned her twelve-year-old was bringing Western magazines into the house. She might have found it encouraging to see that he'd finally outgrown the Oz books, and was ready for something a little more mature than fairy stories. But, Westerns? *Pulp magazines?*

Naturally, a respectable middle-class parent would frown on these cheap publications, offspring of the defunct dime novel of years past. If I felt any guilt, though, it wasn't for reading the things but simply being seen with them — on leaving the drugstore I usually stuffed the latest purchase inside my shirt, so nobody would have to know. Still, my mother was a good egg who wouldn't really enjoy denying me my current choice of literature, as long as I didn't go behind her back. One day, then, while she was sewing, I sat down and read to her from the latest weekly issue of Street

& Smith's *Western Story Magazine* — "Big, Clean Stories of Outdoor Life." And as if it were yesterday, I can remember the astonished look she turned on me as she exclaimed: "Why . . . they're real *stories,* aren't they?"

Well, gee! I'd like to know what she was expecting. At any rate, she not only let me keep the magazines, she even got me a subscription. Like I said, my mother was a good egg.

Since about as far back as I can remember — long before I managed to bully her into teaching me to read — I'd thought I would like to be a writer. I was enthralled with stories and with language. Listening, I'd wonder what it would be like to put words on paper and then have someone, maybe a total stranger, read them and relive the scenes I'd invented — hear my people talking, perhaps share my feelings about them. Once the notion got into my head, it stuck. As soon as I was big enough to hold a pencil and print my letters, I began trying to do something like that.

And now, in stumbling onto Westerns, a Kansas City, Missouri youngster with an unrecognized hunger for other scenery and wider horizons suddenly knew he'd struck pay dirt. It was as though something told

8

him here were a theme and a subject matter that could never exhaust their fascination. As I grew older, I would became a voracious consumer of practically every kind of fiction, including big, roomy novels where a fellow could just move his stuff in and make himself at home for however long it took. I read *War and Peace* twice, and worked my way through both volumes of the Modern Library edition of Proust. Yet all of this reading was done strictly for pleasure, and whatever writing I might undertake would almost certainly be for the same purpose — after all, I had no grudge against the world that I needed to settle, no literary axes to grind.

So whenever I'm asked, and it happens a lot — "Why *Westerns*, of all things?" — my answer has usually been: "Because they make me feel twelve years old again!" But, of course, the truth is more complicated than that. In becoming a writer you learn the hard work — but, also, the fun — that's involved in developing a plot, and finding characters to fit it, and then moving them around and listening to them talk, living with each of them until you learn just who they are, and how everything they do or say comes out of definite emotion. Once you really believe your own story, there's a chance a reader will, too, and want to stick around and see how things work out.

As to Westerns, chalk it up to blind luck that I happened onto something others apparently enjoyed reading as much as I did writing it. For, through the years, no other type of fiction came even close in starting the creative juices working, and sending me to the typewriter again and again with still another yarn — always a Western — that demanded to be put on paper. . . .

In 1928, though, there was a problem. Editors weren't buying stories from twelve-year-olds! I know I gave them every chance — sending manuscripts out only to get them back, with a promptness that spoke well for the efficiency of the U.S. Postal Service and of the office boy at Street & Smith. Then the following year, when I was thirteen, the stock market crashed. Soon the Great Depression had settled over the land and the cost of mailing a script, along with the mandatory stamped, self-addressed envelope, became prohibitive.

So before I reached high school, I'd been forced to act as my own editor. Each new story would be carefully reread, searching for any sign of growing competence, then I would say — "*This* won't sell, either . . . no

10

sense wasting the postage." — and toss it into a drawer with all the others. I was studying Western history now, and any other factual material that might someday prove useful. The summer I was seventeen I wangled a memorable couple of months with relatives at Dodge City, where I had my first look at the Kansas plains and spent blissful hours poking around Boot Hill and Front Street, where Bat Masterson and Wyatt Earp had walked some sixty years before. But still, no sign at all of that illusive first check.

Later on I was to know a writer or two — Les Savage, Jr., for one — who could claim to have broken into the pulps at the ripe old age of eighteen; I was not to be one of them. The day before I enrolled in college, I told myself I would have to face the facts: clearly I just didn't have what it took. Time then to lay aside childish dreams and find something practical — get a degree and teach Western history, perhaps, if I couldn't write about it. Meekly I promised myself I'd try to be good.

So much for resolution. Just eight months later — *der Tag!* A substandard publishing company (that is, one that paid a half cent a word and only on publication) had held a script for over a year, long

11

enough that I'd completely forgotten about it. Now, like a bolt from the blue, a check for $60, payment in full for that 12,000-word novelette. No accompanying letter, only a notation that the thing would be appearing in the July issue of *Western Novel and Short Stories*, but that was enough to send me at a dash to the nearest drugstore, and — yes, by God — there it was!

According to any standard *I* know, "Brand of the Hunted" by D. B. Newton had to be the worst story published in a pulp magazine that year of 1938. Whoever was responsible had managed to hide it rather well at the back of the book and flanked by columns of boilerplate advertisements — "Throw Away Your TRUSS!" . . . "WANTED — Song Poems" . . . "FALSE TEETH As Low As $7.85" . . . "PILES May Lead to Other Ailments." Only one thing mattered. I was a published author; there was my name, in print at last! In that moment, a decade of disappointment dropped away and all the ambition I thought I'd laid permanently to rest came welling up again, intact.

For me, life would never be the same again.

Of the half dozen stories I was to pelt him with that summer, the editor took only one. But it not only brought me another $50, this time, I was right up there on the cover of *Western Short Stories*:

RANGE WHERE MEN DIED TWICE
Epic Drama by
D. B. Newton

So at last I had escaped the stigma of a *one-story* author! What's more, each of the five rejected scripts carried a brief but helpful critique, handwritten — the first personal word I'd ever received from any editor. Henceforth, and despite the demands of college on my limited time, I saw to it that I always had *something* on that man's desk, and, seemingly convinced that I was serous about this and worth encouraging, he soon began taking practically everything I sent him. And I ask you — where, outside of the pulps, could anyone expect to get *paid* while he slowly mastered the rudiments of his craft?

I was to learn that most pulp magazine editors tended to be dedicated professionals, anxious to develop writers who could give them the kind of material they wanted — although the chances of doing this were slim, as long as the publisher refused to pay more than a half cent a word. Personally I felt obligated to the one who helped me over the first hurdles. Despite the low word rate, I continued to sell to him for as long as I remained in the pulps, a good deal of it being stuff everybody else had turned down. But even in those earliest days I hadn't been above passing him over and giving "first look" at a promising script to another editor who would give me two-thirds of a cent — and on acceptance. I guess I'd have to say, I was faithful in my fashion.

Right now, though, how about doing a fast-forward of seven years or so, up to the mid-1940s, and see how things have been coming along? Well, by now college is behind me; so, too, are some forty months of doing my bit to defeat Hitler and the Japanese Empire, behind a desk at Army posts in Missouri and the Pacific Northwest. I've been writing every chance I got, and have racked up a total of fifty magazine sales and even a first novel. I also have myself an agent, and the editors at four different houses are taking my stories for one-and-a-

14

quarter, sometimes even one-and-a-half, cent a word.

And now, sooner than anyone could have believed — suddenly World War II is over. Discharge in hand, and with a wife and year-old daughter, all at once I'm free to go home, although not to Kansas City, Missouri. Instead I have a place I bought while serving at an Army Engineers training camp, near a little town in the shadow of the Cascade Range of Central Oregon — I'd spent my first furlough in that house, sitting on the porch with Royal portable in my lap and knocking out a story a day, all but one of which had eventually sold.

And now here I am, at the ripe age of thirty, with a chance to show that I can actually make a living and support my family as a full-time, free-lance pulp writer — or, perhaps, only prove that my mother-in-law had been right about me all along!

Actually things could hardly have been more favorable. The livin' was easy, that summertime of 1946 in Bend, Oregon. I could make out very well on $200 a month or less, and meanwhile everything seemed to be on a roll — including the pulp market, with magazines expanding and raising their cover prices as wartime paper

15

shortages eased. (In an "Inflation Note," *The New Yorker* observed that *Dime Western* now cost a quarter!) Altogether, there were a lot of pages waiting to be filled — and Newton was willin'!

Each morning I would head for the one-room structure I had rented from a neighbor, at ten dollars a month, for my office, and the stuff would begin to flow — a thousand, two thousand, even three thousand words a day. (A half century later, I am now living in the house next door, and I still have my office. Sitting today in front of a word processor instead of a typewriter, I sometimes have an eerie feeling that the millions of words I've pounded out, here in this little room, are somehow embedded in the walls and ceiling and at any moment could start sifting quietly and insidiously down around me.)

And so, as those long-ago summer days drifted by, a stream of manuscripts began to flow from my typewriter in the direction of my agent's office in New York, but no need any more of a self-addressed return envelope — I was a professional now! Presently the first checks were showing up in my mailbox; still later the published stories reached the newsstands, sometimes two or even three a month. A couple of writers I've met professed to have nothing but disdain for their pulp yarns — never collected them, or even bothered to glance at them on the rack. I'd have hated to be like that. Then and later, every new work to appear would bring at least one memory of that first ecstatic moment in 1938 — "That's my name! That's me! I really exist!"

How could I not be at least curious to see if I had made the cover and the lead position this time, and find out if the editor had kept my title or substituted something dreadful of his own — "Tin-Badge-Backed Bushwhacker," perhaps, or "Wanted: Four Kill-Crazy Gunslammers," or "The Kid with the Graveyard Grin." And if I discovered I'd been given Nick Eggenhofer, or some other topflight illustrator to draw the story head — that made my day.

Somebody has said that writing is a rat race in which you can't even see the other rats. That didn't bother me too much — I had a method for keeping tabs on the competition, and roughly figuring my current position in the pack. Allowing for pseudonyms and so-called "house" names, I estimated that the Western pulps had some two hundred writers who might be considered "regulars," and perhaps as many more who managed to sell a story now and then but didn't really count. I kept careful records, by six-month periods, and, as more and more of my stuff reached the stands, it was pleasant to watch myself climb from 35th place to 22nd, and then to 18th and even higher.

D. B. Newton would never become a "million-word-a-year" man — if, indeed, there were any such, after the demise of the legendary "Max Brand." Something like 30,000 a month was closer to my average. Certainly for sheer quantity I could never hope to compete with a friend of mine, a dear man named Walker Tompkins whom I was to know when I lived for a time in Santa Barbara. Two-Gun, as his friends called him, drove past our house each morning on his way to work in a trailer whose location he would never divulge, to avoid the risk of interruptions. Santa Barbara has lots of sunshine, of course, but in winter there can also be gray and rainy weather. It was on one such day of overcast, while he was busily battering away at his typewriter, that the lights blinked off and then on again so quickly that he never realized his electric clock had also stopped. The afternoon wore on, he kept typing steadily, an occasional glance at the time telling him it was still early afternoon . . . until, at last, he happened to look toward the window and found solid, black night outside his trailer. Two-Gun's usual quota was 6,000 words; that one, endless day he had done 8,000 without even knowing it — although he did tell me he felt just a little logy when he finally knocked off.

I must confess I had occasional pangs of guilt about my own insufficient methods. Things came to a head, that first year, when I decided I really should get an idea just how productive I might be if, like normal people, I were to put in an eight-hour day — in other words, actually be a "full-time" writer. I set up a schedule, for one week: out to my typewriter promptly at eight, off an hour for lunch, then to work again till five. The result? I could hardly believe it myself. By the end of the week I had turned out three novelettes and a couple of short stories — a good bit more than I usually did in an entire month! So, after a day off, come Monday again I sat down to begin another novelette, and — nothing. I couldn't write a line; the well had been pumped completely dry.

I never cared to try that experiment again. After all, I reminded myself, one of my chief reasons for becoming a writer, in the first place, was to avoid having to find a regular job and become a slave to it — having an alarm clock drag me out of bed each dreary morning, wondering if this would be the day when the boss found out about the dork he had on his hands and gave me the sack. So, all right — maybe I wasn't growing rich. I promised myself I'd eventually figure a way to get better money, probably from novels. But I had put a lot of time and effort into getting where I was, and I intended to enjoy it a while — not only for myself but in tribute to a certain twelve-year-old, whose dream first set me on the road to the place where he had longed to be.

What a thrill it would have given that youngster, every time a new story appeared with our name on it. And how he would have loved this Oregon — the wild places, the smell of the pines, the mountains and lakes and forests practically at our doorstep. I imagine he'd have liked Kansas City more, if only he had been aware that *this* lay ahead of him. And, while I was wishing for him, what a shame he couldn't have known, somehow, about the person he was one day going to marry — the perfect mate for a would-be writer, who wouldn't expect the moon but get along happily on what he was able to offer; who would teach herself to type in order to copy his manuscripts, and even have suggestions sometimes when he ran into a snag with a plot; who would give him two wonderful daughters, and share the music and the books and all the other good things that were to be a part of his future. . . .

It was just too bad I couldn't tell him any of this. But by the same token, neither could some other D. B. Newton from the future say a word to prepare *me*, unknowing as I was, for the ominous cloud that even now loomed somewhere just below the edge of the horizon.

III

A writer for the pulps couldn't help but wonder just how long they were going to be around. The oldest, *Argosy*, had begun life in the 1890s as a story paper — *The Golden Argosy for Boys and Girls* — and after many changes in title and format had finally died, to be reborn briefly as a "slick." Street &

Smith's *Western Story*, the pioneer in its field, had first seen the light of day in 1919, and, if it had long since ceased to dominate, it was still hanging on, cut back from a weekly to once a month and reduced almost to pocket size.

Still, every magazine stand was loaded with pulps of every kind: love stories, science fiction, adventure, mysteries, you name it, with Western titles appearing to outnumber any other category. Surely the end couldn't be any time soon. By 1948, in my third year as a full-time free lance, I was becoming more and more pleased with things and with my own development — the stories shaping up well, the words flowing easily. Along with my usual sales, I now had a standing order from one editor for a 20,000-word novelette a month, while another had taken a full-length novel and ordered a second, both of which would be placed as hardcover books after serialization, eventually going onto paperback reprints and foreign language editions — a very large step toward my ultimate goal of doing nothing but book-lengths. Meanwhile, our second child was on the way. What more could a fellow ask for?

But when things begin to look *too* perfect, sometimes one should be ready to duck. For all at once, rumors were starting: the pulps seemed to be in some kind of trouble — possibly even terminal. According to the version I heard, a major publisher had brought in the cost accountants and been informed that he was losing money with every copy he printed. And almost immediately the chill set in.

Within weeks Street & Smith announced that they were killing off their entire string; thirty years after its founding, it would be my melancholy privilege to have a novelette occupy the last spot in the final number of my old favorite, *Western Story.* (Later I would also give the *coup de grace* to the venerable *Blue Book,* with one of my novels featured in its concluding July, 1956 issue.) Other magazines I had been writing for, like *Western Aces* and *Western Trails,* abruptly went under the axe. The ones that remained began a drastic retrenchment — cutting costs, reducing frequency of publication, and, for the very first time, resorting to reprints. Some gave their authors token payments of a few dollars for this recycled material; one editor paid nothing, but instead each story he re-used was prominently labeled "A Time-Honored Classic!" For myself I'd have been just as pleased to have a little cash and make do without all that honor.

By this time the flow of checks from New York had fallen to a trickle. There was no such thing as unemployment insurance for free-lance writers — we would not even be taken under the Social Security umbrella until 1951. I was starting to think I would have to go out and find a proper job — but, doing what?

Yet experience had taught me that when one door closes, another always seems to open — although it may take its own precious time about it. So it happened now. Just when things looked their bleakest, all at once my agent had surprising news. The paperback publishers, with hardly an exception, were suddenly in the market for original novels, Westerns included. They would issue contracts, and give an advance, on the basis of a 70-page "partial" and an outline. And they were wide open for business.

Well, all *right* — something like this was exactly what I had been waiting for. In fact, I had already served as the guinea pig in an experiment along these lines, a couple of years before. The leading paperback house, Pocket Books, had contracted for an original D. B. Newton Western, with which to challenge the hard-cover publishers' monopoly in new fiction. When *Range Boss* appeared in January 1949, it had proceeded to go through printing after printing, eventually racking up a dandy sale of 450,000 copies — I had been living mostly on royalties from this during the lean period while the pulps started downhill.

For various reasons Pocket Books didn't immediately follow up on their idea, but the ice had now been broken. A year later, Fawcett had come out with a line of "Gold Medal" originals, and now the rest wanted to get in. Today, of course, a full half century later, original fiction in paperback has long since become a major branch of the publishing industry, and, since it was my little Western that started it all, I venture to think D. B. Newton rates at least a small footnote, somewhere in the record.

Of course, I wasted no time taking advantage of the new state of things. Abandoning the sinking pulp ship without qualm, I went to work and over the next year placed five books with as many different publishers. Later, on returning to Bend after a brief stint in Hollywood writing television scripts (let's not go into *that!*), I would narrow the list of my publishers to three and over the next dozen

25

Bremen Public Library

years would write everything for them, under various pseudonyms. It was the beginning of a new career; I had never had it so good.

Do I see a hand going up in the audience? Somebody wants to ask: All well and good, but what about after that twelfth year was up? *Then* what happened to you? Trust me — we'll get to it. But first I really have to say something about the Western Writers of America.

When the pulps sank into oblivion, a lot of familiar bylines disappeared along with them, and not without at least one suicide — Walt Coburn, for many years a top-paid pulp writer, apparently could no longer see any future for himself. A number, though, had been busy making their way to high ground, and safety. I'd run into a few of them hanging on for dear life in Hollywood, and my friend Walker Tompkins, after so many years of tremendous output, now admitted that — "Westerns sort of bore me." — and proceeded to forge a new career for himself in non-fiction.

But most of the survivors followed a route similar to the one I had taken. Whereas, until recently, only a few people had been selling Western novels, almost overnight there appeared to be a whole new generation of us, with dozens of titles beginning to pour off the presses. The conclusion seemed obvious: As the mystery writers had done before us, it was time to organize — call attention to ourselves, perhaps help increase the sale of our books through reviews and advertising. At least it was worth a try.

A group consisting of novelists Nelson Nye, Thomas Thompson, Wayne D. Overholser, Norman A. Fox, and Harry Sinclair Drago combined their energies, and invited me to join in. Being widely separated we had to work through round-robin letters, each with five carbon copies — no e-mail, in those days — yet we somehow got the job done, and, when in 1953 Western Writers of America, Inc. was launched with a limited membership consisting entirely of professionals, I would become a board member and also the first secretary-treasurer — a post I was to hold for ten years. Today, WWA still flourishes and continues to grow, although most of those who were in at the beginning have passed on by now. As the last survivor of its six founding fathers, I am proud to be an honorary member of the organization I helped put together, almost half a century ago.

Through WWA and its annual conventions, I've been able to know personally most of the Western authors of my own generation, and even a number of those that I used to read and view with awe, back when I was twelve: S. Omar Barker, Robert Ormond Case, Stephen Payne, L. P. Holmes, Frank C. Robertson, William McLeod Raine. . . . For me, it was quite an experience to find myself accepted by them now, not only as a colleague but also a personal friend.

I'd just like to add, while I'm on the subject, that with very few exceptions the professional writers it has been my privilege to know have seemed to me a rather special breed — interesting, keenly intelligent, well-informed, and approachable. They were also dedicated craftsmen, seriously concerned about their readers and the quality of their work — far more than whatever money it might bring them. Yet, like other creators of "popular" fiction, they were entirely too familiar with the scornful label of "hack writer." I can remember Frank Bonham, one of the most talented of my colleagues, saying in an indignant letter: "Why don't they ever talk about hack grocers, or hack bankers?" Why, indeed? It's guys like those who are *really* in it "just for the money!"

But I believe I see that hand, again. I spoke about twelve good years — and *then* what? Well, in the writer's changeable market, few set-ups last as long as that one did, and, when the old door closed again, it really slammed. All of a sudden the whole publishing industry seemed to be in a feeding frenzy — hard-cover houses swallowing one another whole and being engulfed by foreigners with money, the paperbacks being taken over by conglomerates run by people from Wall Street who knew little about the business, except that they were determined not to waste time with anything except best-sellers. Naturally they couldn't care less about things like Westerns, which had always been depended on to bring publishers modest but reliable returns and help offset their losses from all the best-sellers that never made it.

So, almost overnight, instead of having three publishers I was left with none at all, and this time, in all the turmoil, I couldn't imagine any other door that could possibly open. Frankly, I was ready to give up — but even this time, I was wrong. Once again, changing conditions were able to produce unexpected opportunities — this time, in the person of a brand new figure amid the confusion, an entrepreneur known in the trade as a book "packager."

Lyle Engel's thing involved contracting to provide a publisher with a fiction series, Engel to hire the writers and take care of all the editorial work and publicity, the publisher responsible for no more than printing and distribution. It was a good deal for all hands, and it worked. Naturally when Engel wrote offering me a six-year contract, on better terms than I had ever been able to get through an agent, I accepted without hesitation.

For the first time — at the very end of my career — I would have security and a guaranteed good income to carry me until retirement at seventy. I knew a happy ending when I saw it. I took this one as a reward for all these years I had spent living by my wits. I liked the "Stagecoach" series, I worked well with Engel's editors who treated me with considerable respect, and although I couldn't do the entire series as I was originally supposed to — it turned out Bantam wanted six books a year! — I turned in some pretty good work. But I refused to extend the contract when it ran out. After forty long years of freelancing, I was ready to hang up the old typewriter, at last. . . .

Finally, then, what can I say about the

pulps? Just why they came to such a sorry end, I've never clearly understood. Perhaps television and comic books had something to do with it. Yet even in their last days, they could still produce a few more good writers — notably, Elmore Leonard who would turn out some outstanding Western novels, before letting himself be lured to more lucrative fields on the best-seller list. Toward the very end, *Ranch Romances* lingered on a while in lonely splendor, its publisher still expecting a revival. Finally even he gave up, and pulled the plug. By 1971, an era in popular publishing was finally ended.

Although my memories of it are pure nostalgia, I have to recognize that I picked up some bad habits during my initial stint in the half-cent market. Traces of overheated prose and clumsy plotting would show up later, causing one better-paying editor to complain to my agent: "Sometimes he's good, and sometimes he's pretty hack!" (I saw days when I thought those words would make a fitting epitaph for my headstone.) But there were also invaluable lessons to be learned in the pulps. Nowhere that I know could one have better training in a firm control of material and a strict economy of means. In skilled hands, descriptive and introspective passages would be deftly hinted at, without breaking into the smooth flow of narrative; dialogue, although held to a bare minimum, could depict character, convey emotion, and forward the plot, and still manage to sound very much like normal speech. Such discipline came to be second nature for a talented pulp writer. Would it be catty to suggest that some people on the best-seller lists could have benefited from similar training?

Today, eight bound volumes of magazine stories, together with seventy novels, are ranged along my bookshelf. They represent a lot of hard work — I won't pretend writing is such jolly fun that I would have done it anyway, even if I hadn't needed to earn a living. And yet there is a lot of satisfaction involved, too. It isn't granted every man to see the fruits of his life and labor neatly lined up in a row in front of him. Even if I don't always remember characters and plots, I still have vivid impressions of when, and where, and under what circumstances most of these things were dredged up and captured on paper.

Once in a while I like to take down a book — perhaps one written thirty years ago, open it at random, and sample a couple of paragraphs. Often I won't recognize a single word, yet it's obviously in my style and sometimes I can even say: "D'you know, this isn't half bad." Not long ago, I reread one of my books with absolutely no recollection of anything that happened from one page to the next. As I approached the final chapter, I found myself thinking, a bit anxiously: "I sure hope I've got something up my sleeve, here . . . this thing could use some kind of surprise ending. . . ." And when I got to that ending, sure enough . . . it surprised the hell out of me!

When an author can do that to *himself*, I guess I'd have to say he'd learned his job.

The contents of this volume all date from that period, right after the war, when I was enjoying success in the pulps without any hint that they were about to die, or that the golden glow suffusing my world just then would prove to be a sunset. I've added a few comments that I hope may be of interest, but you aren't required to read them — there's no quiz scheduled later.

And in case it happens to be your first encounter with pulp fiction — be kind.

For, who knows? If I'm lucky, you might even recall the words my mother said, that day so long ago: "Why . . . they're real *stories,* aren't they?"

D. B. Newton
Bend, Oregon

Reach High, Top Hand!

The only thing I can tell you about this sentimental little piece, after all the years, is that it remains my favorite of just about everything I've written. Even my agent liked it! ("I completely share your enthusiasm," he wrote. "It's a swell character story.") All the time I was working on it, I remember going around in a sort of daze, totally absorbed with Sam and Myra Wills, and, when it was finished and I read it to my wife, at one point she suddenly exclaimed — "Look at me!" — and I saw tears running down her cheeks. Today, in a more cynical age, I would hardly expect *that* kind of reaction, but coming as it did from the one person who really mattered, I felt I had had all the reward I would ever need.

I

The railroad depot at Sage Flats, Wyoming had a new stationmaster who was no friend to Sam Wills. Unfortunately, too, because on a warm day like this the depot platform was one of the few comfortable places in town. Even when a summer sun baked the vastly rolling wastes of gray sage and sand and bunch grass, and the twin lines of the U.P. tracks were eye-punishing streaks of brightness running moltenly east and west between Green River and the far-off divide at Laramie, a breeze from low hills on the north horizon always managed somehow to breathe along this shadowed platform and make it ideal for a pleasant nap.

But today, barely an hour after stretching out on an empty baggage truck with a half-filled mail sack for a pillow, Sam was suddenly startled awake by a rough hand on his shoulder and a voice that said: "All right, move on now! The Limited is due by in ten minutes and it don't look good for the town to have bums sleepin' all over the depot!"

Sam did not argue. He pulled his battered hat down over brown locks that were already becoming tinged with gray and, with hands shoved deeply into empty pockets, shuffled away from there. The blue-clad stationmaster watched him go, scowling in distaste.

Over on the siding, a milling of dust and noise above the loading chutes drew Sam's attention. While he dozed, a small shipment of cattle had come in from one of the ranches on the flats and was moving into the pen prior to being prodded up the ramp and into the cars. Something from the past stirred deeply within him as he leaned his shoulders against a corner of the depot and looked and listened to that familiar scene beneath the white-hot Wyoming sky. Behind him the station man's sharp voice called out: "I said move on and I meant it! Get clear away!" But Sam Wills hardly heard. He was already moving across packed earth and beneath blasting sunlight toward the activity in the pens.

Now he could smell the dust and the sweat. He could see the horsemen and hear their cussing as they prodded the last of the big steers through the gate. Sam sauntered over to the fence, swung up, and leaned across the top rail for a look at the bald-face critters bellowing and stirring within.

They were B-in-the-Box cattle. Good beef, too, Sam Wills considered, appraising them with a cowman's eye. Another tidy penny for the box safe in old Harry Benton's office. He thought this idly enough, without any hint of rancor, although rich Harry Benton was Sam's father-in-law and the trouble between them was of thirty years' standing. It got so, after so long a time as thirty years, you could come to take a thing like that for granted. Sam never bothered any more. That was just about his strongest characteristic — not bothering.

Now, satisfied with his look at the cattle in the pen, Sam hopped down from the fence again and, as it would happen, straight into the path of a horseman who came loping along the side of the pen. The first he knew of it was a blow from the muscled shoulder that drove him hard into the rails. He caught his balance, turned as the horseman brought his mount out of a stumble, and then reined about.

The rider was old Benton's foreman, a solid, black-haired man by the name of Tedrow. He shouted at Sam: "What's the matter with you? Too drunk to keep out of a man's way?" And then he saw who it was he had run down and a look of wry amusement wrapped his dark features.

"Well, well," he grunted. "The great cowman himself! What you doing down here, has-been . . . studyin' to get your old job back? Figurin' how you used to do things better in the old days?"

Sam, his shoulders in the faded old coat pressed back against the corral poles, looked at the man in the saddle without answering. There were things he might have said — that he had likely been rodding B-in-the-Box before Cal Tedrow even won his first spurs as a green cowhand. But this probably did not even enter Sam's head. He had long been out of the habit of talking back to anyone.

Now other 'punchers had appeared out of the dust and confusion of the loading pens, and they were watching Sam and their boss with grins on sweaty faces. Cal Tedrow liked an audience. He took this one into the joke with a broad wink, jerked his thumb at the man on the ground. "You know, I hear the boy used to be pretty sharp in the old days. He was a top hand that reached too high and look where he landed! Say, Sam, how much washing did the missus take in last week?"

Sam shoved away from the fence. He only meant to put his back to this crew and walk away from their mocking laughter, but Cal Tedrow must have misconstrued his intentions. The foreman's face went quickly hard, and he barked: "Don't try to start nothin'!" And with a quick thrust of a boot caught Sam in the chest and shoved him back and down. Then he looked at the others and, whirling his bronc', went larruping off through the drifting dust.

In another moment Sam Wills was alone. He got up slowly, slapped the loose, powder-dry dust out of his worn clothing, and dragged on his battered hat. There was the beginning of anger in his stolid, aging face, but it had settled into apathy again as Sam left the loading pens and chutes behind him and headed for the false-fronted buildings of Sage Flat's main street.

It was a warm day all right, one to drain the energy from a man. You almost thought you could hear the paint blistering on the houses of town; and beyond them, far off across a gray expanse of rolling sage, the low-lying hills to northward seemed to shimmer behind curtains of heated air. A ragged clump of tumbleweed came scooting along the rutted street on a hot breath of wind, and tired ponies at the hitch rails stamped fretfully as blown dust whipped and stung their sweaty hides.

Ambling up the warped plank sidewalk, Sam blinked into the heat haze and thought how nice a drink would feel in his dry throat, but he didn't have any money and his credit was no good in any of the town's three saloons. Just to make sure he stopped under the meager shade of a wooden awning and felt through all his pockets.

Clean empty!

No point in approaching Myra again, either. His ears still stung from the tongue-lashing he'd received the last time he'd ventured to ask his wife for money. He shrugged philosophically and moved on along the street.

Harry Benton's own saddler was racked before the hardware store. That was sort of interesting. The store had belonged to Sam at one time, long ago right after the big trouble with Benton when he'd had to quit working cattle, and turned to other ways to make a living.

But no B-in-the-Box mount had ever gnawed the store's hitch rail the few months Sam owned the place, for Harry Benton had blackballed him, and naturally the rest of the range had danced to Harry's tune. Sam was forced to go out of business, and that had sort of been the beginning of the end. He usually didn't think much about it any more, but right now, because of that scene with Cal Tedrow, there was a stirring of anger in Sam against B-in-the-Box and everything connected with it.

Maybe that was why he refused to step off the sidewalk as Benton came out of the store. They met head-on.

Harry Benton was an old man, but his spirit was as high as ever. In the days when Sam Wills ramrodded for him, he had been solid, and stubborn, with a shock of hair as fiery as his temper. The stubbornness remained; for the rest, Harry was bent with time and his head was white, and only the blazing eyes — although a little dimmed — were much the same.

As he saw Sam Wills now, those eyes took on a kindling of wrath and scorn that was all he ever had for this son-in-law of his. Sam stood his ground, and for a moment they were halted like that — the wealthy cattle baron and the derelict confronting him, unshaven, in his broken relics of clothing.

"Well!" old Harry bit out. "You steppin' out of my road, you whelp? Or am I gonna have to kick you out of it?"

His words carried. A face or two appeared to watch with interest this encounter in the hot and empty street. It was Sam Wills's place, now, to step meekly into the dust and let the most important rancher on the flats have the walk to himself.

He had never failed before in such a situation. Yet, somehow, the things that had happened to him today had built an unfamiliar core of resistance within the derelict. From somewhere came words of mild defiance.

"I reckon the sidewalk was built wide enough for two men at once!"

"*Men?*" Benton spat the word. "When have you counted yourself in that class? What man could fall as low as you've come . . . and dragged my daughter with you."

A sudden mask dropped over Sam's features. Without a word he shoved past Benton. Behind him he heard Harry's cry of fury. "You come back here! I ain't finished talkin'. . . ."

In the middle of a word the voice choked off. Sam stopped involuntarily, turned half around. He saw Harry's face, distorted and purple; he heard the gasp that dragged through the old man's lips. Then suddenly he was hurrying back. He got there just as the taut body slumped forward.

Sam caught him, found almost no weight in the rancher's wasted body. Harry was fighting for breath, his mouth gaping, the silvered hair streaming down into his face as the expensive hat fell and rolled on the splintered walk at their feet. He got one word out: "Heart. . . ."

In desperation Sam looked around him.

Other men were coming. Sam saw the open door of the hardware store near at hand and, supporting Harry awkwardly, got him inside. The proprietor was not there. Sam sighted a packing box and dragged the sick man over, let him down upon it with his back against the side of the counter.

Head lolling, Harry croaked out: *"Bottle. . . ."* One thin hand was trying to gesture toward the pocket of his coat. Sam dug into it quickly, found Benton's medicine and the silver spoon he always carried. Sam had seen him pour out the dose and make a face over it, many times. Now with fumbling fingers he got the bottle's cap off, brimmed the bowl of the spoon. "Here you are," he grunted, and he put the spoon to Benton's lips.

At that moment a spasm ran through the thin body. The jaw, suddenly slack, dropped open, and the head sagged forward. The medicine spilled futilely, untasted, over Harry's lifeless chin and his clothing, and Sam straightened slowly, the empty spoon and bottle in his hands.

Harry Benton would never need another dose of his heart medicine now.

The things that happened those next few minutes were a jumble and confusion to

44

Sam. Men came hurrying in from the street with a clomp of boots and rattle of spur chains, raising an alarmed and excited babble of voices. Almost at once they had the store packed, and the concentrated smell of strong men and horse sweat was nearly unbearable. But somebody had sent for the doctor, and, when he came, they made room for one more.

"I knew it!" the medico kept saying half to himself, as he stooped to Harry's sprawled, limp form. "I told him all along he'd go out this way. And with this heat we's been having. . . ."

It seemed a little indecent for them to crowd around the dead man that way. Sam had been quickly shoved into a corner by the front window where he stood shuffling from one foot to the other, thinking someone might want to ask him some questions. Nobody seemed to. The sun came in through the plate glass window like a furnace blast, and the sweat crawled down Sam's spine. He was miserable.

Finally they picked up all that was left of Benton and carried him up the street to the doctor's office, and after that the crowd in the store thinned out some. Sam moved outside, too, glad to get away from the concentrated heat of that plate glass window. He felt lost, as though there was something he should do or say, but no one had invited him to make any statement although there had been many a hard look thrown his way and he'd heard more than one remark about what a shame it was Harry Benton should die like that — from a heart attack brought on by quarreling with his no-good son-in-law.

And then Sam thought of Myra, and he quailed inwardly. Myra would have to be told, and no putting it off, either. Somehow he had forgotten that part of it, until just this moment. With great misgivings, he started for home.

He met his wife within a block of the house. For someone else, with that eager interest most people have in being the first with bad news, had already been to her, and she was heading for the doctor's office. She had on a faded dress; her thin face was pale in the hard glare of the sunlight. A pang of regret for many things touched Sam when he saw her.

"You heard about it?" he asked clumsily, and fumbled to take one of her work-roughened hands. "I'm sorry, Myra. . . ."

She barely paused in her quick stride. Her jaw set as she looked at him coldly. "Sorry? That's a new one!" she said bitterly. "You killed my mother . . . and now Dad!"

"That ain't hardly fair!" Sam protested.

She jerked her hand away from him. "I don't want to talk to you! I don't want to hear your voice or see your face, either. Not just now . . . it'd be too much!"

Her voice broke in a sob. She stepped past her husband and continued on her way.

Sam looked after her for a long minute, and then he gave his characteristic shrug that meant: "What the hell!" He went on to the house, turning in at the littered yard of packed bare earth, stepping up to the sagging porch, shuffling across the threshold of the two-roomed, sparsely furnished shack. He felt at a loss, purposeless. He moved one of Myra's washtubs off of a chair at the rickety kitchen table and sat down. One hand drummed idly on the table top as he stared through the window at clothes drying on the line outside. A tang of sage came on the hot, dusty air that breathed faintly across the open sill.

Presently he shoved to his feet again — restless, weighed by an undefined depression. A drink was really what he wanted. Sam went suddenly to the cupboard, shoving aside Myra's ironing board with its pile of waiting clothes, and fished down an old cracked teapot from the topmost shelf. There were a few crumpled bills stuffed inside it. Sam glanced around furtively, then quickly removed one, and shoved it into a pocket. He went out again through the front door and turned along the street that led to the heart of town.

II

On the steps of the Shorthorn Bar a voice calling his name made him turn with a guilty start. Homer Lowndes was coming toward him across the dusty street, his tall and cadaverous form dressed immaculately. He loomed a head taller than Sam as he hitched his long legs up the steps to the saloon porch. He said crisply: "I saw you from my window, Sam, and I would like to have a few minutes of your time. It's a matter of some importance."

Sam scowled. He didn't much care for Lowndes, mainly because the lawyer was a deacon of the Methodist church and had been a leader in the often-voiced opinion that Sam Wills should be run out of town. Sam also had an inborn distaste for the two big buckteeth that thrust out below his upper lip on the rare occasions when Homer Lowndes allowed himself the luxury of a smile. But the lawyer was not smiling now. Something told Sam he had better not decline.

They went across to the two-story brick building that housed Homer's office, the lawyer's gaunt body preceding Sam up the dark stairway to the second floor. He used a key on the office door, thrust it open, and stood aside to usher his visitor in ahead of him. That was Homer Lowndes for you: lock everything up tight as a vault just to run across the street and back.

The bare elegance of the office furnishings oppressed Sam, made him snake off his hat and run stubby fingers nervously through uncombed hair.

Lowndes went to the bookcase whose gleaming doors housed his thick and musty law books. A clink of glass on glass, a gurgle of liquid, brought Sam's head up then in a quick surprise. He stared as the lawyer brought a tumbler partly filled with amber whisky and set it on the edge of the desk beside him.

"Might as well have your drink and get it over with," Lowndes muttered. "Then maybe you can put your mind on what

I'm going to tell you."

It was a good brand of whisky, and Sam downed it and put back the glass with shaking fingers.

"Thanks," he grunted, still not looking at the lawyer squarely.

Lowndes waved the word aside with an airy gesture. He folded his lean body into the chair behind the desk then, and he got down to business with characteristic abruptness. "So your father-in-law is dead!"

Sam only nodded, waiting.

"You're aware, I suppose, that Myra is Harry Benton's sole survivor . . . which means that she stands to inherit the B-in-the-Box ranch, lock, stock, and barrel. I don't doubt at all that you've had that fact in mind all these years."

His voice was dry and caustic as he added that last, but Sam was somehow too astounded to take offense at the meaning Homer put into it. He said slowly: "Why no, I didn't know that. Harry said a long time ago that he was going to cut her off and leave everything to charity."

"Harry Benton made two wills," Lowndes went on, as though Sam had not spoken, and, opening a drawer of his desk, he brought out a couple of legal documents and placed them on the blotter in front of him, neatly, side by side. He speared a thin, bony finger at the first of these. "This was drawn up more than thirty years ago . . . before Myra left home to marry you and before his wife died. By its terms the ranch and stock were to go to the mother . . . or in case of her decease, to Myra. All very simple."

The long finger rose, hovered above the second document, and then pounced upon it. "But this one, drawn five years afterwards, supersedes the other. There has been none later. It is Benton's last will and testament. And let me read you one paragraph from it."

He picked up the document, opened it, cleared his throat, sliding the dry upper lip back from the ugly teeth. He found the place, and intoned in a sing-song voice: "If at the date of my decease my daughter, Myra Benton Wills, has become a widow, or if, within a month of the reading of this will, she becomes a widow or seeks legal divorce from her husband, Samuel Wills, then my estate shall pass to her *in toto*. If, however, at the end of said month, she has not sued for divorce, or if the divorce be not granted, then she is to receive one hundred dollars and the rest of the estate shall pass to the benefit of such charitable institutions as is hereinafter provided in this my last will and testament."

The voice ceased. Lowndes folded the document and placed it again beside the other will, and then he lifted his eyes and looked at Sam. "You see his purpose? Even in the grave, Benton will not give over his attempt to dissolve your marriage to his daughter. This is his last move . . . this choice he offers her. Which do you think she will take? Which," he added, slowly and deliberately, "do you think she *should* take?"

Hot words that had been trembling to spill from Sam's lips melted away to nothing. There was that in the probing voice of the other that made him turn square and face the truth. And the picture he saw — the picture of himself, and of what these thirty wasted years had meant — was one that hurt.

"You're right, Homer," he grunted then bitterly. "And so was Benton, thirty years ago, when he wouldn't give his consent to Myra marrying me. I'm no good for her!"

Lowndes shrugged a little, frowned thoughtfully at the bony yellow fingers folded before him on the desk top. "Well, we might as well be fair. You're a good cowman, Sam. You had made Harry a fine foreman, but because you had the audacity to marry his daughter he kicked you out and blackballed you so that no other rancher hereabouts dared hire you."

He looked up again, and there was a strange glint, almost of friendliness, in his sharp eyes. "You see, I do know quite a bit about your story, Sam, even if I am a newcomer in Sage Flats. At one time I imagine I made things rather hot for you . . . before I started inquiring around and began piecing together what I learned.

"Sam, if you could have left this region, you'd have had no trouble to make a good place somewhere else. But Missus Benton came down with a stroke, brought on by all the family argument, and Myra insisted on being near her mother. So you gave up cattle and opened a hardware store. It failed. You tried one thing after another, and every time Harry Benton broke you. And still Myra's mother hung on and on . . . for over ten years more."

Sam sighed. "That's true enough, Homer, but it's no excuse. If I'd been any good, Harry couldn't have licked me. I just didn't have the backbone. Because Missus Benton did die, finally, and then it was already too late. That was my chance to break away, to try for a fresh start. Myra was willing and anxious then to go. But I just didn't want to! I was a failure, and I'd got used to it. I'd got. . . ." He glanced down at himself. "It's got down to this . . . and I stayed there."

"I know," the lawyer agreed. "You'd become a worthless, no-good bum who'd let his wife break her back at other people's washing just to keep the pair of you alive. They tell me she was a very sweet and pretty girl when she lost her head over you thirty years ago, Sam. Those years certainly haven't been easy on her. But now. . . ."

He picked up the document he had read, looked at it, and then at Sam. The latter's mouth hardened. "Yeah, I guess I know what you mean. Well, you needn't worry, Homer," he added bitterly. "When you think about the life I've given her, there's no doubt in my mind which choice she's going to make. She despises me, I know that well enough. And I promise I won't give any trouble or fight the divorce. In fact . . ." — he looked at Lowndes sharply — "I'll even make a deal. For fifty dollars I'll leave town right now and never come back, and she can claim desertion or whatever else she wants to call it. All the money she's ever going to have, it ought to be worth that much to her to be rid of me!"

The lawyer raised an eyebrow curiously. "Where will you go?"

"To hell, most likely," Sam told him. "I been headed that way a long time now."

The bony hands spread in a brief gesture. "I could suggest this to her. Or advance you the money myself. Yes," he went on, "it's a very intelligent solution . . . a bribe for you, clear title to a ranch for your wife. There's just one thing. Myra is only a woman . . . not even a young woman, any more. How is she going to hold on to that ranch once she owns it?"

Sam shrugged. "She's got a foreman. She's got Cal Tedrow."

"Precisely!"

Their eyes locked. Each read his own thought reflected in the other's. Sam said: "Then you don't like Tedrow, either?"

"I don't trust him. Harry Benton scoffed whenever I tried to warn him, but I am reasonably sure Tedrow is not above stealing cattle from his own employer. Now, if a woman should come into control of B-in-the-Box, seems to me it would be a field day for him. He'd rob her blind!"

Sam Wills frowned. "What's on your mind, then?"

"Just this . . . in spite of everything, I'm confident that the one person in this world still most interested in Myra's welfare . . . in seeing her established and her ranch set in working order . . . that person is a man named Sam Wills. Deny it, if you like. Nevertheless, I'd like to offer an alternative suggestion to the one that you just made." He picked up the document he had read aloud, looked at it, then dropped it into a drawer and shut the drawer with his knee. "Let's just leave that where it is for the time being." He picked up the second will — the old one. "I shall file this original will, and I'll announce it as Benton's final testament. Under its terms your wife can then take possession of B-in-the-Box with no provisos.

"Now, here is my proposition. Today. . . ." He looked at a calendar on the wall. "Today is the seventh. Exactly three weeks from now I am going to the ranch for another look through Benton's papers, and there . . . quite by accident . . . I shall discover the later will. You, Sam, will have until that day to set matters straight at the ranch and replace Cal Tedrow with a dependable foreman . . . one who you know will serve Myra faithfully after . . . after the true will has been made public."

Sam hesitated. "That don't give me much time."

"I'm sorry. By suppressing that will for even three weeks, I am stepping outside the letter of the law, a thing I've never done before in my career. There are many people hereabouts, I'm sure, that know or suspect its existence . . . I would not dare delay any longer in producing it."

Sam got slowly to his feet. The lawyer did likewise. A hard gleam was in Sam's eye. He said: "Except for one thing I would tell you to take your proposition and stuff it. If you want to know what I think, I got good suspicion you've got an eye on that ranch yourself. I know lawyers, and I know there's a reason for you being so damn' solicitous about my wife's welfare. I wouldn't even put it past you to try and marry her yourself, Homer, once you're rid of me, if B-in-the-Box came with her.

"Well, good luck to you, if you can swing it. But me, I resent being a tool for anybody. I'd tell you to go to hell . . . except I can't resist an opportunity to stand up to Cal Tedrow and tell him he's lost his job."

Lowndes's face showed no anger, only its normal cold frostiness. "You'll go through with it then?"

"Yeah," said Sam. "But only for three

57

weeks!" And there was a fire in him that had not been there in many a long year.

It was a breathless day with no relief from the high sun's torment when Sam Wills hired a livery stable team and wagon and drove Myra out of Sage Flats to take over her father's ranch. They didn't have much to say to one another that day. Sam, with the ribbons in his hands, looked side-long at his wife from time to time, sensing the tumult of emotions that must be concealed behind her tired eyes and thin, stony features.

The big house, sitting on a hill with pop-lars tall and green about it and the barns and corrals and outbuildings behind, would be a matter of memories for her. Sam thought: *She was born in that house, and she left it for me because her dad and mother wouldn't have me. And now she's coming back . . . thirty years older, and no one there to greet her.* A sudden excess of pity flooded through him, and Sam wanted very much to say something to his wife — just a word or so. But communication had long ago become a difficult thing between these two. Sam merely shrugged and, halting his team under the shade trees, jumped down into the grass and came around the back of the wagon, reached up, and gave his wife a hand to help her down. She said: "You going to see to the team?"

He glanced at the wagon. Beyond, he could see men lounging about the door of the bunkhouse. The B-in-the-Box riders were staying close today as the new owners moved in. Sam grunted: "I'll have one of the hands run the rig back to town."

But he had taken only a few steps in their direction when Myra called him. She was at the top of the steps now, in the shade of the verandah, and he thought that her voice sounded almost a little frightened. "Maybe . . . maybe you'd better come with me, Sam."

Somehow relieved at having put off his encounter with the ranch crew, Sam came back and moved slowly up the broad steps. He took the key from Myra, unlocked the door, and shoved it open. Myra stepped inside. Sam followed.

The last time they had gone through that door together — even now he could remember the delicious terror of it as, fortified with the courage of youth and of a fact accomplished, they had walked in timidly and shown Harry Benton the brand new wedding ring on Myra's hand. Sam wondered if she felt this, too, wondered if that was the reason she called him back and wanted him with her now.

But quickly the spell had passed, and again they were two shabby, aging people wandering through the empty house. Sam didn't try to talk, but let her take the impact of each well-remembered room in silence. She paused a long time in the doorway of the bedchamber where her mother had died. After that they went down the stairs again and into the low-ceilinged living room, and here Myra lowered herself stiffly to one of the pair of comfortable, leather-bound settees. Sam stood by the cold fireplace, staring at the cougar skin on the hardwood floor.

The sound of sobbing jerked his head up suddenly. Myra had her head bowed against her hands, and he watched awkwardly, not knowing what to say as her thin shoulders jerked to her weeping. But she didn't stop, kept right on crying as he had not seen her do in many years. On an impulse then he moved to her, put a hand upon her faded hair. "Please, Myra!" he mumbled. "Ain't any good cryin'. . . ."

Suddenly she had stopped, and, reaching up, she seized his shabby coat sleeve and drew him toward her. "Sit down, Sam." He obeyed uneasily, his shapeless hat upon his knee. She was very serious, but not cross now as he had grown accustomed to finding her. "We've got to have a talk . . . about everything."

"Yes," said Sam.

"It's not easy, what I want to say. Coming here like this to my home after all these years. I feel old and lost. And yet . . . there's a chance now, Sam. A chance to make something of the little time that's left, and maybe forget what's come between."

He could say nothing, merely sit and look at her tired and patient face.

"I'll need help, Sam," this worn and graying woman beside him was saying now. "I can't go it all alone. Won't . . . won't you try, now, again? We've hurt each other, I know. I held you back when you might have gone ahead . . . but you. . . ."

"You don't need to say it," he muttered. "I know my shortcomings, I reckon." He stood up. "I'm no good, Myra, and it ain't likely there's much left in me worth saving. But I used to know something about a ranch . . . I'm goin' outside now," he added gruffly, "and size up the crew."

He was glad to escape from her, and her tired, accusing eyes. Dragging on the shapeless hat, he went out through the

dark front hall and upon the broad verandah, closing the big door behind him.
And there were the men of B-in-the-Box,
gathered in the shade of the bunkhouse,
waiting motionless with their eyes upon
him. Sam steeled himself to face them.

III

Under the hard glare of the sun, he went toward the silent group. Nothing had changed
much around the ranch headquarters, he
had time to notice, since the days when he
had been foreman here at B-in-the-Box. The
same buildings, except for the fine new barn.
The big house itself had a new wing that had
been completed only a year or so before; the
extension contained Benton's office and a
spare storeroom or two.

There were ten riders on the payroll.
Two or three got to their feet as Sam came
up, but the others merely lounged and
stared at him, and he stood facing them, a
scarecrow of a man in his battered
clothing. Most of them were armed, but
Sam's gun and belt had long ago gone as a
trade-in for booze.

Big, dark-haired Cal Tedrow stood leaning against the side of the door, hat pushed back. Sam felt that here was the most effective place to affirm his authority. He cleared his throat, said with a firmness of tone he had not used to any man for a long spell of years: "You want to quit now, Tedrow, or wait to get fired?"

The foreman straightened, putting his feet down flat upon the earth; his dark face shot forward. He began to swear at Sam Wills in a flat, monotonous voice. The others heard him in silence, watching the faces of the two intently as though waiting to see how this would develop. "You worthless, drunken bum! You can't fire me!"

"Your pay stopped five minutes ago. You better draw it and ride," Sam said.

"Yeah?" Tedrow spat into the dust. "We'll see about that." He came away from the door, and Sam tensed, thinking the man was coming at him. Sam's liquor-softened body would make no match for Tedrow's whang-leather toughness. But the foreman did not want a battle. He went straight past Sam Wills toward the house. He pounded at the door. Sam knew then what was in the other's mind.

Myra opened the door, looked blankly at Tedrow. And then the latter was saying, in a voice that carried clearly to the men before the bunkhouse: "Ma'am, you're your own boss, but I'm telling you flatly you can't run this ranch without a damn' good ramrod. I've served your dad for three years . . . I know this ranch and I know its problems. And now that character," he added, with a contemptuous glance at Sam, "tells me I'm through here. I won't accept that from anyone but you, direct."

There was a silence. Sam, with all these cowhands looking on, stood there and endured Tedrow's glance, and he endured the humility of having his own wife weigh him in the balance, publicly, in front of the hired crew.

But then Myra said in a voice that sounded thin and without too much conviction: "My husband is in charge of operating the ranch. If he thinks best to do this, then it stands."

"You're making a bad mistake, Missus Wills!" Tedrow stated angrily. "That man ain't capable of rodding a spread like this. He's a has-been . . . a no-good drunk. Your dad built a fine ranch. He'll tear it down in a year's time."

"We don't need to argue," she cut him off. "If you will step into the office, I'll pay you the money you have coming."

Tedrow went dark with cold fury. "All right," he bit out, "I will!"

She held open the door for him, and he entered, moving stiffly, not removing the big hat from his head. And slowly, deliberately, six of the men before the bunkhouse came to their feet, and they, too, moved toward the porch.

Sam caught one of them by the arm, dragged him around. "Where are you going?"

The man looked at the other five, back at Sam. "I dunno about them. Me, I'm drawing my time. I just don't care to work here no longer."

Sam stood aside and watched the B-in-the-Box crew melt away and leave him standing there in the hot sunlight with bowed shoulders and empty hands.

The last man had been paid, and Myra returned the cash box to the office safe where old Harry Benton, distrusting banks, had always kept his money and papers. She came out into the dark hall of the new wing and found Sam waiting, not able to meet her eye directly as she faced him. The front door slammed shut behind the last of the crew.

Sam muttered: "Thanks for backing me against Tedrow."

"You're my husband," she retorted rather sharply. "I couldn't very well have done anything else . . . it wouldn't have looked right. But. . . ." She looked at him closely, in the shadowed hall. "Are you sure it was the best move? You see what happened."

"Yeah, I see. I had my reasons, though," Sam added. "Right now I'm going to saddle up and take a look around . . . see how large a crew we really need to run this ranch. After that I'll go out and find them."

Starting for the corral to find a mount, he halted in sudden surprise as he noticed three cowpunchers still lounging in the shade by the bunkhouse. He headed in their direction. "Ain't you three gone yet?" he demanded in a sour tone.

One got to his feet — a tall, lean youth, who could make a quick move without seeming to put any effort into it. "Then are we fired too, Mister Wills?"

Sam looked at the three of them. "No . . . not if you ain't of a mind to quit. I just thought everybody left with Tedrow."

"Uhn-uh," said the youngster. "We three don't like Tedrow."

"I see." Sam was thoughtful. "What's you fellows' names?"

"Bob Redpath." The others identified themselves as Norrell and Lang.

"Set down, Bob," said Sam. "I guess you boys see what I'm up against. I have to take over this spread . . . cold . . . and run it without any crew to speak of. I don't know anything about the shape the range or the stock are in. And . . . ," he added slowly, "it's been a long time since I thought much about such things. . . . Now, you fellows got any suggestions?"

Norrell and Lang exchanged glances. The latter said: "Shucks, neither of us been on the payroll but just a few weeks. But Redpath's ridden for B-in-the-Box nearly a year now."

"The spread's in pretty good shape, Mister Wills," Bob Redpath spoke up. "There are a couple of things, though. . . ."

"Well?"

"We been losing some cattle," said the young man earnestly. "Not heavy . . . just a trickle, a few head now and then. Once or twice, though, Tedrow would have us make a good-sized gather, and then we'd leave them alone for a night and next day they'd be gone. Speaking mighty plain," he added, "Tedrow and some of his pals was generally away from the bunkhouse on those nights."

Sam looked at him sharply. "Like that, huh? Did you ever say anything about this to Harry Benton?"

"Couldn't. None of the hands ever was able to talk to the boss except through Tedrow . . . that's the way Benton run this ranch. Common cowhands was too far beneath him."

Sam nodded, for surely he, more than any other, had felt the weight of old Benton's autocratic notions.

Redpath said: "And it was the same about the dam."

"What dam?"

"Well, that's the other thing I meant to tell you about. You see, B-in-the-Box has a good graze, but it ain't getting the water it needs. And there's a place I've noticed along the creek where it seems to me a dam could be thrown up pretty cheap and backfill a natural little reservoir. Then, with irrigation ditches put out from there. . . ."

Sam got to his feet quickly. "Wait a minute, Bob," he said. "Let's just saddle up and go take a look at that place. You boys," he added to Norrell and Lang, "hang around a spell, will you?"

Complete as his memory was of the whole stretch of that range, Sam could not have named a place for a dam until Redpath took him to the spot and pointed it out. "Well, I'll be jiggered," Sam muttered. "It wouldn't take much to close off this narrow point and the hills behind it form a perfect cup. Yeah . . . a good idea, come to think of it. Seems like the creek's smaller than in the old days. Maybe the springs back in the hills are giving out, and in that case we'd better start thinking about impounding this water while we can."

"I'm glad you agree," said Bob Redpath modestly. "Seemed to me I was right."

Sam looked at him thoughtfully. "There's a head on your shoulders, Bob. And from remarks you've let drop I fancy you got your share of savvy about cattle and horses, too. How would you like a try at rodding this outfit?"

The younger man turned toward him slowly. "Me? Fill Tedrow's job?"

"I'd like you to take a whack at it. Your first chore will be to build you a crew."

"Why. . . ." Bob looked both confused and pleased. "I'd like it fine, Mister Wills . . . I really would. Only. . . . Why do you want a foreman at all, if I ain't being too personal? Why don't you rod the B-in-the-Box yourself?"

Sam could feel the color rising in his face. His fingers tightened on the reins. He started to say: "I ain't gonna be around long enough." He changed that to — "I got my reasons." — and abruptly reined his bronc' about and headed him back across the swells of sage and bunch grass. Bob fell in beside him. The new foreman looked puzzled.

Next morning Sam and Bob took the buckboard into Sage Flats. Before they left Myra gave Sam a list. "Here's some things I'll be needing. I think you can get most of them at Logan's, and we'll put an order in to the mail order house at Kansas City for the rest."

He took the paper, glanced at the items. "Good night!" he exclaimed. "You're really going to make the place over, aren't you?"

"I laid awake most of the night, planning," she admitted, and there was a tone in her voice and a color in her thin cheeks that Sam could not remember having found there in years. "This house is a gloomy place. Dad didn't seem to care how it looked. But I'm going to put up some new drapes and liven things a little bit." Almost shyly she added: "Do . . . do you think I'm being silly?"

"Good Lord, no!" he blurted. "Seems to me you're just enjoying yourself, Myra. It's high time you was." And then she smiled at him.

It lasted just an instant, that smile, but it was compounded of many things — of understanding, even of forgiveness. It took away the years that were piled about her eyes and her mouth, and it smoothed the harshness from her brow, so that, for the moment, this person smiling at him was the girl that he had loved all those years ago.

But the moment passed quickly, and Myra was turning away from him to the iron box safe. "I'll give you the money now," she said briskly and, opening the cash box, began counting out a handful of bills. Then suddenly she faltered, made a move as though to stuff the money back into the box.

Sam blurted out: "That's all right . . . I'll tell Logan to charge it to you. Not so much danger that way of me getting sidetracked at the Shorthorn Bar."

He saw her jaw go firm. With quick determination, she shut the lid of the box and handed the money to him. "I like best trading in cash." She hesitated. "I've given you a little extra. Why not stop in at the clothing store and buy some new duds? A rancher ought to look the part, you know, and that outfit of yours has seen its best days. . . ."

The money rode heavy in his pocket all the way to town. He had little to say to Bob Redpath.

When they nosed their team and buckboard into a hitch rack before the general store and Sam swung down to snub the reins, he happened to glance at the brick building across the way, and there he saw the lean and yellow face of Homer Lowndes at the open window. Sam looked away quickly.

Bob joined him on the board sidewalk. "What's the program, Mister Wills?"

"I dunno. I got some shopping to do first. Maybe you can nose around and see if there's riders in town looking for work. Sign on any that look good to you."

His new foreman agreed, and they parted. Sam went into the general store. Old man Logan scowled when he saw who it was.

"Another scorcher today," said Sam, as he handed over the list and the merchant scanned it though his glasses.

In answer, Logan only raised his brows in a sideward glance at him, and with a sour grunt moved away.

He set out the goods perfunctorily, gave Sam back the paper, and snatched the money that was handed him. He made change and turned his back without a word.

Sam gathered up his bundles and dumped them grimly into the rear of the buckboard. It positively hurt, he knew, for the good people of this town to have to deal with him in any way — to accept now as an equal the derelict they had never noticed before, unless to throw him out or sic the dogs on him.

And, of course, they were right. Those who had despised Sam Wills had always secretly pitied his wife; now his change of station was due to her and her alone. It was Myra's money, not his own, that he was spending today.

As he hooked the buckboard tailgate, a sudden commotion down the street broke in on Sam's reflections. A fight had started. Two men were in the dust, slugging it out, while others came yelling and shouting to watch, the planks of the walk drumming under their feet. And then one of the combatants went down, and through swirling dust Sam caught a better glimpse of the other, standing over him. It was Bob Redpath.

Sam started in that direction as fast as he could run, but liquor had broken his wind and the fight was over before he reached there. The man Bob had licked was getting up, slinking away through the crowd with a hand clamped to his jaw. Bob turned to a bunch of men on the post office steps, fists clenched, and bareheaded. "Any more of you want the same?"

There were no takers. A few turned hastily and walked away, but another spoke up quickly: "I've changed my mind about that job, friend. If you'll take me, I'd like to sign on."

Two or three others echoed his words. Redpath nodded. "All right," he said. "Get your horses and meet me in ten minutes." Then, as they scattered, he turned away, ignoring the curious glances of the onlookers, and he came face to face with Sam Wills. "Oh . . . howdy," said Bob, grinning sheepishly.

"Been hiring riders?" said Sam. He glanced at the bruised knuckles Bob was wiping on his shirt front. Bob followed his glance, tried to laugh as he flexed the hand.

"Little argument," he said carelessly. He would talk no more about it.

Bob and Sam headed for the buckboard.

Within a few minutes four cowpunchers with trail-stained clothing, and soogans and warbags strapped behind their high-cantled saddles, had ridden up singly and joined them. Bob introduced them to Sam, who allowed that the B-in-the-Box foreman had signed up a good bunch of men.

"I've finished my shopping," Sam said then, indicating the load of goods in the back of the wagon. "So we might as well be heading home. Unless," he suggested idly, "you'd like a drink first?"

Bob Redpath gave him a sharp look, ducked his head quickly. "Ain't particularly thirsty," he muttered. "But I'll step inside with you."

"Oh, no." Sam took the reins. "I was just thinking you might want one." He clucked to the horses.

IV

"What were you fighting about?" Sam demanded suddenly, when they were about halfway to the ranch.

He saw the confusion that gripped the youngster. Bob tried to tell him: "It wasn't anything. . . ."

Sam cut him off. "Maybe he said he wanted nothing to do with an outfit run by the town bum. Was that it?"

Redpath colored. "Did I . . . ?"

"No, you didn't say anything of the kind," muttered Sam. "I just guessed it. Well, that's a stigma this ranch won't have to put up with forever."

At the B-in-the-Box, Redpath showed the new hands to their quarters. Sam unloaded the buckboard. Myra was delighted by the things he had brought. "These are just right!" she exclaimed, unrolling a bolt of flowered drapery goods. "They'll make up into nice curtains and put a touch of color into this drab living room. See?"

She spread it at arm's length to show the effect. And something about her face, peering at him excitedly above the brightly colored goods, touched him deeply. "Gosh, Myra," he blurted. "You ought to get you a dress made out of something like that. It makes you look younger . . . like when you was a girl!"

"Why, Sam." Her cheeks colored with pleasure. She dropped the goods across one arm and raised her free hand, self-consciously, to smooth her faded hair. She stopped then, expression changing. "I told you to buy yourself some clothes," she said in her old tone of suspicion. "What did you do with the money?"

"Oh." He dug into his pocket, pulled out the bills, and looked at them. "Guess I just forgot," he mumbled. He tossed the money on the table. "Bet you thought I'd get plastered with that, didn't you?" He shrugged, turned abruptly, and shuffled out of the room.

"Wait!" Myra cried. "Sam, I'm sorry, I. . . ."

But he would not come back, and her voice was cut away by the door's closing.

Time was running out, however, and the three weeks' grace Homer Lowndes had granted him were almost over. A few days before the end of that period the lawyer himself dropped by. He was the first caller Myra had received since inheriting B-in-the-Box, and his coming filled her with an obvious and almost child-like excitement.

She served him tea and cake in the old swing on the verandah, wearing a flowered dress she'd found at the store in Sage Flats shortly after Sam offered his suggestion. The change it made in her was startling. Lowndes, recovered from his first astonishment, responded with an unctuous charm and showed his buckteeth in a yellow smile that Sam, who observed the scene from time to time around the corner of the house, found revolting.

Before he left, Lowndes found a chance to draw Sam aside. "How is everything going?" the lawyer wanted to know.

"To schedule," Sam told him. "She's got a dandy foreman now, and the ranch is in good shape."

"Cal Tedrow?"

"I hear he's still in the neighborhood with a half dozen hardcases that quit their jobs the same day I fired him. I hope he doesn't give any trouble. Otherwise, Myra should be able to get along quite well after . . . after I leave."

"Good!" Lowndes hesitated a moment. "I must say, Wills, that your wife is still a most attractive woman. I would never have dreamed what a change this inheritance could make in her."

Sam only shrugged, but after Lowndes had left, he cursed and let off steam by kicking an empty can across the dusty ground. "The damned hypocrite," he muttered. "Got his cap set for her already . . . and the ranch, too. And here my hands are tied, and he knows it."

One result of the lawyer's visit, however, was to break the ice with the people of Sage

Flats. The wives of other ranchers began dropping in to call on the woman who had formerly done their cleaning and washing. Myra received them all graciously, and what was past seemed now forgotten. Today she was owner of the district's biggest cattle ranch. And with every day that passed she appeared to grow younger, more like the girl she had once been.

After one of these visits, Sam came up the front steps to find her seated alone in the verandah swing, and she stared at him with a strange look in her eyes. "Sam!" she exclaimed.

He stopped, put a shoulder against the pillar beside the steps. "What is it?"

"Just now . . . sitting here this way . . . I was reminded of that first day, a long time ago. Do you remember?"

He nodded, slowly. "Yeah, I remember. . . ."

★ ★ ★

Coming up those same steps, tall and brown and strong in his youthfulness, and she, sitting in that same swing, brown hair loose about her shoulders, eyes bright, and a charming color in the fresh, soft curve of her cheek. She had spoken his name; with a touch of his hat brim he'd started past toward the door, only to have her call him back again.

"Are you mad at me, Sam?"

He stared at her. "Mad at you, Miss Benton?"

"You never even speak to me any more. I'm sorry if I've done something to offend you. . . ."

Consternation was in him, and he swallowed twice before he could speak. "Gosh, Miss Benton! How could you offend anyone? I been pretty busy, that's all. Your dad's waiting in the house to see me, right now."

"Oh. You better go along then." And the sun came out in her face. "I only wanted to ask you about the hurt foal."

"Why, I'll be glad to take you down to the pasture to see it, later on, if you'd like."

And that was all — just the few, half-stumbling words, and the unspoken thing that passed between them, going deeper than any words. And then the brief, sweet moment ending as Harry Benton came striding to the door looking for his foreman — and the quick suspicion that flashed into the older man's face as he found the pair of them together and read the lost looks in their eyes. . . .

"Yeah," said Sam, and ran his fingers through graying hair. "That was a good many days ago."

"You coming up the steps just now reminded me," said Myra. She rose, went to her husband, and then she kissed him, swiftly, and stepped back. She laughed at the look on his face. "Do you mind so much? I just felt like doing it. . . ."

He couldn't answer. It had been a long, long time since any show of affection had passed between these two.

"I told you to buy some new clothes, Sam," she said suddenly. "I meant it, too. I want you to go right into town and do it . . . this very afternoon! And I'll not have any excuses this time."

A turmoil rode within Sam as he took the trail to Sage Flats under the hot sun. It was not going to be so easy to go away and give up everything. Not the ranch — losing that would mean very little to him. But Myra — Sam realized the truth. He still loved his wife, and, in spite of everything he thought, there was still some tenderness left in her heart for him.

He knew a sudden wild impulse. Defy Homer Lowndes and the second will! Let him produce it — and then let Myra decide. Perhaps — but that would solve nothing. The old problem would be with them again. Myra would be left without her father's ranch, and with a weakling of a husband on her hands.

Sam was swinging down from his bronc' as this truth struck him, his fingers fumbling to knot the reins about the hitch rack before the Shorthorn Bar. A moment later, without quite knowing how he got there, he was leaning on the mahogany with a boot on the rail, and his voice sounded to him like a croak as he ordered: "Whisky!"

The barkeep, knowing him from the old days, gave Sam a hard look, and automatically he dug into a pants pocket, his stubby fingers finding the money Myra had given him. The clothes he needed wouldn't take all of that. He fished out a bill, slapped it down on the bar, and then his first drink in weeks was in his hand and he emptied the glass quickly, set it down gasping for breath.

Above the saloon's swinging doors, across the white-hot blast of the street, he could see the windows of Homer Lowndes's office. How long was it since he had sat in front of Homer's desk and drunk the stingy glassful of liquor Homer offered him? It must be — Good Lord! Day after tomorrow, the three weeks would be up. Then Lowndes would produce that second will, which even now must be waiting in the drawer of his desk where Sam had seen it placed.

A sudden sweat broke out on Sam's forehead as an idea struck him with brutal
force. "You damn' fool," he muttered
softly. "Why hadn't you thought of that?"

*Get to that office, perhaps at night. Pick the
lock on the door some way. Find that will and
destroy it — and then let the ghost of Harry
Benton — and Homer Lowndes, too, try to do
anything about it!*

The idea was so sound, so foolproof,
that it turned Sam all a-tremble. He
needed another drink to steady his nerves
and clear his brain so he could think about
it. He would have to do this very carefully,
not take any chance of being caught. He
motioned to the bartender, got his glass
filled again. "Leave the bottle set there," he
ordered as an afterthought, and lifted the
amber liquid to his mouth. . . .

V

"Hey, Mister Wills! Sam!" The hand was
shaking him again. Sam tried to sit up, but
the pain in his head was too much. Bob
Redpath's urgent voice faded out. Lying
back, Sam tried to figure out where he was
and what was happening. He must have

passed out completely; next thing he knew Bob was back and a hand was under his head, raising him, and there was a pungent, steamy odor in his nostrils.

Bob said: "Come on, drink this, Sam. It's strong, black coffee. It'll do you good."

The last thing in the world he wanted just then was coffee, but the thick china mug was against his lips, insistently, and he gulped it down. He gasped over it, with the bite of the hot liquid eating at the fog that filled his head. Then here came the cup, full again.

"More," insisted Bob. "Drink it up."

"No," groaned Sam, trying to push the cup away. "No, please. . . ."

But it went burning down his throat. He shook his head, ran the back of a hand shakily across his mouth, found the scrape of beard stubble. And then his eyes came open blearily, and the face of Bob Redpath swam slowly into focus. "Where . . . ?" Sam muttered thickly. "What . . . ?"

"You're in Sage Flats," his foreman told him. "Right at the edge of town. I saw your bronc' grazing and found you here in the weeds beside the road."

Sam tried to sit up, to look around, but the effort was too much, and he collapsed against Bob. He ran a furry tongue across his lips. "A drink!" he begged brokenly. "For the love of. . . ."

"No! You've already had too much. I got a whole pot of coffee from the eat shack yonder, and you're gonna drink every drop if it takes that to sober you up. Come on, now!"

There was no resisting that firm voice or the hands that forced the cup against his lips. Sam let the scalding liquid pour into him, then a spasm seized him, and he rolled over face down into the ditch and was sick. He lost all the coffee, and everything else, until his stomach churned on emptiness, and a great weakness and trembling took him.

"Good enough," said Bob grimly. "Now we'll shove some breakfast into you and you'll be good as new."

"Lemme alone!" moaned Sam, his fingers digging at the sandy soil. "I wanna die!"

The other jerked him up, clear to his feet. "Now listen! You got to sober up and pay attention to me. There's been trouble. Cal Tedrow."

That name served to clear Sam's head. Staggering uncertainly on swaying legs, he blinked at the other. "What's he done?" he demanded. "He hurt Myra? Damn you, what's he done?"

"He just turned broncho, is all. Him and his crew made a try last night for that hundred head we're holding for the Wagon Gap shipment. Luckily, I had some men spotted there, and they busted up the raid . . . killed a couple of his riders, and scattered the rest. The sheriff's got a posse on the trail now."

"When . . . when did you say all this was?" Sam demanded.

"Last night." He added dryly: "It's early morning now, you know."

Then, with a groan, Sam saw the pieces begin falling into place. "And I went and fell off my bronc' trying to get home," he said bitterly. "And lay here in a ditch all night . . . while this was going on."

"I found you hadn't been in your room," said Bob. "That's how I came looking for you and caught sight of your bronc'. Now, we got to get you back on your feet *pronto*, and head for home."

"Like this?" Sam looked down at himself, at his clothing foul with filth and mud. He remembered, shoved a hand frantically into his pocket. It was empty.

"Drunk it up!" he exclaimed, self-hatred twisting his wan, bearded face. "The money Myra gave me for new clothes. I can't ever face her again, Bob. I'm no good! I didn't even. . . ." He almost said: I didn't even have the guts to do the job I planned, and rob Lowndes's office. But he held it back.

"Now listen to me, Mister Wills," said Bob earnestly. "I happen to have money with me. We'll get some breakfast. Then, as soon as the store opens, we'll buy you those clothes . . . you can pay me back later. And we'll tell your wife something to explain where you were last night."

"No, no," Sam mumbled, shaking his head in misery. "There's no point in it. Why waste your time, kid?"

But Bob Redpath had a stubborn quality in him, and, when the two of them came to B-in-the-Box in mid-morning, Sam was wearing a new shirt and riding pants, and boots and hat. Sam rode with head sagging, his spirit low.

Myra was waiting in the yard for them, consternation showing in her as she saw Sam's wan, sick face. "Is he hurt?" she demanded.

"No, Miz' Wills," Bob explained. "Your husband's pretty well worn out, is all. He was in the saddle all night trying to overtake Tedrow's crew . . . that's why he never come home."

"Help me get him into the house!" Myra

87

exclaimed. Still weak and shaky, Sam had to let them ease him down from the saddle and then, one on each side, support him as he stumbled up the steps and into the coolness of the house. And then he was in his own room, on the bed, and the new boots were being taken from his feet. "Thanks, Bob," Myra said. The door closed, and they were alone.

On a chair by his bed, Myra had a hand on his hot, dry forehead. And she was saying: "You shouldn't have tried it, Sam. You're not as young as you used to be. And you wouldn't have had a chance if you'd happened to catch up with that gang. But I'm proud of you just the same." She added: "You look mighty nice in your new outfit, too, Sam. But now, you get some rest."

Sam twisted feverishly, overcome with shame. "No, no," he protested. "It ain't true . . . it ain't. . . ." He wanted to blurt out the facts.

"What is it, Sam?" said Myra.

He shook his head. "Nothin'," he muttered. "I dunno what I'm saying."

"You get some sleep," she ordered. At the door she paused. "Can I bring you a little something to eat first? You must be starved, too."

"No! Just . . . leave me alone."

For a long time he lay there, wrestling with a problem that was too much for him. And then at last he slept, a troubled rest, and, when he awoke, night had come again and all was stillness in the dark of the room.

He pawed aside the blankets, dropped his stockinged feet to the floor, and sat up on the edge of the bed. His head ached sharply; he waited a moment for it to clear.

He had slept all day. And tomorrow was the deadline Homer Lowndes had set for him. Well, he knew now what he had to do, and he knew that, somewhere, he had found the strength to accomplish it. He was ravenously hungry, but there was no time to think of food. He got up, padded across the room, and found the lamp on the dresser. He located a match, lighted it.

A clock beside the lamp said ten thirty; he would have to be in town by midnight for that was when the westbound stopped at the depot and took on water at the tower.

A sick-looking face, clouded with day-old beard stubble, peered back at Sam from the mirror above the dresser. He looked down at himself, at the new clothes. And then, in a corner of the room, he spotted the bundle of mud-caked rags that someone must have found tied to the cantle of his saddle, and brought in while he slept, and left here.

Moving hastily, Sam undressed and got into the clammy wreckage of his old clothing. The new garments he rolled up and tied in a bundle, and then as an afterthought he dug out paper and pencil from a drawer of the dresser and leaned to scribble a hasty note:

Bob:

I can't pay you for these but maybe you can sell them and get part of your money back. You shouldn't have bought them. You shouldn't have wasted your time or your lies trying to save me.

The rods is the only place for me and that's where I'm headed. I'm taking one of the horses but I'll leave it at the stable back of the railway station. So long, Bob. When Lowndes comes out tomorrow you'll find out why I'm doing this — for my wife's sake! I'm afraid she might not have made the right choice — that she thinks I'm worth keeping. You and I, though, we know different. We know the truth about me!

I leave the ranch in your hands. They're good ones.

Sam Wills

He folded this, tucked it into a pocket of the shirt where Bob would surely find it. Then, with the bundle under his arm, he tiptoed out.

Bob Redpath slept in the bunkhouse with the rest of the hands. Sam knew that most, if not all, of the half dozen B-in-the-Box riders would be gone from the ranch tonight — some guarding the cattle that Tedrow had almost got away with, others riding with the sheriff's posse if it, indeed, was still in the field. Sam stole out of the house without waking his wife, and then across the dark ranch yard. The bunkhouse door was open. He set the bundle of clothes where Bob couldn't fail to see it, and then he made for the corral.

A number of horses was in the pen. He would find saddle and bridle and blanket in the tack room of the barn, next to it. Sam quietly eased open the barn door, moved into the big room redolent with the odors of hay and grain and animals. The tack room was up front. Sam walked into it — and straight into a gun barrel that rammed hard against his belly.

Tedrow's voice said: "We was beginning to think maybe you weren't headed this way after all, Sam."

He sucked in breath, sharply. "Tedrow," he muttered. "What are you doing here?"

"It's as good a place as any, ain't it, with the law out in the hills looking for us?"

"You're through in this country," said Sam. "Don't you know that?"

He heard the fury behind the other's reply: "Yeah . . . thanks to you, you worthless bum! But me, I don't care to leave empty-handed . . . not when there's a safe full of cash that I might just as well tap, first. That's why we doubled back and stopped off here."

"Are you talking about . . . ?"

"Shut up!" the ex-foreman growled. He added: "Search the guy, Nick, and see he ain't got a gun on him."

Rough hands seized Sam, felt for a weapon. "Nothin', Cal."

"All right," said Tedrow. "Start walking, mister. And no noise."

Halfway through the big building they hauled up suddenly. One of the men whispered: "Somebody coming."

"In here . . . quick." Sam was pushed bodily into a stall, and the others crowded in after him. A man's figure blocked out the opening of the barn's doorway, then Bob Redpath called softly: "Sam. Mister Wills!"

The gun in his ribs, and the harsh breathing of Tedrow against his ear, held Sam taut and silent. The man at the door said: "Are you still here, Sam? I woke up, and I found the note you left. You're making an awful mistake, Sam. Believe me, you are."

The silence ran out; no sound except the scurrying of a rat somewhere in the hay. Suddenly Bob came running by them, and into the tack room. He came out again, and they could tell he was lugging a heavy saddle with him. And then he had left the barn, and the one called Nick said tightly: "Maybe we should 'a' stopped him, Cal. Maybe he guessed something."

"No he didn't," Sam said hastily. "He just decided I had already left, and he's saddling a bronc' to ride to Sage Flats and try and head me off."

Cal Tedrow said: "All right. We'll just wait here a few minutes."

And presently a horse left the corral, and the sound of its hoof beats drummed away to silence, and then Sam knew that except for himself and Myra, and maybe the old crippled cook, the ranch was now deserted.

"OK," grunted Tedrow. "Let's go!"

They moved across the darkness of the yard — Tedrow, and Sam, and two of Harry Benton's renegade hands. When they reached the new wing of the house, Tedrow said: "We'll try this side door. If it's locked, we can force a window."

But the door was open, and they trooped through it silently. Tedrow closed and locked the hall door and said softly: "Light a lamp, somebody. We'll just make ourselves at home."

Nick got the wick burning. He was a big-boned, towheaded waddy; the third man Sam recognized as a skinny hand who was generally known as Rooster.

Sam faced Tedrow now in the lamplight, and he knew he made a shabby, unimpressive appearance. But he said stoutly: "You can't get away with it!"

"Cut out the nonsense!" growled the ex-foreman, and he shoved Sam around toward the iron box safe in the corner of the room. "Get over there and open that tin can for us, real quick."

Sam shook his head. "But I . . . I don't know the combination to that safe."

"You don't?"

Rooster snorted. "He's lyin'."

"No . . . no, maybe not." Tedrow looked

very sour. "Come to think of it, if that wife of his has got any brains in her skull, she wouldn't tell this booze hound how to get to her money."

"Then what'll we do?" demanded Nick.

"Fetch the woman in here," answered Tedrow. "We can make her tell us the combination."

Sam choked out: "No. . . ." But no one paid him any attention.

Suddenly Rooster was saying: "Boss, I think I can open this crackerbox by touch. Just be quiet a minute and lemme hear the tumblers fall. . . ."

He was on his knees in front of the safe, a look of pained concentration on his bony features, working the dial with deft, lean fingers. The other two were watching him, waiting, all their attention on Rooster's effort.

Sam was thinking of Harry Benton's will — how it said that Myra would have to be a widow to inherit B-in-the-Box. He was thinking just then that there was more than one way to make a widow out of a woman. And the thought made him suddenly reckless, suddenly indifferent to whatever might happen to himself.

Nick was standing next to him, eyes trained on Rooster and the safe, and the gun butt in Nick's holster was thrust, invitingly, almost into Sam's fingers. Very calmly Sam pulled it out, and, before Nick could do more than give a startled squawk, the barrel of his own weapon was laid across the side of his head and he dropped cold, striking a corner of the roll-top desk. The safe had swung open, and Rooster was reaching for the metal cash box as Nick's fall interrupted him. He whirled, startled, and the box dropped to the carpet followed by a snow of papers. Rooster was digging for his own revolver. Sam squeezed the trigger. The concussion of the shot was terrific in that closed space. Sam had not fired a gun in years, but he had a feeling that his bullet had gone home even before he saw Rooster sag against the safe.

Then Tedrow hit him with a heavy fist that took Sam across the side of the face. Sam went down. His fingers opened, letting the gun drop. But in agony he held on to consciousness and would not go clear under. He was rolling as he hit the floor, and he just missed the toe of the boot that Tedrow aimed at Sam's face. He caught that boot in his hands, instead, and with what little strength he had in him Sam gave Tedrow's leg a jerk.

It was just enough to throw him off balance, to swing him around clutching at the desk for support. His hand struck the kerosene lamp, sent it crashing over in a spray of broken glass and burning oil. And then he, too, hit the floor, and Sam threw himself at him.

Somewhere in the house he heard Myra screaming, calling his name. He could not think about that. Tedrow was more than he could handle — a tough frame of bone and sinew, and hands that could beat and batter the other man's soft body. Sam endured that punishment, tried to hold Tedrow, and drive home a blow that could have some effect on him. His fists bounced off the man like rubber, harmlessly. Tedrow had lost his gun, but he wouldn't need it. Grappling there on the floor of the office, Sam could see him faintly — black hair streaming into a sweating face, eyes glistening.

But how *could* he see? Sam knew, then. The lamp! It had smashed, and burning oil had ignited dry timbers. Flames were running halfway up the ceiling, in that corner. They had caught the drapes Myra had hung at the window, and found here new fuel. The whole wing would go, the entire house. . . .

Desperation gave Sam new strength to

battle the darkness that Tedrow's blows were putting inside him. He felt the man's cheek splat beneath one knuckle-bruising blow — that had been a good one. He broke loose, rolled, felt the edge of the heavy desk cutting into his shoulder. Tedrow, coming to his knees, dived forward.

At the last second Sam twisted, let the man go past him against the desk. Tedrow dropped with a groan. At once Sam was on him, pounding Cal's head against the desk — again and again, until the man was still.

Staggering, he came to his feet in a nightmare of leaping flames and dancing shadows. Beyond the door of the office Myra was calling his name. "Stay back!" he cried through the thin partition, his voice a croak. "Get help . . . water! Before this fire spreads!"

On the floor were the huddled shapes of three men. He couldn't leave them here. Sam grabbed a chair and smashed the window. Air rushing in fanned the flames to new fury, and the curtains swayed, dripping fire. Sam got a grip under Tedrow's armpits and dragged him to the opening. Somehow he shoved him through the opening. There were two others left.

Firebrands were swirling around him, and

he was staggering, coughing on wood smoke, when the last man was saved. After that he went to hands and knees, groping, found the cash box where Rooster had dropped it. There were papers, too — deeds, letters, old tally books. He couldn't save them all. But he got an armful of them, and the box, and then he stumbled to the window, and he went through it head first, out of that room choked with smoke and flame. He dived through the shattered window as though into cool water, but it was hard earth that received him.

VI

He was in his own bed again. The biting smell of wood smoke was everywhere. His face and his hands felt stiff and hot with burning fire; he stared dumbly at white bandages, not quite registering yet what had happened, or how he came to be here.

Myra said: "I taped up the blisters with tea leaves. That ought to take the burn out of them."

Sam saw her, then, kneeling beside him. It was daylight. "Did . . . did you get the fire put out?" he demanded anxiously.

"Yes . . . the cook and I . . . and some of the boys were close enough to see the reflection in the sky, and they rode in fast. We lost the new wing, but the rest of the house will be all right with some patching."

Sam said quickly: "You got the money?"

"Oh, yes! And Cal Tedrow and the other two . . . they've already been taken in to jail. Oh, Sam!" Tears were in her eyes and her voice. "I'm proud of you. The world will know, now, that I haven't been mistaken in you all these years."

"Now, wait," he stated miserably. "Night before last. . . ."

"Forget night before last," she retorted, smiling. "Did you think I'd never seen you with a hangover before? But you can't explain away what happened in the office. Why, I wouldn't trade you, Sam, for any man I've ever known."

What he might have said to that was broken off by a voice sounding in the doorway. "Am I interrupting something?" It was Homer Lowndes, his yellow features broken in a smug smile of pleasure, and then Sam remembered what day this was.

"Well, well," said the lawyer, and the look he laid on Sam was a sardonic one. "Looks like our little man has turned into a hero overnight. Yes, sir, the whole damn' range is talking about you."

"Skip the humor," growled Sam, and he braced himself. "Just hurry up and tell us what you come out here for this morning."

The face dropped its smiling mask. "All right, I'll do that. From what I was told by my predecessor in the law office at Sage Flats, there's reason to believe that Harry Benton must have left another will . . . later than the one I filed three weeks ago. I've been worried about it. So I came here today to make a final search and see if I couldn't find it among his papers."

"Another will?" repeated Myra blankly.

"You heard him," Sam muttered. "Well go ahead and look, damn you!"

"Oh, I already have," said Homer blandly. "You know, that was a bad fire you had last night. If such a will ever did exist, it must have got burnt to ashes. I couldn't find a trace."

Dumbly Sam Wills heard him, and it took a long moment for the meaning of what the lawyer had said to strike home. But then he caught the wink Homer gave him, and he thought: *Good Lord! The old devil's got a heart, after all.*

Lowndes was saying: "Even if Harry did

intend a different way of disposing of his estate, seems to me this was still the best way it could have worked out. I reckon the ranch is in good enough hands." He smiled at both of them. "Good day, Sam. Good day, Missus Wills. I won't be bothering you any more."

Sam lay back on the pillow, and his wife's hand was on his shoulder. Sam did not say anything. He was too full of wonder and happiness for speech.

The Taming of Johnny Peters

From its beginning, the Western has been enlivened from time to time by a stream of genial humor, often bordering on farce, that first appears in Mark Twain's tale of the jumping frog, to resurface in the Wolfville stories of Alfred Henry Lewis, in Owen Wister, and in bunkhouse banter among the ranch hands of the Flying U and the old Bar 20. (Asked why he smokes so many cigarettes, one of Mulford's cowpokes answers: "I like the way they strangle me.") During the 1920s, pulp magazine readers cherished the comic writings of Roland Krebs, Ray Humphrey, Robert Ormond Case, W. C. Tuttle, and perhaps the best of them all — Alan LeMay. (Try *Bug Eye* and also *Useless Cowboy* which was the source of Hollywood's *Along Came Jones* with Gary Cooper — for me, still the funniest Western-movie spoof of them all.) More recently, in novels, we've enjoyed Charles Portis's *True Grit* and Elmer Kelton's *The Good Old Boys*, and have seen humor and tragedy effectively blended in Larry McMurtry's Pulitzer Prize winner, *Lonesome Dove*. On not quite so lofty a level, here's one of my own efforts in a comic vein, from the 1940s pulps. I had fun writing this.

I

Johnny Peters, night wrangler for the Big M trail drive, Kansas-bound, was but seventeen and as green as they come. This was his first trip up the Chisholm, and in preparation he had blown in more than he could afford on a fancy outfit.

He had shiny, gooseneck spurs, with rowels like silver dollars. Brand new boots and jeans. A red silk shirt with blue piping on the cuffs and pockets, blue neck cloth, and pinto horsehide vest and cream-colored Stetson. The kid's saddle was a second-hand rig but not too bad bunged up, and he kept it oiled and polished. And there was a wide belt and holster, and a rubber-handled Colt six-shooter that he'd had out of leather a couple of times, plugging away at prairie chickens and a hawk or two. But Sam Martin, his boss, had called a halt on gun-firing near the herd. Caused stampedes, he said.

He cut a real figure of a cowpuncher,

though, did Johnny, with all the slick sur-
faces shining like mirrors when he forked
his buckskin gelding. Only trouble was, he
held the night wrangler's job, and that
meant loose-herding the cavvy after dark
and spending his days sleeping in the
bedroll wagon — or trying to — and
helping the cook rustle wood, water, and
cow chips for the cooney sack. Which was
the closest Johnny Peters had got so far to
being a cowhand.

The cook he worked for was a tough
character named Peewee Long — six foot
two, with arms the size of another man's
leg and a mean disposition. His eyes had
lighted with unholy joy the first time they
spotted Johnny; in fact, having the kid
around to browbeat seemed the only thing
that made being a cook bearable for him at
all. It was especially fun to roust Johnny
out of uncomfortable sleep in the jouncing
bedroll caboose, and put him at some work
or other.

Like today, when he closed a ham-like
fist around the youngster's ankle and all
but hauled him bodily out from under the
canvas. "On your pins, cowboy! Got a big
chore for you!"

Johnny groaned, and clambered out of
the wagon. The only man in the outfit, he

figured, expected to work all night and all day, too. Maybe the boss had him confused with two other fellows. . . . But he never yet had made an issue of the thing, mainly because the cook gave the impression that it wouldn't be wise to open his yap.

He said: "What do you want done, Peewee?"

The boss had picked his spot for the night camp, and the chuck wagon was drawn up near a spring where there was a nice stand of cottonwood and willow. By the time the herd caught up and went on to the bed ground, supper would be on the fire. Already the sun was dragging low over the flat, flat prairie. Coming toward the end of a hot, sultry day on the Chisholm.

Peewee shoved a slab-like thumb toward the trees stirring in a faint breeze down by the creek. "Some down timber, there . . . could make firewood for the next several days. I want you to chop me up enough to last."

"Our axe is busted," Johnny Peters said, scowling at the trees. Fine job for a cowpuncher!

"Don't matter. I spotted one of them nester places just off the trail, a few miles back. They're bound to have an axe. Go

106

borrow it . . . and don't take all day, either!"

Johnny said, casting about for some way out of this: "I been told some of these Kansas sodbusters don't cotton to us Texans. Maybe they won't loan me their axe."

"You heard me!" the big guy cut him off. "Get goin'! I don't want to see you back here, empty-handed!"

So Johnny Peters hauled out saddle and gear and piled them onto his buckskin that trailed the wagons on a whale line. He gave his hat a brush with his sleeve, tucked in the tail of the red shirt. Minutes later he was jingling off across the level land — a skinny, towheaded youngster who sported a few dozen hairs so far toward a mustache, his trappings all a-shine in the late sunlight.

Within him, fruitless rebellion stirred. Johnny Peters, ace cowpuncher — off to borrow some nester's axe and use it chopping firewood for that ham-fisted cook!

The homestead was about what he'd have expected: a sod house and barn, already beginning to settle in on themselves, a few chickens running around. There were people in the house — in fact, some sort of discussion seemed to be afoot. A tumble of voices issued through the open door and window, pitched high with emotion and showing no regard for parliamentary procedure. Johnny drew up at a little distance to think things over, some distance from the dooryard, and sat there considering and blinking into the torrent of sound the way you do into a high wind.

He couldn't make out anything that was said, but there must be at least four men inside there and a couple of women. And every one of them spitting mad and trying to yell down all the rest. Johnny Peters frowned a little. "The way those folks are rowin'," he muttered, "was they an axe in the house, I don't think it would be such a good idea to remind anybody of it."

Listening to the racket, he shifted uneasily in saddle and hooked one knee over the horn while he got out the makings and rolled a smoke. He wasn't much good at that yet, and he spilled tobacco all over him when the paper disintegrated. Thoughtfully he brushed the ruins of the quirly off his pinto vest and ran the back of a hand across his mouth.

Next to the house he spotted a woodpile and an axe canted against it, the head gleaming in the late sun. He looked at it a long minute, but, after all, he couldn't just ride up and take it, and something made him mighty reluctant to mix, even by the slightest amount, into that free-for-all tongue ruckus raging in the shack. He didn't want any nearer to that than he already was.

Suddenly something went *smash!* And the wreckage of a china plate came scattering out through the window. The voices surged to new heights. At that, Johnny Peters discreetly unhitched his knee, shoved his boot with the shiny spur rowel into stirrup, and, speaking to the buckskin, started away from there at a good clip, looking back only when he was a quarter mile away.

All in all, he hadn't seen hide or hair of the people in the nester shack; he doubted if, engrossed as they were in their wrangling, anybody had noticed as he rode up and then left again. And, all in all, he was just as pleased to leave it like that.

But he had reckoned without Peewee. When he came back to the wagon, the cook was standing beside the big wheel waiting for him, huge fists planted on his hips, a dirty apron wrapped around his middle. Peewee looked over his outfit. "Where's the axe?" he demanded harshly.

Johnny opened his mouth, closed it

again. For a minute he looked at Peewee, and Peewee Long glared back, face turning an ugly color. Johnny Peters swallowed, finally.

"I knew I forgot something," he muttered.

And he turned his bronc' around and started off across the prairie again. A screech went up behind him. "Why, you no-good, dumb kid!" the beefy cook shouted. "You dare to come back here without an axe, I'll. . . ." He went into lurid details.

Presently the voice dropped behind Johnny, and there was silence except the swish of dry grass about the hocks of his pony. Johnny was sweating a little and feeling pretty low. Trouble, front and back of him. And hard to tell which looked the most dangerous. He knew for sure he didn't want to mix into that nesters' battle, but he didn't want the bully cook mopping up ground with him, either.

So he came in on the nester shack again, and the voices were still yelling without any let-up. The sun was dragging down, and a red tinge hung in the long, slanting light. Johnny pulled in and this time swung himself from saddle, kept his bony legs working right across the hard-packed dirt to the open door. The angry voices tumbled around him. He knocked a couple of times on the doorpost, but he didn't think anyone could hear that. He cleared his throat and said: "Hi, folks."

Nobody heard that either, because just as he spoke, his voice was drowned by the crash of a chair being booted across the room. A big bear of a gent, prowling back and forth in front of the far window, had kicked it aside when it got in the way of his pacing. There were three others, all as big as the first one. They were all of them striding around in there, great hulking figures that seemed to fill the crowded space, and they were waving their arms and bellowing all at once.

The one who had kicked the chair looked like he might be the old man of the other three. Now he yelled — "Shut up!" — and suddenly the others quit their hollering.

A heavy silence fell. The old man stood glaring around at his sons. He had a foul-looking pipe stuck into a parting of his heavy black beard, and he jerked this out with a hand about twice the size of Peewee Long's. Pointing with it at somebody across the room, he said: "There's been altogether too much talk around here. But this is final . . . no Tompkins woman is throwin' herself away on no dirty cowpuncher! Just git the notion out of your fool head, Suella! And let's not have no more fuss about it!"

Johnny followed the line of the pipe stem, and saw the girl. She was a little thing, gingham-dressed, pretty in a corn-yellow haired way, and she was standing with her head up, leaning back against the edge of a crude homemade table. There was a second woman in the room, too, rocking back and forth in a rocking chair in the corner. She was old and shriveled-up looking — maybe the mother of the girl and the three younger men.

The girl said stoutly: "Paw, I'd even marry a Injun to get away from this ornery household! I'm just plumb sick of it here. But that ain't the point! There ain't no cowboy on my string . . . I'm not fixing to run away!"

"Quit lying!" said one of the younger men. "Rafe heard what he heard and seen what he seen! He knows you was in the thicket last evening with some gent you called Bill . . . somebody who's coming back today to fetch you away, with all your belongings, and take you somewhere and marry up with you!"

"Yeah, don't try denying it!" put in Rafe Tompkins, glowering at his sister. "I know the guy was a cowboy because I seen the size of his hat and heard his spurs clinking. Had I been a-wearing my gun. . . ." He patted the huge hogleg strapped in a holster to his thick, overalled leg.

"The hell with shooting such a skunk!" yelled the third brother. "Farmers and cowmen don't mix and ain't ever going to. If that sneaking cowhand so much as shows his face here again. . . ." He looked down at his spread fingers, a wicked grin on his bearded mouth as he slowly twisted the thick fingers into hard, tight balls. And then he lifted his eyes, and, still standing that way with his fists clenched and his brute shoulders leaning forward and bulging with taut cords of muscle, he looked and saw Johnny Peters in the doorway. A grunt exploded between his lips.

The rest of them turned then, and silence clamped down like a lid on a box. With all their eyes on him, Johnny Peters stood there resplendent in the sunset in his red silk shirt and horsehide vest, his spurs flashing light. He put up a hand, touched the brim of his big new Stetson. " 'Evening, folks," he said.

Nobody answered him for a long moment. The old woman in the corner kept creaking her rocker back and forth, jerkily, but no one else moved. Then the brother called Rafe straightened slowly. He said: "You want something . . . *cowboy?*"

"Why, yeah," said Johnny. He didn't like the man's tone, but he answered pleasantly enough. "I come to try and get. . . ."

With a roar the old man smashed his pipe down on the puncheon floor. "You come for Suella, maybe?" he shouted. "You come fixing to take an old man's only daughter from him . . . from her home, and the folks that love her. Why, you low-down. . . ."

Johnny got the drift then, and it sent him backing out of the doorway on shaky legs. "Hey! Wait!" he cried. "You got the wrong cowpoke! I'm just a stranger here. I ain't the one you think!"

But he never had a chance to make that stick.

"Oh, Bill! Bill, darling!" The girl in the gingham dress was running at him, dodging the hand one of her brothers flung out to stop her. Before Johnny Peters knew what was happening, both her arms were around his neck. "They found out, Bill . . . they won't let me do it. You'll have to go without me!" And as he tried to yelp some-

114

thing, she slapped a wet kiss on his mouth and then whispered tensely: "Get on your horse, mister, and ride! Please!"

"I ain't your Bill darling!" cried Johnny desperately, tearing loose. "I never laid eyes on you before!"

One of the brothers let out a bellow of rage. "So *that's* your game!" he thundered. "Crawling out from under your promises already! Why, I'll rip your hide!"

"Go it, Milt!" called one of the others, and then Milt Tompkins was charging out of the shack, pushing his sister to one side while his big fist reached for Johnny Peters.

Johnny ducked and it scorched air. The rest of the farmers were pouring out of the house now, although that old woman never budged out of her rocker in the far corner of the room. Maybe she was growed to it. Suella Tompkins had her hands pressed against her cheeks, a look of terror in her pretty eyes, but Johnny was too busy all of a sudden to pay her much attention.

A second swipe from Milt's fist caught him solidly in the chest and sent him back-pedaling, until he tripped on one of his big spurs and sat down, hard. Dust *whooshed* out from under him, and a couple of the scrawny chickens that had nearly been caught went scattering and squawking.

Milt came on, swinging a heavy farmer's shoe. Dazed as he was, Johnny managed to roll with the kick, and it missed by inches. Then he had his hands and knees under him and scrambled up, still moving away.

Behind Milt his father and the others were circling, trying to get in and join the murder. Four of them! Johnny Peters faded back fast, all the time trying to make them see they were making a bad mistake. But his frantic words did no good at all. Milt got a second blow across, and Johnny's head rang like a bell as it connected. He drew another bruising wallop, in the ribs, before he could break away from the slower-moving, clumsy Tompkins crew.

He wanted to get to his bronc', but a glance showed him they had him cut off from that direction. Next moment Johnny happened to catch sight of a man who leaped out the barn door and went sprinting away around the corner of it, un-observed by any of the Tompkins men.

Something told him who that gent had to be. But he was too out of breath to make a noise, and, before he could call the Tompkins' attention to him, the man from the barn had got clean away into a thicket of brush and trees lining a gully not far from the buildings. He had a horse tied there and in a matter of seconds was up and heading north at a clean gallop that quickly faded away.

And still none of the Tompkins family seemed aware of him except for Suella, who had been watching her Bill darling make his getaway with tense anxiety in every line of her young and shapely figure. Seeing he was safely gone, she simply turned around and went back into the house. Johnny Peters was left to face his doom.

The men folk had him pinned behind the well now, circling frantically around it as they tried to corner him. Once they did, he didn't see that he had a chance of saving life or limb. *Plague take that girl, anyway!* he thought bitterly. Johnny was young, and no one had ever warned him that a female with a pretty face and figure was capable of hanging the Injun sign on an innocent man as heartlessly and without conscience, as Suella Tompkins had just now hung it on *him*. . . .

Blam!

A deafening roar ripped the late afternoon apart. Everybody jerked around, and there was Suella, back again, holding a double-snouted shotgun. One of its muzzles dribbled smoke as, just overhead, a stinking black balloon slowly dissipated. Into the echoes of the weapon's blast the girl yelled a warning: "Don't make me use the other barrel! Paw, I want you and Rafe and Job and Milton to back off and let this fellow alone. He ain't Bill Cary."

"We're apt to believe that, I guess," her brother Rafe snorted. "After you throwin' yourself at him, and a-kissin' him?"

But Johnny had seen his chance, and he snatched at it. He turned and bolted for his horse. Big Rafe was right at his heels, outstretched fingers grabbing for him, but Johnny ran like a jack rabbit and threw himself into saddle. It so happened that he came at the buckskin from the off side, and being a good cow pony the bronc' objected to that and started bucking. But every buck jump took him farther from Rafe's reaching grasp, and, somehow, Johnny hung on and got settled in the hull.

Belatedly then he remembered the rubber-butted six-gun in his holster. He pawed at it a couple times and dragged it out. "Git back!" he shouted. "Git away from me, all you hellions!"

And sight of the gun did haul up the angry quartet in their tracks, to stand staring at him with hungry looks on their faces and hands yearning to rip him in two.

Panting, Johnny sat in saddle and felt the blood trickle down from his nose. Suella came running barefoot through the ranks of her men folk, the shotgun dragging down her small hand.

"You especially!" Johnny snapped at her. "You're poison, and I don't want another thing to do with you!"

But she grabbed his stirrup and hung on, looking up at him in her gingham dress, her yellow hair down in a cloud around her shoulders, her big blue eyes troubled. "I'm awful sorry, mister," she panted. "Honest I am!" At the same moment, he saw she had a folded piece of paper, and with a sneaky movement she tucked it into the top of Johnny's boot and after that, smiling a little frightened smile, moved back away from his horse.

Her father gritted tightly: "Mister, if I ever git my hands on you. . . ."

"Aw, shut up!"

Johnny Peters had all of that family he wanted, and with his horse between his legs, distance was a very attractive thing just then. He said: "If me and any of the Tompkins ever meet up again, it won't be any of *my* doin's . . . that's a promise. Good bye, and the hell with you!"

He raked the buckskin with his big spurs

and lined out toward the blood-red sunset. He was a couple of miles away before he realized he'd forgotten something again.

The axe!

"Don't bother comin' back without it," Peewee Long had warned him. With a groan Johnny Peters pulled in and sat wondering what he ought to do. He ran a wrist across his mouth and got blood in the red silk sleeve. He for sure wasn't going back to that homestead shack again, and on the other hand he couldn't face Peewee empty-handed. It was what you'd call a dilemma.

Then something made him think of the piece of paper Suella Tompkins had tucked into his boot top, and he leaned over and got it out. The thing, he saw, was a note, hastily pencil-scribbled in a round, girlish hand. On the outside fold it said: Pleez find Bill Cary and give him this. Probly headed for Plains City. Pleez as it is a mater of life and death!

Scowling, Johnny unfolded the scrap of paper and read the note inside:

Bill deerest,

I'm glad you made it out of the barn all rite. They wood have killed you had they of noen.

If you receive this be in the thiket tonight at nine thirty I will be there packd and redy to ride and get married up with you.

Love,
Suella

Disgust filled Johnny Peters as he finished reading. "Of all the unprincipled females!" he snorted. "She deliberately sicced her men folks onto me so as to give her boyfriend a chance to sneak out of hiding . . . and now I'm supposed to deliver his mail!" He shook his head. "She must think I'm the world's most complete idjit!"

But though his impulse was to wad up the note and throw it away into the prairie grass, somehow he didn't. Something in the note had given him a sudden inspiration.

"Plains City," he muttered. "Now, I wonder how far that might be? If it ain't too much of a piece, I could maybe ride there and buy an axe. And in the meantime, should I run into this Bill character I suppose it wouldn't hurt me none to just hand him the note. After all, that gal is depending on me." He added grimly: "And maybe I'd like a closer look at this Bill Cary, anyway. Maybe I ought to kind of

121

sock him in the nose on general principles, for the beatin' I took that was supposed to have been his!"

That consideration made up his mind for him. He tucked the note into his shirt pocket and kicked up his bronc' again, this time swinging north and wide of the Tompkins homestead. It was getting dusky, but he calculated he could pick up Bill Cary's trail, and it would likely head him straight toward the town he wanted. After that, he'd just see what he would do about things.

He found the tracks without any difficulty, and, before the light got too dim to follow them, they led him into a wagon trail angling off across the Kansas flatlands. With this to guide him, Johnny Peters made better time. Some of the slow prairie dusk was still in the sky when he sighted a glimmer of lamplight ahead of him.

Plains City was not much — a mere handful of sod and tarpaper buildings, scattered antigodlin fashion across the wastes. Johnny looked them over, hunting a hardware store or some such place that might still be open and where he might be able to buy an axe. He only knew for sure he would have to finish his business here pretty *pronto,* because he was already going to be dog-gone late getting back to the Big M herd. Peewee Long wasn't above letting him go out on nighthawk duty with an empty stomach, if the cook got mad enough — and he was most likely pawing the ground by now.

But right offhand Johnny didn't spot what he was looking for. He did see a line of horses, though, racked in front of a cheap-looking saloon. And in the filter of lamplight through its doors and windows the bronc' on the near end looked like it might be the one the gent in the barn had ridden away on. Well, it wouldn't take long to find out. Johnny Peters swung down at a neighboring tie-pole and rang his silver spurs into the deadfall.

There were about a dozen men in the smoky, lamp-lit room, some playing cards, others lined along the pine-plank bar, drinking. A nondescript bunch — they might be a crowd of frontier riff-raff, or they might be cowhands from some tough trail crew that had been paid off at Ellsworth and were drifting south again.

As Johnny stood in the doorway, looking them over, he drew hard stares from the men. One of those at the bar squared around and grunted in a flat voice: "Well, how about it, kid? Were you wanting anything in particular?"

His voice lacked friendliness. Johnny said: "Why, yeah. I'm looking for a fellow named Bill Cary."

He saw suspicion run quickly into the eyes staring at him. The one who had spoken exchanged a quick glance with his neighbors, then speared Johnny with a harsh question: "What you want with Bill?"

"I . . . I got a message for him."

There was a moment's silence while the whole room seemed concentrated on the slim kid in the doorway, and Johnny Peters felt definitely uncomfortable. Then the man who had questioned him shrugged and said: "Try the eat shack. Two doors up."

Johnny murmured his thanks and got out of there hurriedly. One tough crew, he thought, and apparently friends of Bill Cary's. Maybe he had better reconsider and not give this Bill *hombre* the bust in the nose he had contemplated. On the other hand, it occurred to him that maybe he hadn't ought to deliver Suella Tompkins's note, either. If the crowd he ran with was any indication, Bill Cary wasn't the type for a young female like

Suella to go eloping with. . . .

But then, Johnny asked himself, just why the hell should that cut any ice with him? What business was it of his who that nester brat threw herself away on? After the near murder she'd gone and wished off on one Johnny Peters that evening. . . . Deliberately he moved up street until he spotted the eat shack and, through a flyspecked window, saw Bill Cary eating at a table near the door.

Yes, it was the gent from the barn — a slim, darkly handsome young man on closer inspection. Just the kind that would appeal to an ignorant homesteader's girl. Fishing out the note, Johnny strode inside and tossed it down on the oilcloth table cover.

Bill Cary stopped eating to look at it, and then he lifted cold, smoky gray eyes to flick across Johnny's features. "What's this?" he grunted.

"What's it look like?" retorted Johnny. "A note from that Tompkins girl."

"Oh." The man gave his full attention now. "You must be that fellow I seen her throw to the wolves, to help cover my getaway." And he snickered.

Color poured up into Johnny's face. "I see you laughing," he said tightly, "but I ain't heard the joke yet! If you think there was anything funny about. . . ."

"Oh, set down!" grunted Cary, and turned his attention back to the note. He picked up a coffee cup and emptied it nonchalantly while he worked his way through Suella's badly spelled message.

Left standing there across the table from him, Johnny didn't know why but he accepted Cary's order. He pulled out a chair and let himself into it woodenly. He got out tobacco and papers and began another attempt at a cigarette. When it went to pieces on him, he brushed off the crumbs, stuffed the makings back into his pocket.

"You gonna keep that date to get married?" he asked.

The good-looking gent shrugged. "I wouldn't mind," he grunted, "but right now I'm broke. Got on a tough streak of cards last night and lost my roll. I rode out there this afternoon to tell the gal the deal was off, but her folks was waiting with shotguns and I just managed to sneak into that damn' barn before they caught me."

Johnny frowned. "What are you gonna do about this note? You wouldn't stand her up, would you . . . leave her waiting there in the thicket tonight at nine-thirty?"

"I ain't goin' nowhere near that farm full

of wild men," grunted Bill Cary. He gave Johnny a searching look. "Say, kid, how about you taking her back a message for me?"

"Whoa, now!" Johnny Peters started up. "I'm no more ready to commit suicide than *you* are! Remember, they think I'm the one that. . . ."

The dark-haired man waved a hand. " 'S all right. Relax. I see what you mean." He was considering Johnny with greater interest now, and with amusement in his dark and cynical face. "Just who the hell *are* you? Some guy looking for a job?"

"No," said Johnny. "I got a job . . . with a trail herd, going through to Ellsworth." He didn't specify just what the job entailed, but it was somehow mollifying to have a grown-up fellow paying him this much attention.

Bill Cary gave the kid's fancy rigging another glance. "You're sure made up like a fine cowhand," he admitted. "What outfit did you say that was?"

"The Big M. from Texas." Johnny told him some more about the herd and where it would be bedding down that night. "Which reminds me," he exclaimed, starting up from his chair, "I got to be getting back. The cook . . . I mean, my boss will be wondering what become of me. Important special errand, he sent me on."

"I see." Cary tossed silver onto the table, and got up, too. His manner was friendly enough now, although his eyes had a look as though he might be thinking distant thoughts of his own. "I'll just walk along the street with you," he said.

It was pitch dark when they left the eat shack. "Is that a pretty good-size herd you're handling?" Cary asked offhandedly, sauntering alongside Johnny.

"Two thousand head."

"How many riders?"

"Eight."

"Uhn-huh." They had passed the saloon, where raucous laughter and talk flowed out upon the night. Except for him and Cary, no one showed on the street just then.

The kid stepped to his buckskin, reached to snag the stirrup. "Well," he said, "this is where I leave you."

"You're damn' right!" And before Johnny could duck the half-seen glimmer of the barrel, Bill Cary's stealthily drawn six-gun came crashing down hard on the kid's skull.

He came to in wet and silent darkness, with a headache that felt like somebody splitting his cranium open under regular blows of mallet and wedge. Johnny Peters lay for a long time wondering where he was and what had happened to him. Finally, as his head began to clear some, he remembered vaguely walking along with Bill Cary while the gent pumped him for information about the Big M trail herd.

He fumbled at his hair, found blood where the scalp was broken. There was cold dampness on other parts of his body. Gradually he figured it out that he was lying in an alley somewhere, half propped against an overturned rain barrel. The barrel must have had water in it, and whoever had dragged him back here had accidentally kicked it over in the dark.

Johnny pushed himself to his feet and leaned against the wall until strength came back a little. His six-gun was still in its holster, undamaged, but water and mud had wrecked his nice red shirt with the blue piping and the pinto horsehide vest. Right then he wasn't able to worry much about his regalia.

Sometimes a kid grows up in a minute or two, and something like that happened to Johnny when that six-gun crashed against his skull. Because now he was thinking like a man, and understanding a lot of things that had passed completely over his head not long before. He thought he knew, now, why Bill Cary had been probing him for information about the Big M. He knew, too, why the night seemed so unnaturally quiet. . . .

Staggering along the alleyway, he gained the street and saw that the line of horses that had been racked in front of the saloon was gone, along with the men who had been roistering inside, last thing he knew. He didn't think he needed to be told where they were off to.

Bill Cary had admitted to being broke and on the make for quick money. Those friends of his were all toughs of the same stripe, and they would outnumber the Big M crew nearly two to one. Easy enough for them to hit Martin's resting herd, if they were of a mind to, and bust it up. Start it stampeding, smoke it out with the defending trail crew, and then, later, gather up as much of the scattered herd as they wanted and dispose of it with some crooked buyer or Indian agent.

Thinking like a man, Johnny Peters figured this all out for himself. He also tried to figure out how long he'd been lying in the alley, dead to the world. That wasn't so easy. But it would have taken some time for Bill Cary to get his men together and outline his scheme, and even then it wasn't likely they would ride directly against the herd. Probably they'd wait until the bulk of the crew was in the blankets and the first watch out on the bed grounds.

Anyway, by the youngster's reasoning, there was at least a chance of getting there before it was all over — maybe even in time to give the alarm.

His buckskin was still tied where he had left it. Johnny piled into saddle and went out of that sleepy town hell for leather, pointing as best he could toward the unsuspecting trail herd.

The buckskin was tiring when Johnny sighted the lamp-lit window of the Tompkins shack, winking at him across the plain. He would have liked to stop and try for a remount, but he wasn't fool enough to do it. He gave the nester place a wide berth, instead, and kept going, easing in now and again to let the horse take a breather while he listened tensely for any sound of gunfire or running cattle.

It all looked quiet enough when he sighted the Big M cattle bedded down under stars, and a thin sickle of new moon gave the campfire a cherry glow with the cocoon-like shapes of riders asleep around it. Maybe, after all, he had made a big mistake — maybe all his reasonings had been wrong.

But then he asked himself again: why would Bill Cary have pumped him with all those questions? And then given him the business with a six-gun barrel?

So, Johnny pounded in on the campfire; the blanketed figures began to stir. All at once he was sawing reins as the blocky shape of Peewee Long rose before him and the cook's raucous voice bellowed: "By God, it's tooken you long enough to fetch one measly little axe! Where the hell . . . ?"

"Don't bother me," grunted Johnny. He leaped down from saddle and shoved past the cook. "I got to see the boss."

"*I'm* talking to you!" The cook caught Johnny Peters by a shoulder, and the red silk ripped as he was jerked around.

In desperation Johnny dragged back a fist and let fly. His knuckles rammed straight into the midst of Peewee's ugly face. Caught off-balance and taken by surprise, the cook yowled and went stumbling backward, to crash into a pile of tinware stacked up on the tailgate of his chuck wagon.

Johnny about choked, staring at what he had done. His hand ached like he had smacked a stone wall; otherwise, he wouldn't have believed it had really been he that knocked the bully cook for a loop.

But before he had time to wonder about it, Ed Martin was striding out of the darkness, amid an angry chorus from cowhands who had been rousted by the clatter of tinware.

"What the hell is this, Peters?" the boss demanded, taking in the ruined condition of Johnny's muddy clothes, the lather that covered his panting horse. "Have you been drinking?"

"No, sir!" As Johnny blurted out his news, he saw the man's expression slowly turn from anger to incredulity and then to grim concern. The kid ended with: "Maybe I'm talking through my hat, but that's how I added it up. And I got here as quick as I could."

"A good thing, too," Martin said bleakly. "Wouldn't be the first time I've heard of night hawkers starting a stampede, so as to gather up as many head as they can handle and sell 'em for whatever they're able to get." He raised his voice then, issuing orders. "We'll take no chances. Everybody hit saddle! My God, if there's someone with an eye on *this* herd . . . they'll get a fight!"

There was excited talk as the crew broke out of blankets and ran for the night horses that were kept saddled and waiting for them. Johnny Peters, so exhausted suddenly that he felt weak in the knees, tottered over to the chuck wagon and dug a tin cup from the stack, got the big coffee pot out of the coals, and drained off two shots one after the other. He tossed his cup into the wreck pan and was starting to walk away when an angry bellow filled the night.

"Hold it right there, cowboy!" shouted Peewee. "Everybody knows my rules. You're to sand out that cup you just used, understand?"

Johnny turned, and Peewee got a better look at him in the firelight. The cook's blustering voice broke off. One hand nursing his jaw, he quickly faded back into the shadows as Johnny stood staring. Slowly the truth dawned. The kid said aloud in awe: "Be dogged if I ain't got the big guy buffaloed! How come I never thought to try hitting him before tonight?"

Hurriedly then he roped himself a fresh bronc', switched saddle and gear to it, and swung astride to ride out and join the rest of the crew that were swinging in a bunch toward the bedded cattle. Johnny had left the campfire behind, and the night was black around him, when a puff of breeze from the east brought him the faint pulsation of hoof beats.

He hipped quickly about in saddle, but once again there was only the utter blackness of the prairie night and no sound at all except for his bronc's swishing through deep grass. But he knew what he had heard, and of a sudden Johnny Peters was slapping in spurs, galloping to catch up with his boss and the rest of the men. They turned as he overtook them, and he was gasping out what he'd heard.

"They're coming in a bunch, boss . . . from behind us! Must be a mile away."

Ed Martin snapped quick orders. "We'll ride to meet them. Keep them as far away from the herd as possible. It's the only way we can hope to avert a stampede!"

And the bunch swerved east to meet the raiders. Johnny Peters, riding with them, had his gun in his hand, and a cold sweat was pouring off him. This was it! This was the real thing — big adventure on the trail! He was suddenly kind of sick of the whole idea. . . .

Then a black mass of horsemen swept across a slight rise, under the dim sickle moon, and the two groups came together.

Big M got in the first shots, taking the raiders by surprise. After that it got really hot — horses milling up dust, guns making patterns of flame and mingled thunder.

A bullet picked Johnny's cream-colored Stetson right off his head. He fought his scared and bucking bronc' with one hand, tried hard to hit something with the gun in his other. In the yelling, milling confusion he wasn't sure most of the time which way was up.

But the whole thing only lasted a matter of minutes. Surprised at the sudden resistance they met, and badly crippled by that first volley of firing, the toughs who had ridden with Bill Cary broke suddenly and scattered, leaving some of their number on the ground. The Big M crew left saddles quickly to round up these prisoners. Among them was Cary himself, cursing and hugging a wounded arm.

They dragged him back to the campfire. Somebody kicked up a blaze, while part of the crew rode off to quiet the herd, which had been brought to its feet and set milling by the gunfire. Ed Martin and the others crowded in around the prisoners with grim expressions on their faces.

Cary spotted Johnny, and he cursed again. *"You!"* he gritted. "I should have

136

done more than just slugged you!"

"That's damn' right," declared Martin. "Johnny Peters is one of my best riders. I'm gonna see that he gets a bonus and a better job out of this night's work!"

Johnny blurted, staring at his boss: "You mean . . . you're splitting up me and Peewee?"

"No more hauling water and firewood, Johnny . . . you're too valuable to waste on them chores. As for *you*," he added, turning to Bill Cary, "I ought to run you in, but it ain't worth the trouble. The boys have caught some of the bronc's you varmints rode. If you know what's good for you, you'll pile onto one of them and get going . . . while we're in a mood to let you."

"Sure, sure," grunted Cary. "Just let me get my pants into a saddle and I'll be clean out of this country. . . ."

Johnny cleared his throat. "I got some riding to do myself, Mister Martin. That is, if it's all right, I mean. I'll try not to be gone more'n an hour."

To which Ed Martin answered gruffly: "I guess, after tonight's work, just about anything you want around here you can have, kid!"

Johnny mounted up again. It was close to nine-thirty when he came in on the

Tompkins place. He was quiet about it, and thankful for no more light than what the stars and the sickle moon could give. He rode into the thicket and tied his horse.

"Bill?" came Suella's whisper. "Is that you?"

Johnny didn't answer. He waited until she was close . . . and then he grabbed her and kissed her, hard. She broke away finally.

"You ain't Bill!" she gasped. *"You got a mustache!"*

It was the first time anyone had ever called the fuzz on Johnny's lip a mustache. But he kept his voice firm. He said: "No, I ain't Bill. I'm Johnny Peters . . . the cowpoke you almost got murdered today. I figured I had that kiss coming."

"Y-yes, Johnny," answered the girl.

"And I won't stand for any more trouble from your paw or them brothers of yours. I went pretty easy on 'em this afternoon, but another time I might not be so lenient. That plain?"

"Yes, Johnny."

"OK. You get 'em prepared along them lines against the next time I come ridin' through this country."

She moved toward him, and he kissed her again. Then he pushed her away gently.

138

"Go back in the house, Suella, and get you some sleep. Can't have my girl looking peaked."

"Good night, Johnny," she murmured faintly, as though in a daze. "I'll be waiting."

Jingling back toward the bedded down Big M herd, Johnny Peters counted over the events of the day, and his mood expanded until it seemed to embrace the whole star-studded night, even if he was still a mite bewildered by the suddenness with which everything had happened. He got out tobacco and paper, worked with them a while as his bronc' jogged along under sickle moon.

"For a gent that does everything so dog-gone well," he grunted finally, tossing the makings away in disgust, "it's a wonder I roll such a damn' poor cigarette!"

But he wasn't of a mind to let it bother him.

Tinhorn Trouble

The "anti-hero" — a person cast in the rôle of protagonist although he lacks most of the qualities a reader is usually expected to admire and identify with — seldom showed up in the Western pulps. Max Brand's con-man, Geraldi, was a notable exception. For some curious reason the Western story had become saddled, early on, with the notion of a morality tale — right and wrong, good against evil — a concept that seems oddly at variance with the *real* West, where the ultimate issue was actually one of sheer survival, by almost any means. But even in the wake of movies like *The Wild Bunch* and *McCabe and Mrs. Miller*, established myths still remain largely intact. The pulps never wavered in their respect for the familiar moral stereotype. When we wrote for them, we tacitly accepted a strict, if unwritten, code whereby each character in a story, and his actions, had to be weighed and assigned an appropriate reward or punishment. The hero and all the other good people picked up the marbles; the truly evil had to be killed or, if a secondary villain, possibly sent to prison in-

141

stead. As for a weak character who might at some point waver and briefly go over to the wrong side, he must at the very least repent his mistake and be shown at the end feeling very, *very* sorry! Obviously, by such a code Frank Camrose, my tinhorn gambler, is something of an anomaly: coolly supercilious, ethically dubious, something less than a gentleman — actually to be the hero of his own story, he was about as "anti-" as anyone could get. All the same, he struck me as someone it might be fun to write about and still perhaps manage to sneak under the wire. So I went right ahead, and apparently we both got by — "Tinhorn Trouble" is the result.

I

The crate on which Frank Camrose sat, swinging his silver-headed walking stick, contained mining machinery consigned to the new and roaring Montana gold fields. Below him, at the foot of the muddy dock, a yelling mob trampled and fought for space aboard the packet, *Pride of Omaha*, that was warping in toward the landing with its decks already filled to overflowing. Gold fever! It was a madness that seemed to have touched every man along this wild Missouri River frontier — every man, apparently — except Camrose himself.

They were fools, he reflected as he disdainfully watched the noisy struggle. What few ever saw the fabulous yellow dust of the new strikes would most likely lose it all into the hands of wiser, sharper men. Often enough, those hands had belonged to Frank Camrose.

Now the *Pride of Omaha* had thrown out a landing boom. As sweating stevedores began hurrying freight ashore, the captain and purser were having a job of it to keep back the mob until shifting of cargo would determine how many additional passengers could be taken aboard. Camrose shrugged, adjusted the hang of a fine box coat, rose leisurely. In a pocket of his fancy Marseilles vest was a cabin ticket, purchased at the local office, which absolved him from joining in that sweaty scramble. Besides, unlike these others, he took no particular interest in his nearing departure. It was distinctly someone else's idea.

He threw a cautious glance back toward the warehouses that lined the wharf street. Yes, the tough pair was still there, watching him. Seeing his look, one of them patted a holstered gun and flashed Camrose a toothy, evil grin. He turned away angrily and leaned for the carpetbag at his feet. But then he stopped, straightening quickly.

A light carriage had halted not far from him, and a single passenger was alighting. Camrose had a civilized taste for beauty, and he could hardly believe what he saw there against that background of muddy wharf and raw Missouri River port.

In hoop skirt and mutton-sleeve waist, and little feathered hat atop crisp black curls, she made as neat a figure as he had ever seen in St. Louis or the East. She had a lovely, heart-shaped face, and eyes that were frowning now — as though half in fright.

They looked at Camrose, and he started a hand toward his hat brim, but the glance had been an unseeing, abstracted one that moved past him, went on to rest in apprehension on the swarm of jostling, shouting men at the foot of the wharf. The carriage driver deposited a light trunk on the ground at her feet; she fumbled in her reticule, found money for him, and he drove away and left her looking very much alone.

Camrose knew an opportunity when he saw it. He was just about to step forward when suddenly a horseman came bursting out of the street above the docks and tore down on the girl, in a drumming, mud-spattering gallop.

Frozen, Camrose could neither move nor shout warning. But at the last moment the girl glanced about and saw the rider almost upon her, reaching far out as if to seize and sweep her up. Somehow she managed a leap backward. The hand caught her arm briefly and flung her heavily into the mud. Plowing to a halt, the rider swung his mount and came at her again, leaping from the saddle.

And by that time, Frank Camrose was in motion.

He plunged forward, walking stick glinting silver in the sun. Its heavy knob smashed against the back of the attacker's neck as he leaned over the girl, and with a grunt he collapsed. Disgust on his handsome, clean-shaven features, Camrose used cane and boot to roll the limp body away and free the girl.

For a moment she could only stare dazedly at the immaculate hand he offered. Her expensive clothes were ruined now, the feather of the little hat dangling brokenly beside a white and frightened face. When he had her on her feet, she still clung to him, and Frank Camrose didn't hurry to release her. "It's all right," he told her soothingly. "The danger's over."

"But. . . ." Alarmed brown eyes peered at him. "The man . . . !"

"Do you know him? Ever seen him before?"

"Never! I'm sure of it."

He was a lean, red-faced derelict — mere frontier riff-raff. Lying unconscious there in the mud, his gaping mouth showed yellow buckteeth, and blood dribbled from the long, sharp nose. Camrose was reminded of a gray rat he'd clubbed once in a waterfront rooming dive, and revulsion touched him.

"Let him lie," he said. "The fellow was probably after whatever he might find in that purse you're carrying."

The incident, brief as it had been, seemed hardly to have drawn any attention at all on the busy wharf. Camrose asked: "You're boarding the *Pride*?"

"Yes." She fumbled with her reticule. "I have a cabin ticket. But. . . ." She glanced toward the noisy mob.

"Just stay close to me," Camrose assured her. "We'll get you safe on board. . . ."

He managed his own carpetbag and her small trunk with one hand, using the cane in the other to force a way for them through the crowd. When they reached the gangplank, they found the boat officials having considerable trouble to keep it clear.

One huge, black-bearded fellow in particular was bawling drunken argument, towering over the captain with ugly face thrust forward. Camrose scowled as he and the girl halted, unable to pass.

"Move aside, please!"

The man gave no sign of heeding.

Camrose lifted the walking stick, prodded him sharply with the end of it. "Don't you hear me? One side!"

With a bellow the big man turned. Camrose caught the stench of sweat and cheap grog-shop whisky, saw danger in the stare that raked his slight, flashily dressed figure. "Who the hell do you think you're shovin', sweetheart?"

The girl cried out as a single swipe of the man's big paw had sent Camrose reeling, spilling luggage as he went heavily to one knee. Head ringing, he came stumbling again to his feet.

But a hogleg revolver had appeared in the boat captain's hand, and was shoved hard into the big man's middle. "Enough of that!" snapped the official. "Stand aside and don't make any more trouble, you understand? Your turn aboard comes after the cabin passengers . . . and only then."

"Captain," said Camrose coldly, brushing himself off, "you'll do best to keep this whole crowd of riff-raff off your boat!"

That brought a chorus of howling rage, but the captain's gun was there to hold back the crowd, and Camrose, contemptuously ignoring them, proceeded to collect the luggage.

When their tickets had been checked in the purser's book, he and the girl went up the gangplank and made their way to the cabin deck. At the door of the girl's compartment, Camrose deposited her trunk.

"Thank you," she said. "You've been most kind."

He bowed a little, smiling. "The name is Camrose. If there's anything further. . . ." The sudden freezing of the friendliness in her eyes halted him.

"No, Mister Camrose," she said. "No, thank you. You really needn't bother!"

It was a curt dismissal. She didn't offer to tell her name.

The girl knew about him! It was the only explanation — she must have heard something of the trouble that had led to his hasty departure from that river town. But, on the other hand, when you considered the help he'd just rendered. . . . Well, such were the wages of gallantry.

Although the *Pride of Omaha* had once been known as a luxury boat, quarters were now badly cramped. Camrose looked over his compartment with a scowl, dropped carpetbag and stick into a corner, and hung up his tall hat. The mattress looked reasonably comfortable. He saw a sign tacked up: **Gentlemen will remove their shoes before lying on the berths.** Ignoring it, he stretched out comfortably and hoisted his booted legs onto the blanket.

Staring at the deck overhead, he considered the future and found it little to his liking. Days of solid boredom on this crowded sternwheeler and then the raw, sordid squalor of a Montana mining camp. There would be some card-playing in the men's saloon, of course, and at their destination a chance of dipping into a flowing stream of gold dust and lining his almost empty pockets.

Given a chance, he would far rather have been heading for St. Louis or some other point of civilization. He'd long since had enough to last him, of mud and noise and the reeking, brawling frontier. Unfortunately, there were no downriver boats scheduled for another forty-eight hours, and the men with the guns hadn't been in a mood to wait that long to be rid of him.

So here he was, aboard the *Pride* — and most likely the only passenger who was not anxious to be under way. He thought about the girl again, wondering what could be taking her north to the gold fields. But these were idle questions, and, before he had worked long at them, Camrose felt his thoughts going fuzzy and presently he fell asleep.

When he woke, the shadows of late afternoon were in the cabin, and he could feel the rhythmic throb of the twin engines pulsing throughout the big boat. They were moving. Through the porthole Camrose saw the slide of flat, brown water and the brush-choked bank. The ringing of a bell came to warn him that the evening meal was about to be served in the saloon.

In the washroom he cleaned up, brushed

his clothes, removed a bit of dried mud from his gleaming boots. Again taking hat and cane, he strolled out upon the deck, his pace quickening when he saw the crowd about the door of the saloon. Inside the long room, tables had been set up and laid for supper, but most of the seventy-five places were already taken. A large number of men were gathered outside waiting to get in, and a waiter held them back, explaining patiently: "I'm sorry, gentlemen. Only ladies and their escorts at first table. . . ."

Camrose scowled, biting his lip. He certainly had no intention of waiting for a place at a scanty second table. Then inspiration hit him, and quickly he was turning away on the heel of a polished boot.

The girl was just stepping from her cabin, and he met her with lifted hat and flashing smile. "Aren't you interested in eating? They're serving already."

She tried to prevent his taking her arm, but he had it. "I think I know the way," she said a little frostily.

"Of course." But he did not free her arm. "Still, you know, it's a pretty tough crowd on board. And after what happened on the dock. . . ." Under the cool scrutiny of her gray eyes, he decided perhaps this was a time for frankness. He smiled again, audaciously. "Besides, I'm hungry and they won't let me in unless you're with me."

"Oh." Suddenly, amusement broke through. "Well, at least you're honest about it," she said. "Maybe we should hurry."

A few minutes later Camrose was pushing his way through the crowd and taking one of the last places at the long table, the girl beside him. Her little trunk had afforded a change from the mud-stained garments, and there was nothing in her cool, assured manner to tell of the fright she had suffered only short hours before. As she ate, she kept rather silent, aloof, and Camrose studied her covertly. Finally he said: "It seems to me, if we're to be dinner companions on this trip, we could put things on a more sociable basis. Do you realize I don't even know your name?"

"Better not be too sure of yourself," she warned, looking at him directly. "No one said anything about our having *every* meal together!"

Camrose put on an injured look. "You wouldn't make me join that hungry pack there, outside the door?" He added: "Besides, you ought to have an escort."

"Oh, but I have one," she corrected him. "It looks like you cut him out this time, but it's not apt to happen again."

"No?"

"Tom Redmon is a pretty capable man," she said, a hint of amusement in her eyes. "He's been a miner, and he's got the hands and shoulders of one. You may be seeing something of him between here and Goldport."

"That sounds like a discreet warning," grunted Camrose. "Am I to take it this . . . mucker . . . has you labeled, and no one had better cut in on his exclusive rights?"

She colored slightly. "I didn't say anything like that! Tom is an old friend . . . a family friend, who's worked for my father almost as long as I remember. He naturally has protective feeling toward me. I'm afraid he might not care to see the two of us together . . . if you understand what I mean."

"I think I'm beginning to." It was Camrose's turn to show anger.

She went on quickly, before he could say more. "I want to make myself plain, Mister Camrose. I happen to have heard something of who and what you are. You helped me today, and I really appreciate it . . . but still. . . ."

"You've made it plain enough!" Camrose pushed back his chair, flung his napkin to the table. He added stiffly: "There's no need going into details. . . . Good evening!"

He stalked out of the saloon, pushed through the waiting ranks of the hungry bystanders, took a quick turn about the deck to settle his roused anger. It was seldom that Frank Camrose permitted himself a loss of temper, but the hint of scorn in the girl's remarks had touched deeply.

For a long time he stood glowering at the tumult of frothy waters that the big paddle wheel lifted and churned at the stern of the boat. A snag dropped past, lifting above the water those treacherous pointed arms that could rip the hull out of a craft if an unwary pilot ran over it. A glaze of red smeared the Missouri's muddy surface where sunset was reflected out of the wide western sky.

Calmed somewhat by the beauty of the evening, Camrose turned back at last to his own cabin. Strangely enough, when he started to close the door behind him, it would not come shut. He turned to see where the trouble lay.

"Easy does it, bucko," grunted a pleasant voice.

Camrose had been caught entirely off guard. For a man of such bulk, this one had moved soundlessly and he had got half through the door before Camrose knew he was being followed. Now the man stepped into the cabin, closed the door himself, and put thick shoulders against it, smiling a little.

Dusk was in the room, but the man's teeth gleamed whitely and there was a glint of light on the revolver in his huge fist. When Camrose got a lamp burning, it showed him cold black eyes in a craggy, battered face under thick, graying hair. Heavy lips grinned at him. The man was dressed in store clothes that stretched tightly across wide and muscular shoulders.

"Set down," grunted the intruder. "Or keep standing, just as you feel like. We have business to talk about. You know who I am, Camrose?"

Still standing by the lamp, Camrose said: "I've got a notion. I think you're Tom Redmon."

"I suppose June Lang told you."

"If that's her name."

Redmon eyed him coldly. "I suppose you never heard of Lang and Stoddard, either?"

"Who hasn't? They're the ones involved in this strike at Goldport where we're all headed." Camrose frowned. "Though, come to think of it, seems to me I heard old Bill Lang had died not too long ago."

A snort burst from big Tom Redmon. "Don't try puttin' on an act with *me*, Camrose. I know what you think you're up to!"

"Oh?"

"I can generally spot a tinhorn on the make . . . even if I hadn't heard about you getting run out of that town back there, when they caught up with your blackleg tricks. But now, you're onto something new. You already figured who June Lang was . . . you've most likely made a fair guess as to how much she stands to inherit, once she reaches Goldport.

"Well, I talked to June, less than an hour ago," he went on, not giving the other man a chance to answer. "She told me what happened at the boat landing . . . you saving her from a purse snatcher, and seeing to it she made it on board. Nothing wrong with *that*, I suppose. All the same, she's on to you. And I promised her I'd see to it you wouldn't be trying to push things any further."

Frank Camrose had heard him through

without giving any sign of a reaction. All he said now was: "You take quite a lot on yourself, don't you?"

Redmon's craggy features colored slightly. He moved a step nearer, the gun still firm and level in his hand. "You'd better believe it! I've known that family a lot of years. I worked for Bill Lang . . . now I work for his partner. And with Bill dead, it's my responsibility to see his girl reaches Goldport and takes over her share of the company."

"It's nice you feel so responsible," Camrose remarked, with the slightest hint of mockery. "Really a shame you weren't on hand today to save her from being robbed, and get her past that mob at the gangplank. Not exactly good judgment, would you say? Leaving an opening for someone like me to step in, and put Miss Lang under obligation. . . ."

Anger struck a spark in Redmon's opaque stare; his grip tightened on the gun. But what he said was: "Talk ain't getting us anywhere . . . why don't we quit beating around the bush? Every tinhorn I ever knew had his price. So, what's yours?"

"To *you*," Camrose answered shortly, "I don't think I have anything to sell!"

It came then — not a bullet, but a blow

of the barrel that would have smashed his face if it had landed. But a sharp intake of breath telegraphed the move before it started, and Camrose ducked away from it, let the weapon go past him by a scant inch or two. At the same moment his right arm was coming up, clenched fist jabbing sharply.

It caught Redmon in the throat, sent him back on his heels with head rocking upward, and that way the massive jaw was exposed, and Camrose measured his next blow exactly. His knuckles connected. The big miner hit the cabin bulkhead and slid down, black eyes glazing.

Camrose swore at the pain of his bruised hand, and leaned for the gun Redmon had dropped as he fell. He jacked out the shells and tossed them onto the berth. The empty gun he threw down beside Tom Redmon's slumped, half-conscious form. He stood a moment frowning down at him, then, with a shrug, took his walking stick and tall hat and, blowing out the lamp, stepped from the darkened cabin.

III

Stars were out, and a moon was on the verge of rising above the bluffs of the eastern bank. Since it would be a full moon, giving ample light for navigation, the *Pride of Omaha* was continuing its course past the usual hour for warping in and tying up to the bank during the treacherous time of darkness.

Pondering that scene with Redmon, and nursing his sore hand, Camrose stepped into the carpeted, brightly lighted saloon. It was a place of busy talk and movement. The long dining tables had been removed, and card games were under way. A considerable crowd of the *Pride*'s first-class passengers lined a bar where white-coated tenders were busy with the first rush of evening trade.

Camrose elbowed to a space at the highly polished counter and, while he waited for the attention of one of the bartenders, took a cigar from an elaborate pocket case and bit off an end. He was reaching for a light when he suddenly changed his mind and, stowing the smoke away again, pushed quickly forward through the crowd.

Across the room, June Lang had just entered. She looked up quickly, and the hostility was plain in her eyes as she saw him, but he came straight toward her. "Miss Lang. . . ."

"I see you've learned my name," she said shortly. "Been asking questions, I suppose. I'd much rather you didn't discuss me."

Camrose felt his jaw muscles tighten a little. "Discussing you was not my idea," he corrected her. "Your friend Redmon practically insisted on it. He invited himself into my cabin and went on at some length about you and your reason for making this trip upriver. He also mentioned your father's partner. . . . Not that it's any of my business, but I wonder just how well you happen to know this man Stoddard."

Something in his tone must have prompted her to answer. "Why, I met him with my father once . . . two years ago, not long after he'd joined the company. That was in Saint Louis, where I was going to school. I've never been to the Montana headquarters. But, why did you want to know?" she asked.

"Simply because I *do* know him," he answered. "And I'd have to advise you not to trust that man any further than you just have to."

160

"Any further than I'd trust *you?*" she suggested. Her manner had turned suddenly frosty.

"All right. Perhaps you could say it takes a tinhorn to recognize one . . . but I'm serious about this. I hold Deck Stoddard as one who wouldn't let anything get between him and something he wanted. And, with your friend Redmon on his payroll. . . ."

Quick anger lifted her breast, her eyes smoldering. "Now you've said too much, Mister Camrose! I *have* known Tom Redmon . . . practically all my life. Whatever you're hinting at is not likely to affect my opinion of *him*. So now, if you'll excuse me. . . ."

And she was gone, moving abruptly away from him across the threshold of the smaller, ladies' cabin and closing the door firmly behind her. Camrose took a step to follow, but a notice tacked below the glass caught his eye: **Gentlemen Not Allowed Except on Invitation of Ladies.** It didn't add — *This means you!* — but at the moment it seemed to point directly at Frank Camrose. With a baffled shrug he turned away.

At the bar he caught the eye of one of the white-jacketed attendants and had his evening drink, then got the cigar out again and fired it up. He was still there when Tom Redmon came stomping in through the far door of the saloon, pausing to scowl furiously around the long hall.

Even at that distance Camrose could see the ugly bruise beginning to discolor the man's blunt jaw. But if he was looking for Camrose, Redmon missed him at the bar. He saw June Lang through the glass door of the ladies' cabin, and deliberately he opened that door and went in to her.

Camrose left the bar, traveled down the long carpet for a look through the glass. June and the man were seated together on the long, leather bench that ran along the bulkhead, talking earnestly. As Camrose watched he saw the girl touch the bruise on Redmon's jaw, saw the miner shrug aside some question she asked. Redmon was scowling at the toe of his boot, listening to what the girl had to say.

Repeating everything I told her, most likely, thought Camrose in disgust. If Tom Redmon was up to any crooked work, he would have warning now and be on his guard all the more carefully. . . .

At one of the tables a stud game was forming. Camrose introduced himself, shook hands all around, and took a seat where he could watch anyone who entered or left the ladies' cabin.

But his mood was sour, and it didn't help the run of the cards. With his mind elsewhere he lost pots he should have taken, let another man bluff him out of a pair of kings that ought to have been sure winners. No one would have thought this was the same Frank Camrose whose success at poker, proving too phenomenal, had led the men of that town back yonder to pull guns on him, relieve him of his winnings, and put him forcibly on the first boat that touched the wharf.

Presently he saw Redmon and the girl come out of the ladies' cabin and leave the saloon together, her hand confidingly on his arm. Camrose stayed in the game another twenty minutes, and then, as a large piece of his dwindling roll went down the drain of a losing hand, tossed in his cards and went out upon the deck, angrily twirling his walking stick.

The moon was well up the sky now, putting a chilled brightness upon shore and trees and sliding waters. At the stern Camrose stood alone, watching the frothing churn of the big paddle wheel, and letting the beauty of the night take the edge off his irritation. A man in his position, he reflected, had to keep control of himself or he would end up broke. He had to put this other business completely from his mind.

It was at this instant he heard movement behind him and turned — just in time to meet the rush of a figure out of the shadows of a cabin bulkhead.

Another moment, and he might have been hurled across the railing, down upon the blades of the paddle wheel. As it was, he barely managed to brace himself before the force of the attack struck and bent him half across the rail. The heavy-headed walking stick clattered to the deck as he clawed for balance. His assailant stepped on it, and it rolled, hurling him to one knee. That gave Camrose the fraction of time he needed to recover his balance.

Then the man was lunging up at him again, and in the moon glow Camrose had glimpsed his face — the same gaunt, rat-toothed man he'd tangled with earlier in that encounter on the wharf! A glimpse was all, before they came together in a desperate struggle.

His opponent was lean, wiry, and tough as hickory. If he was armed, he had forgotten it in the fury of attack; there was no weapon in the hands that reached for Camrose's throat. On that deserted section of the afterdeck, the grunt of panting breath, the scuffle of boots, were the only sounds.

Those hands almost got their grip on Camrose's throat, and then with a jerk of his head he tore loose from them. A savage jab of bent elbow caught the other squarely across the face, sent him stumbling. Camrose barely had time to brace himself before his opponent was coming at him again. But as Camrose straightened to meet him, there was a sudden sound of running feet, of voices shouting, men hurrying toward the scene.

The attacker didn't stay for that. Breaking away, he was darting into the shadows. Camrose loosed an angry shout and went after him.

He came abreast of a dark companionway that led to the freight deck, heard running feet retreating into the lower shadows. A heavy chain, intended to keep the crowd below from mingling with the cabin passengers, had been wrenched from its fastenings. Without stopping, Camrose ran madly down that ladder.

Here the throbbing engines made their racket. As he threaded his way among piles of cargo and stacked cordwood, there was no sign of the quarry, and Camrose suspected he had already lost his man. Then all thought of pursuit was jolted from him, as without warning a group of men rose up to bar his way.

"Here's one of 'em!" shouted a voice.

Light from a deck lantern, washing over the scene, showed the hard faces, the rough clothing of the gold-rush mob. A big paw reached for Camrose, and he shook it off, demanding: "What is this? Out of my way! I've got business to take care of!"

Drunken laughter greeted him. "Business?" someone echoed. "Down here amongst the scum of the boiler deck, and in them clothes?"

"The swells chain us off from their own part of the boat," shouted another, "but they think they can come gawkin' any time they feel like it, like we was in a damned zoo or something. . . . How about it? *I* say this is another case for the Kangaroo Court of the Missouri!"

"Bring him along!"

The cry was taken up by a dozen throats. Cursing, Camrose tried to back free. But they were on him from all sides, and the sheer press of numbers bore him down and pinned his arms helplessly. Fuming and struggling, he had to let himself be hauled away along the deck, toward a cleared space where others of the mob were formed in a shouting circle.

Chagrin at losing his quarry gave way to alarm as he heard the raucous yells greeting the arrival of a new victim before the self-appointed judge of the court. "Make an example of him!" yelled one who stood on the rail, waving a half-empty bottle. "Let's see how he looks with his head shaved!" He reached, knotted huge fingers in Camrose's hair, and yanked viciously.

Camrose was fighting them again, in sudden desperation, but his struggles were futile. One sleeve of his fine box coat gave with a ripping of seams. A moment later, subdued and panting, he stood before the packing-case bar, helpless in the hands of two of his captors.

"Well, damn me for a. . . ."

The "judge" came leaping down from his seat, heavy cowhide boots shaking the deck. A burly, whiskered face was thrust into Camrose's. "Look, boys! It's sweetheart . . . and without the nice cap'n to hide behind. Remember me, sweetheart?"

Camrose remembered that scene at the gangplank, his own unwise remark to the boat captain, the hatred he had seen born in the eyes of the gold-rush mob. And here he was, powerless in their eager hands. . . .

Contemptuously he returned the big

leader's stare, bleeding lip twisting a little as the reek of bad river whisky hit him full in the face. "If you think you can make me crawl," he said, "you'll find you're mistaken."

Fury swamped the brute pleasure that had shone in the man's eyes. A curse broke from him, and then the man's huge fist came around. It caught Camrose squarely on the side of the head and hurled him against one of those who held his arms.

But though a buzzing of pain was in him, he caught himself and came back and, surprising his captors, was able to jerk free. He landed one swinging blow that seemed to bounce off the brutish face like rubber, then, its momentary surprise overcome, the mob fell upon him with a mingled shout.

He fought back with both fists and boots, trying to hold out against impossible odds. Sweat and blood ran into his eyes. The blows rained from every side as drunken men crushed in, all trying to find a target.

It was only seconds, but it seemed an eternity before he was beaten to his knees, strength and consciousness running out of him. A boot struck him in the head, and he fell face forward against the splintered deck.

IV

It was the nudging of a boot toe, also, that brought him aware, rolling him over like a half-filled grain sack. Bright sunlight hit his closed eyes and stabbed an ache into his slowly waking brain. He seemed to hear a voice from a considerable distance: "Roust out of it, you, and answer me. You carry wood, or not? Answer, damn it!"

He got his eyes open, squinted painfully. A man in the uniform and cap of a boat's mate stood over him. "I said . . . do you carry wood?"

The question didn't make much sense to Camrose. He raised a leaden hand and touched his face. He mumbled: "I don't know what you mean."

"The hell you don't! Either you show me a first- or second-class ticket, or you get on your pins and start rustling wood with the rest of this scum."

With a groan, Camrose forced himself to a sitting position, one hand against the deck to brace him. "Of course, I have a ticket," he grunted, fumbling for his leather wallet. Finding nothing, he dug deeper until his fingers hit the bottom of an empty pocket. He tried other pockets, before dazed senses registered the fact that his wallet was gone. Stolen, while he lay battered and unconscious!

A snort burst from the curling lips of the mate. "Quit stalling! You're gonna tote wood. Just because you laid yourself out in a drunken brawl won't get you out of it!"

He hooked a rough hand under the other's arm and hoisted him up. Camrose put his back against a bulkhead to hold him until strength returned. His clothes were tattered ruins, and he could feel the raw cuts and swollen bruises on his face. Some cool water in the washroom would take the edge off the burning, help to clear his tortured brain. But when he took a tentative step toward the companionway, the mate jerked him around.

"No, you don't! I'm keeping an eye on you until I see you hit the gangplank. And that's right straight in front of you. Get moving along, now. *Pronto!*"

Mists of morning were rising from the silent river, and melting under the early sun. The *Pride of Omaha* was tied up at a level, muddy clearing of the timbered bank, where a wood-hawk had piled his cords of hardwood to trade with the river captains. A landing boom had been thrown across to shore, and the third-class passengers — the ones who could pay neither for food nor bed and had contracted to rustle wood for their passage — were already toiling back and forth with new fuel for the *Pride*'s diminished boiler-room stacks.

Head still spinning, Camrose went down the loading boom. Even solid ground felt unsteady under him. He wanted to go away and sit down somewhere and wait until he had a grip on himself. Later, he could face the problem of the future.

There was considerable activity at the wood yard. As usual, passengers had come on land for a morning stroll while the *Pride* was being wooded, and the dresses of women made colorful contrast with the drab rawness of the shore. Under the eyes of one of the boat officers, Camrose fell in with the stream of wood carriers moving up toward the cord stacks, and made a pretense of picking up an armload of the fresh-cut hickory lengths.

Then, seeing his chance, he threw the stuff aside and slipped into the brush, moved back among the trees where the new sun had not fully dispelled night mists and shadows. Here he dropped onto a stump and sat shivering in the clammy chill, gathering his strength while he tried to think about his next step.

It was a bleak moment for Frank Camrose, gentleman gambler. His pockets were empty, his ticket gone, his fine clothing in tatters. If he managed to reclaim the carpetbag from his cabin on the boat, he would have a change of clothes and, more important, the hundred dollars in gold that made up his stash — that final reserve which, by his superstitious gambler's code, must never be set at risk, for if that went, too, his luck was certain to vanish with it.

Any other options seemed to run out, as he sat here with the Missouri River at his back and, confronting him, half a continent of howling, empty wilderness. Body aching in every muscle, his spirits at their lowest ebb, at that moment Camrose hardly knew where he would find the courage to get his feet under him again, and face bleak reality.

A sound of voices and of movement through the rank brush forced itself on his attention. His head lifting, he turned to stare dully as two men came toward him through the river mist. One was Tom Redmon, the other, the same rat-faced tough he had already twice encountered in the past twenty-four hours. The latter carried a gun in one bony hand. Redmon had his weapon tucked behind his waistband. They both halted the instant they caught sight of Camrose.

"Well . . . so here you are," Tom Redmon grunted. "You don't look so good this morning."

Camrose made no answer. He was trying to work though the astonishment of seeing this unlikely pair together. It raised all kinds of wild speculation, but none that seemed to make any sense just then.

The one holding the gun said: "How about it, Tom? Do I give it to him right here? Or do we take him into the brush first?"

"In the brush, of course," Redmon answered, and the opaque eyes turned to flint. "You should know this is much too close to the boat. You messed things up real good for me yesterday, Dugan . . . lettin' that girl get away from you. This time, I intend to make sure you do something right."

Camrose settled a hard stare on Tom Redmon. "I'll be damned! It finally begins to make sense . . . that business on the wharf was something more than a purse-snatching, wasn't it? It's Miss Lang, herself, he was after!"

Redmon shrugged meaty shoulders. "I

should never count on Dugan. He was supposed to pick her off before she got anywhere near the boat . . . but, of course, he missed connections and had to go chasin' after her . . . right onto the wharf, in front of everybody."

"I would 'a' had her," the other man objected sullenly. "Except for this son-of-a-bitch horning in. . . ."

Camrose ignored that. To Tom Redmon he said coldly: "Just what was your idea? To keep her somewhere, I guess, until Deck Stoddard had time to make good his hold on her father's business. But you must have seen that, in the end, she'd need to be put out of the way, to make sure of her . . . the same way he made sure of Bill Lang."

Their stares locked, for a long moment. Then the big man grunted harshly to his companion: "We're wasting time. Get on with it . . . that boat's gonna be ready to shove off before we know it."

"Right." Waggling his gun barrel, Dugan told the prisoner: "You heard. On your feet, mister . . . and start walking."

Strength had returned to Camrose, and his legs were under control as he came up off the stump. Even with a gun trained on him, and both men watching his every move, he took a moment to send a searching glance about him, as though seeking some way of escape from the thing he knew would soon happen to him.

That was when he saw her.

June Lang stood half hidden by the dripping branches of a fog-shrouded tree, near enough she could not possibly have missed a word that had been said. Her eyes were dark stains in the shocked pallor of her face, and now a startled exclamation from Dugan brought Tom Redmon around to face her.

The big man found his tongue. "June! I told you to stay on the boat!"

"Yes." Her voice was barely more than a whisper. "I know you did. You were so insistent, it started me wondering about something Frank Camrose tried to tell me yesterday. And . . . I followed you. . . ."

Dugan said gruffly: "I'd say she must have got herself an earful!"

She nodded. June came slowly forward, her stare pinned on Tom Redmon as she demanded: "Is it true, then? Did you and Deck Stoddard kill my father?"

"*N-no!*" He all but stammered the word. "Not *me*, Junie . . . never! Deck was the one planned that part . . . he handled it all himself."

"And next, it will be *my* turn?"

"Honest to God, Junie. . . . No, listen to me!" He lunged a stride toward her and, as she started to draw away, reached and trapped one of her wrists in a heavy paw. Frantically Tom Redmon protested: "You got to believe . . . all the time . . . I been trying to make sure you wouldn't end up getting hurt!"

"Let go!" All of a sudden she was struggling to break free, but he caught her other arm and hauled her against him. Only the threat of Dugan's revolver could have held Frank Camrose in check, where he stood helplessly watching.

"Please . . . hear me out!" Big Tom Redmon was breathing heavily, intent on the effort of persuasion. "You maybe never noticed, but I been powerful interested in you for a long time now . . . since you first give sign of turning into a woman. But it's been no use, not even after all I've went and done for this family. Bill made it clear he meant you to be a lady, not have anything to do with a roughneck the likes of me.

"When I realized that, it was like the whole world had fell in on me! You got to believe, it's the only reason I would ever have thrown in with Deck Stoddard . . .

and even now it ain't too late. Even now there's ways he can be stopped. *Legal* ways, the pair of us working together. Like if we was man and wife, for instance. . . ."

With a cry she broke loose from him and stumbled free, the horrified look on her face seeming to halt Tom Redmon in his tracks.

And Frank Camrose, unable to stand there and watch any more of this, elected to take a gambler's chance.

He went at Dugan, reaching for the gun. Caught off guard with his attention divided, Dugan was slow to react — slow enough to let him get a hand on the weapon just as it went off, harmlessly driving a bullet into the mud at their feet.

But now Redmon had become aware of what was happening, and he came whipping about, pawing at the revolver in his own waistband. A jerk at Dugan's arm had thrown the man off balance, and at the same moment a looping swing of Camrose's fist caught him squarely in the middle of his rat-sharp features. Dugan reeled backward, just as Redmon thought he saw a chance at Camrose and squeezed the trigger.

Dugan backed straight into the bullet, his whole body jerking as it took him between the shoulders. He collapsed without a sound and fell loosely against Frank Camrose, who seized the man's lifeless body and gave it a shove in Tom Redmon's direction.

Moving fast, then, he closed with the big miner before the latter could work his smoking gun a second time. Its barrel struck him on the shoulder, numbing him, but he was not to be stopped that easily. He took the pain, and his clubbed fists continued working at the jaw and thick chest of the bigger man, until nothing but empty air met his blows — and the words of the girl finally somehow reached him: "Stop it, Frank! He's through. . . ."

Camrose was left staring at the man's unconscious shape and at his own bruised and bloody hands, while his breathing slowly settled, and from the wood yard and the boat landing below them excited voices lifted across the morning stillness.

In a very few moments men would be coming to investigate the sounds of gunfire. Camrose supposed they would take care of the dead Dugan. Later, perhaps, Tom Redmon might be persuaded to testify against Bill Lang's treacherous business partner. But just now, his main thought was for June Lang. "You better come away," he said. "Let me get you back on board."

He had caught one of his hands in both of hers. "It's a wonder we're either of us still alive!" she exclaimed, gray eyes peering into his battered face. "You did your best to warn me . . . but I refused to listen."

"No good reason you should." Suddenly there were things he needed for her to hear, and perhaps only moments to say them. "You had my number, from the very start," he told her gruffly. "A tinhorn . . . that's Frank Camrose, all right. Of no value to himself or anyone else. . . ." And yet, with that confession made, he could read no hint of scorn in the earnest look she gave him, and somehow the words came pouring out.

"I'm not too proud of myself, right now. I've always been one to sneer at the likes of those boomers down there on the *Pride of Omaha* . . . at least, though, such men aren't afraid to work up calluses, making an honest living any way they can. But here I stand, begging for a chance to finish the only worthwhile job I ever undertook. Please! Let me go on with you, upriver, and try to help settle the score with Deck Stoddard for what he's done to you and your father."

Getting no answer from the girl, Camrose added hastily: "I don't want you to misunderstand. Whatever might come of it, I promise you won't be under any obligation to me . . . ever."

There! He had put it clumsily enough. He could only wait for her reply while voices sounded nearer through the fog-swept timber, shouting: "Where'd the shots seem to come from?" and "Over that way, maybe. . . ."

June slowly shook her head, and Camrose felt his spirits plummet. "You make it sound much too easy," June Lang told him, but then she continued, with the beginning of a smile: "So, can't you see, if you really manage to do all those things . . . why, I just might not be able to get along without you at all, Frank Camrose."

He looked to see if her eyes were mocking him. And he saw, with a quick wonder, that they weren't.

Breakheart Valley

Given a few additional scenes, a subplot or two, and space to develop the characters more fully, this cowman vs. nester story might have been strong enough to support treatment as a book-length novel. Or, not — the thing worked well enough as a novelette, and that was all I wanted from it at the time. On another occasion, I did expand "Reach High, Top Hand!" into a book — called simply *Top Hand* — and it was published in that form. I think I did a fairly good job, and yet I've always suspected the short version was better and should have been left the way it was. There's a lot of sense to the saying: "If it ain't broke, don't fix it!" By the way, don't be surprised if you notice a similarity between "Reach High, Top Hand" and one of the scenes in this story — a certain piece of business involving an office safe. I'm afraid that if something I invented gave good service the first time, I wasn't above trotting it out and using it again somewhere else. On four occasions, in four different stories, I described the Cherokee Strip Land Rush, and each version turned out almost word for word the same as the others — but, why not? It was the same land rush, wasn't it? Besides, I'm afraid I've never really been convinced that anyone, anywhere, actually *read* my stuff — except, of course, the lino-typist — and so I wasn't worried too much about being caught plagiarizing myself!

I

Something about the saddle of a loping horse gives its rider an air of one who owns the earth, or at lease imagines he does. So it was with these three who came along the road from town, side by side, bodies giving easily to the gait of the Bar-Y horses under them. From the seat of his farm wagon, with a scant pile of new-purchased supplies in the rear, Vance Hewlitt saw them bearing down on him. He spoke to his team, and pulled over to allow plenty of passageway.

Hoofs jarred the earth as the trio neared. Hewlitt thought no one was likely to miss the arrogance and vanity of the rider on the near side: Cap Nordhoff and his gear fairly glinted with silver, as the sun struck gleams from the high pommel of his *charro* saddle, the *conchas* fastened to his hatband, or the plugged Mexican *peso* which the Bar-Y foreman wore at his throat to anchor the ends of a blue neck cloth. The man on the far side, then, whose rust-colored mane hung to his shoulders beneath a cuffed-back sombrero would be Nordhoff's perpetual sidekick, Red Riling. They were not a pair for whom Vance Hewlitt had any liking.

Between them rode a girl whose rich golden hair streamed back from her head, unhindered by the neat, low-crowned hat that depended now between her shoulders from its rawhide throat strap. She looked very small in contrast with the bulk of the pair who bracketed her stirrups.

She wore a wine-red silk blouse, blue corduroys, expensive stitched half-boots. She rode with utter gracefulness, and the wind of her riding whipped and ballooned the shining material of her blouse, and molded it smoothly across the curve of her full young breast. Her head was lifted, cheeks whipped to a glow by sunshine and fresh air. No more than her two companions did she appear to notice, by even a glance, the man on the seat of the farm rig making way for them to go by.

But as the trio drew abreast, Vance Hewlitt caught the sideward look the dark-skinned foreman threw him from the corner of his eyes, and saw the mouth beneath the heavy brush of black mustache quirk with ill-concealed disdain. He read the thought behind that look. What followed, although it came with startling suddenness, was hardly a matter of surprise.

There was plenty of room for the three of them to pass, but that made small difference to Nordhoff. As he drew even with Hewlitt's team, he gave a sharp, deliberate yank at the reins, and his gelding almost stumbled, shouldering heavily against the nearest of the work horses.

This was a bony sorrel mare that had once been gored by a bull and whose soul still bore the scars of the encounter. Ever since, a sudden lunge from that blind side was all it took to drive her into a frenzy. Squealing now in terror, she rose, pulling frantically away as she pawed the air with shod hoofs. One of them struck her teammate and instantly started that animal to pitching.

A shout broke from Vance Hewlitt as he stood and pulled back on the leathers, hands suddenly full with his frightened team. He heard Cap Nordhoff's coarse laughter; the big man had pulled in to enjoy the commotion he had started, and now the other two riders were also turning back.

Hewlitt ignored them all. A quick wrap around a grab-iron anchored the reins, and then he was down off the seat and hurrying to reach for the mare's headstall, risking a swipe from a shoe in doing it. But the mare knew his voice. As he talked to her, she gradually quieted, although she was still breathing hard and trembling when he released his hold.

Behind him Cap Nordhoff said loudly: "You sodbusters should have the courtesy to move your broken-down rigs out of the way when a *man* wants by."

Slowly Vance Hewlitt turned. Unlike Nordhoff and his red-headed friend, Hewlitt wasn't wearing a gun. Moreover, there was a special reason why he didn't want trouble with anyone from Bar-Y, today of all days. He kept his voice under control as he answered: "You had plenty of room. You crowded my team on purpose."

"Oh? I'm a liar now, am I?" The dark face turned evil. The man's eyes registered their intent an instant before Nordhoff's spurs prodded home and sent the chestnut gelding straight at the one who stood facing him.

Hewlitt took warning, and he sprang

aside, pivoting on one flat-heeled clod-buster shoe. As Nordhoff went past, he hooked his hand across the instep of the cowman's boot and let the rush of the bronc' tear the foot from stirrup. A quick heave upward and Nordhoff went over, out of saddle, to strike the ground that was still muddy from spring thaw.

He wasn't really hurt, and he came bouncing up again with a bellow of fury. Red Riling, who had started a grab for holster, changed his mind and went spurring instead to catch up the gelding, letting his boss settle with this nester who had had the presumption to unseat him.

Nordhoff waded in, big fists cocked and swinging. Hewlitt let him come, although he was at a disadvantage of some fifteen pounds against the big man's hard, muscular weight, being himself perhaps an inch taller than the Ballard ramrod and of sparer build — lean, almost.

He blocked the man's first swing on a raised forearm, and then drove his own right fist against the side of the jaw. The jolt of the blow ran up into his elbow, and it halted Nordhoff in his tracks.

The big man shook his head as though to clear it. Then he started forward again, and his dark face, beneath a smear of dust and sweat, was distorted with his rage.

"Stop this!"

It was the Ballard girl, speaking in a tone that seemed to expect obedience. When Nordhoff gave no sign of halting, she simply moved her palomino in front of him, forcing him back as she continued: "The man is right, and you know it! I saw exactly what you did. Now, why don't you just let this lie where it is?"

A long moment Cap Nordhoff stood and returned her look with unconcealed animosity. Watching the two of them, Hewlitt sensed something between them that had little to do with the present moment, or with himself. It was more like a clash of wills, which might have been building in the months since Nordhoff had taken up his job as foreman of the Ballard iron.

If so, the big man must have decided this wasn't the time for an open challenge. His mouth closed like a trap. He gave Hewlitt a baleful look as he touched his jaw where the other's knuckles had landed. He would probably have liked nothing more than to continue the fight. Instead, he leaned to snatch his sombrero with its fancy hatband out of the mud. Without another word he took the reins that Riling had caught for him, and swung again into the saddle.

The last fierce glance he shot at Hewlitt, as he and his crony put their mounts into motion, made it clear that nothing had been settled here.

Connie Ballard remained behind. She was frowning as she told Hewlitt: "There was absolutely no call for that. I'm glad I was able to end it."

Still angry, he said briefly: "You needn't have on my account! I'm not at all sure I couldn't have licked him."

"If you had, it might have done him good . . . to find out, for once, he'd picked the wrong target." But the blue eyes, candidly sizing him up, appeared unconvinced.

And a moment later she was gone, lifting her pony into an easy canter as she followed the pair from Bar-Y, but showing no inclination just now to catch up with them. Vance Hewlitt wiped sweat from his face on a shirtsleeve as he watched her out of sight.

So, that was Connie Ballard — daughter of the man who ruled this valley. In the half year since the colony of homesteaders came and staked their claims at the valley's eastern end, all any of them had known of her was an occasional glimpse as she galloped her handsome palomino along the valley trails, head erect as though above noticing these strangers who had dared invade her father's domain. Today had been his first sight of her at close hand, the very first words they had spoken. Hewlitt had no reason to suppose she would remember him, if they were ever to come face-to-face again.

Even so, and in spite of the circumstances, he had to admit now that this golden girl was very nearly the loveliest woman he had ever laid eyes on. The tones of her voice, even in anger, were such that a man was not likely to forget. . . .

He put such thoughts from him, and climbed again to the wagon seat. It was too bad the encounter with Nordhoff had to happen just when he was on his way to Bar-Y as an emissary for the grangers, bringing a proposal to lay before York Ballard. Still, he was in no mood to turn back. The team had quieted. Hewlitt spoke to them, shook out the reins, and got his rig to rolling again in the wake of the vanished Ballard riders.

Some twenty minutes later he turned in at a gateway where the Bar-Y was burned into a slab of stained hardwood, suspended beneath the high crossbar above his head. A spring breeze stirred the poplars lining the lane that led to York Ballard's ranch headquarters.

As Hewlitt brought his shabby farm wagon to a halt and swung down, almost the first thing that caught his eye was the golden pelt of Connie's palomino, unsaddled now and moving gracefully about the corral. The ring of a hammer against heated metal came from the blacksmith shed. Everywhere there was the busy activity of a prosperous ranch headquarters dominated by its fine, two-storied main house.

York Ballard had just emerged from the barn's wide entrance, in conversation with his foreman, and, as Hewlitt headed for them, he was sure he looked just as much out of place in these surroundings as he felt.

The talk broke off. The two men had watched as he pulled up his team and swung down — the rancher's eyes coldly curious, Cap Nordhoff scowling fiercely. There was already a splotch of discoloration forming on the latter's jaw, and Vance Hewlitt's right fist could feel again the satisfaction of putting it there. But when he spoke, it was to the rancher, and without preliminary: "Mister Ballard, in case you don't know my name, it's Hewlitt.

The homesteaders have asked me to speak to you, on behalf of all of us. We want you to hear some of our ideas about the future, and hope to get your approval."

Ballard was not a large man, but one lost sight of that in the fierce intensity of his blue eyes. In a deep rumble of a voice he said: "You never asked my approval, last year . . . when you moved into this valley and filed on land I'd always counted as my winter graze!"

"We were acting within our legal rights," Hewlitt reminded him. "We had no false ideas that we'd be welcome. When, afterward, you brought in Cap Nordhoff, here, and Red Riling and the others, we understood they were to be sort of a cocked gun pointed at our heads . . . a warning not to go too far."

"A good thing you *do* understand that," the foreman put in dangerously.

"All right, Cap," grunted the Bar-Y owner. "Just get on with it, Hewlitt. Come to the point."

"I will." He lowered the tailgate of the wagon, and from the scant supplies he'd bought in town hoisted a heavy burlap bag, which he dropped to the ground at the feet of the cattlemen.

"Ballard, this is seed . . . the finest hardy

alfalfa. I shouldn't have to tell you there's no better stock feed anywhere. With winter over and our housing taken care of, it's time we were getting started on a crop. And this is the one we're all agreed on. It should do well here, give us three or four cuttings a year easily. On the other hand, putting all our fields into alfalfa will need a certain amount of water for irrigation. We'll have to take it from your creek, but we think we have something to offer in return.

"What we're offering," he continued when no one else spoke, "is a guarantee of all the winter feed you have any need for, and at a better price than you're used to paying . . . after all, there'll be no cost for hauling and shipping. And, one more thing . . . each season, once we've made the final cutting, you can feel free to turn your holdover stock onto our fields and use them for winter graze, just as you were doing before any of us came here. Anyway, there's our proposition," he ended. "We'll be anxious to find out what you think."

Ballard's fierce stare skewered him. The rancher said in his rumbling voice: "You appear to have got this all figured out."

"I certainly hope so. We've put a lot of thought into it. Our means are limited, but pooling our resources we have the cash for enough seed to do the job. Assuming, of course, that we have your approval."

He could only wait, then, for Ballard's reaction. Lips pursed, the cattleman scowled at the bag lying on the ground between them. Hewlitt was at a loss to guess at what he was thinking. But Cap Nordhoff was ready to respond. The foreman challenged Hewlitt with a savage look and a question of his own: "And, supposing Bar-Y ain't interested in *any* deal with you clod-busters that doesn't have you pulling stakes and getting the hell out of this valley where you ain't wanted?"

Hewlitt met his scowl with a level, gray-eyed stare. "In that case, I suppose we won't have much choice. Instead of merely plowing a furrow to mark the boundary around our fields, looks like we'll have no choice but to put the money we've saved into three-strand barb wire . . . to fence them off and then hold them, any way we can."

"Barb wire!" Cap Nordhoff turned to his boss. "You hear that? *Now* he's talking like every stinking nester I've ever met up with! It's a pure waste of time even talking to them, let alone thinking about any kind of a deal."

A new voice interrupted, saying: "I don't agree with that!"

Connie Ballard, still in riding pants and wine-red blouse, had come upon them unnoticed, but she appeared to have listened to Vance Hewlitt's proposal and Nordhoff's scornful reply. Now she walked straight up to the big foreman and, with head tilted back to meet his dark look, spoke past him to her father.

"I'd say we've been offered a sound proposition . . . one that should make it possible to hold more of our cattle through the winter, at a reasonable cost, and get the best price for them on the spring market. It could be a profitable arrangement for everyone."

York Ballard slowly turned his head for a thoughtful look at her. "You really think so, girl?"

"I do, indeed." She put a hand on his arm, as she added earnestly: "Dad, don't let Cap Nordhoff do your thinking for you! Those people are in the valley now, and it's clear they mean to stay. Surely it's better to try and get along with them, than to have Cap stirring things up . . . no telling where *that* could lead!"

However much influence this girl might have with her father, Nordhoff's dark expression seemed to indicate he knew, this time at least, he had lost the argument. He shrugged his heavy shoulders and raked Hewlitt with a murderous glance.

And now York Ballard, although without any show of real enthusiasm, gave the homesteader a grudging nod. "Very well," he said gruffly. "You can tell your people their idea's approved. We'll give it a try, this once at least, and see how things work out."

Vance Hewlitt drew a slow breath. "I can tell you, they'll be glad to hear we've made a deal." And he offered his hand to bind the agreement.

But just then, over at the main house, a bell began to clang, and York Ballard turned away from the hand as though he hadn't seen it. To his daughter he said: "Time for dinner already? Come along, Connie. Reckon I'm ready to put away a couple of steaks about now."

Vance Hewlitt felt the hot tide that flowed up into his throat and parched his flat cheeks, as he let the hand that had been ignored drop futilely to his side. Ballard had already started for the house. Connie remained, still looking up at Cap Nordhoff with an expression Hewlitt took to be one of triumph. Now she gave a toss of her golden curls and turned away from the scowling foreman. Her look passed over Vance Hewlitt as though she failed to see him, and she hurried to join her father.

With a muttered curse big Nordhoff heeled about and strode angrily into the barn. Hewlitt was left standing with the bag of seed at his feet. He had had his victory, but it felt like a hollow one.

York Ballard might grudgingly accept a business deal with a homesteader, but he would not shake hands on it; instead he had walked away to his meal, thus violating that other Western code that said a visitor, whoever he might be, should be invited to take a place at table. Apparently *that* was too much to expect from Bar-Y.

As for the girl, she had now used him a second time to score points in what appeared to be an ongoing battle of wills with the bully foreman; otherwise, someone from the homesteader settlement was plainly of little interest to this family. So be it — they were welcome to their Ballard arrogance. Vance Hewlitt had accomplished what he came for. He should be willing to settle for that.

II

The go-ahead had been given, and it meant plenty of work for the homesteaders strung along the river toward the east end of the valley — wearing, dawn-to-dark labor that left little else a man could give his mind to.

The ground must be prepared for the seed that had been ordered. Irrigation must be provided, with ditches to be dug and a method devised to control the flow of water. Almost the whole weight of the project lay heaviest on Vance Hewlitt's shoulders, since it had originated in his brain, and his neighbors — Guy Adcock, Len Ferguson, and the others — looked to him for the leadership to co-ordinate their efforts.

Meanwhile, as spring advanced and the parks and aspen meadows of the bordering hills began to open up, the Bar-Y 'punchers were involved with all the stir of preparations for moving the stock onto high summer range. Already a homesteader, straightening from his unending labor, could stand grasping hoe or plow handle as he watched dark figures on horseback spurring through lifting dust, while the faint chorus of bawling steers rose from the draws and ravines leading into the hills. Sometimes, comparing all this to his own soil-bound existence, he might feel the stir of jealousy.

But it quickly died. The man in the saddle had his freedom, but he could look no further ahead than next month's pay day. The one with the plow, on the other hand, worked with a purpose: the future he was building for himself — and, perhaps, for a wife and family as well.

Unlike most of his neighbors, Vance Hewlitt had no family to share the fruits of his labor. But he was young, with a lot of time ahead of him. He farmed because he liked to watch things grow from the soil.

And he built to last. The log-and-sod roof cabin on the construction of which he'd spent the fall and winter had been put together with loving care, down to the last adze-stroke leveling door sills and window frames, and the up-ended horseshoe fastened above the entrance for good luck.

He sometimes found himself envisioning the girl he would like someday to share this cabin with him, but lately, all too often, he discovered all at once that she had calm blue eyes and golden hair of a richness such as no girl he knew, except for Connie Ballard, had ever possessed. And then he turned angrily upon himself for the time he wasted in such fantastic reveries.

Still, he couldn't help a certain quickening of the pulse that came to him when he rode up to the Ferguson place one morning and saw her, in the saddle of her palomino, talking to Len's wife Mattie before the cabin door. It was totally unexpected. Never before had anyone from the big, white house come near the homesteaders' places.

He rode in slowly, forking the bull-shy mare under a battered hull. It was a handsome sight, sure enough — the golden girl on the golden horse, her shapely figure set off in a loose gray blouse and riding skirt. Mattie Ferguson was holding up the baby for the visitor to see while Connie paid compliments to his smiling mother.

But the scene struck a sour note for Vance Hewlitt. He contrasted Connie Ballard's expensive clothing with Mattie's faded calico and found himself thinking: *the mistress of the manor — calling on one of the serfs.*

This comparison stuck in his mind, and he couldn't get rid of it. As he rode into the dooryard and the two women turned to him, he knew the dark reflection of the thought must be visible on his face.

Mattie Ferguson smiled at him and said: "This is Vance Hewlitt, Miss Ballard. I think you've met."

"Yes, we have," Connie agreed. Her glance was cool, a little speculative, as she met his unfriendly look. "It seemed to me time to get acquainted. And perhaps I'd be allowed to see how things are going."

Hewlitt nodded curtly. "I guess I could show you around. . . ."

They rode along the plowed and irrigated fields, where the last seed was now in place and awaiting the miracle of growth. Connie appeared interested in the system of channels and gates Hewlitt and his neighbors had devised to make sure enough water reached every point where it was needed. But when she asked if he could estimate the amount they had already taken from the creek, he wondered suddenly if this was a warning.

Maybe the Ballards were having second thoughts, worried about this project using too much of the valley's precious water — in the event of a dry season, perhaps. He assured her that irrigation was only temporary, to be ended as soon as things had got off to a good start. Each individual plant, with its deep taproot, would then be entirely self-sufficient. "They're perennials, and they seem to last forever . . . with us doing nothing but collect as many cuttings every year as the ground they're planted in can give us. And in the end, we can plow them under and they'll enrich the soil for us, with nitrates. Alfalfa is great stuff!"

"Will you ever be growing anything else?" she asked.

"Aside from our own truck gardens? Certainly. It all depends on the markets, and how much stock feed your father will need from us . . . or perhaps other ranchers in our shipping area. After all, we plan to make a living . . . and who knows what may turn up, further down the road?"

Connie asked no more questions. He could only hope his answers had been satisfactory.

There was a hill behind Vance Hewlitt's place that would give a clear overview of the whole lay-out, and he took her there. They tied their mounts to a locust branch and stood gazing on the plowed acres, the dancing flash of the creek in the middle distance, the valley floor lifting to the foothill breaks beyond.

"It's lovely here," Connie said.

Looking down at her beside him, Hewlitt saw the soft curve of her cheek and throat, her gaze upon the scene before them.

"This hill used to be just about my favorite spot in the whole valley," she added.

"Before I came along to spoil it for you with a two-bit homesteader's shack?"

She stared up at him. "I wasn't going to say anything like that!" she protested. "Every man has a right to a home. And besides, I don't think you've spoiled it. The little house is charming. You must love your wife very much to put so much care into it."

"I haven't any wife," he corrected her. "Nearly all the others do. Today, you saw the cabin Len Ferguson built for Mattie . . . where she had their baby. It's the first time that pair ever had a place they were able to call their own." He added shortly: "But I wouldn't expect any of this to interest you much."

Connie Ballard studied him, frowning. "Why do you say that?"

"Well, we're hardly what you'd call neighbors. Intruders, is more like it . . . people the Ballards had hoped never to see in their valley. I can understand you keeping to yourself, not wanting to know too much about your neighbors, or have anything to do with us if it wasn't absolutely necessary."

"I'm here now," she pointed out.

"Yes . . . and to tell you the truth, that's what bothers me," he said bluntly. "I've answered your questions, showed you everything you wanted to see . . . now I have to wonder what's going to happen when you report to your father. Will we still have a deal? Or, is York Ballard looking for an excuse to call it off?"

She stiffened, the blue eyes widening. "Did you suppose he *sent* me here? And for such a purpose as that?" She must have thought she saw the answer in Hewlitt's face, for she turned from him abruptly. "Then I think I'd better leave! I apologize for taking your time. . . ."

Before he could protest, she was already hurrying to her pony. She jerked its reins free of the locust branch and swung deftly astride. When she looked again at Hewlitt, he saw that her face was pale. Her voice trembled as she spoke. "I want you to know something, Mister Hewlitt! I *have* been interested in this group of yours from the very first day they came. Out riding, I used to watch from a distance . . . seeing the way you all worked together, how everyone pitched in when someone needed their help. I'm truly sorry I never knew about Missus Ferguson's baby, but I have no doubt the other women were there to do anything and everything for her that she needed.

"It made me happy," she went on in the same tone, "just knowing there *are* such people. I wanted to tell them so, and try making friends." She shook her head. "But, you see . . . I couldn't!"

"I don't understand!" Hewlitt exclaimed. "Why not?"

"Because I was afraid they wouldn't let me . . . knowing who I was, and who my father was! I thought they'd be suspicious, perhaps think I was trying to pry or make trouble. And. . . ." Suddenly her voice broke, and her eyes were swimming with tears. "And *you've* shown me, just now, how exactly right I was!"

In the next moment she was gone, sending her pony from that hilltop that she said had once been the most beautiful spot in her world. Vance Hewlitt was left staring after her, stunned with the knowledge that he had completely misjudged Connie Ballard.

There was no guile here. What he'd taken for coldness had been a lonely girl's fear of rejection by the very people she would have wanted for her friends. And suddenly, now that it was too late, he remembered his own mean-spirited words.

He stood there, abashed and overwhelmed with guilt.

One thing for certain, there was little likelihood he would be given a chance to apologize or try to make amends with Connie Ballard. He would have to live with knowing the thoughtless damage he'd done. . . .

In the days that followed Connie Ballard never returned to the homesteaders' settlement. As before, they saw her occasionally at a distance, spurring her palomino along the valley trails — a flash of golden beauty against the burgeoning green of springtime. Once, Vance Hewlitt's wagon passed her on the town road. He nodded and touched a finger to his hat brim, but her gaze was set straight ahead as she rode by.

At least, there had been no repercussions from Connie's visit of inspection. If she'd given York Ballard a report, it would appear not to have caused any difficulties. Hewlitt could only suppose the arrangement with her father was still in effect.

Then, late one afternoon, Len Ferguson came to him with word of something going on at the Bar-Y stackyard, adjoining Ferguson's claim here on the southern bank of Boulder Creek. The stack feed York

Ballard had brought in last fall had been stored there, under fence to protect it from cattle or deer, and hauled out and tossed sparingly to the seed herd that was held over during the lean months of winter. "Ballard's men have gone and taken down the fence," Len reported, "and now they're moving beef in there. I can't say I like the looks of it. . . ."

Hewlitt interrupted his chores to hoist a saddle onto the old sorrel mare, and the two of them rode to have a look. It was just as Ferguson had said. With the pole fence dismantled, a sizable number of head wearing the Bar-Y were already milling in the big yard while members of the crew worked to pull apart and spread what was left of the remaining stacks so the eager cattle could get at them. Today had been the warmest of the season, to date. Above the constant lowing of the herd and a rising film of hoof-trampled dust and chaff from the demolished stacks, the westering sun gave off more than a hint of what it would be like a few weeks from now.

York Ballard and his foreman and the latter's crony, Red Riling, sat their saddles observing the work, with Cap Nordhoff bawling out an occasional order. All three turned as the homesteaders rode toward them. Vance Hewlitt said without preliminary: "We were somehow under the impression your beef was all on its way to summer pasture, by this time."

"Not these," Ballard answered in his rumbling voice. "I've just landed a military contract, that needs to be filled immediately . . . and it's the quickest way to get some extra meat on them before I have to ship."

"I wish we could have known about this."

Cap Nordhoff turned his head and deliberately spat at the ground. "You know about it now," he said roughly. "Bar-Y ain't required to fill you nesters in on every detail of its business."

Ignoring him, Hewlitt went on: "Len Ferguson is some concerned about his property line." He indicated the single plowed furrow, not far from where they sat, that marked off the beginning of Ferguson's land. Beyond, newly sprouted plants made a dark green carpet, covering the full length of the homestead claims that stretched, without a break, almost to the valley's eastern end. "We had to make a choice between a good crop and fencing to protect it," he continued. "Now, with this herd where you've put it, we have nothing to prevent them drifting over onto our fields."

"Why would they do that?" Ballard retorted. "There's more feed, right under their noses, than they can hope to eat in the short time they'll be here."

But Vance Hewlitt persisted. "I don't think you understand. Right now is a critical period for us, while all these plants are getting their taproots set deep. Once it's done, there isn't much of anything can hurt a good stand of alfalfa . . . but until then a cow's hoofs can do a powerful lot of damage . . . and, as you know, every penny we were able to scrape together is down there right now, in the ground!"

The rancher had listened to this, as though in growing impatience. "Not being a farmer," he said now, with a shrug, "I'll have to take your word for all that. As I recall, though, we *did* have an agreement." And as he continued, although he spoke to his foreman, he still regarded the pair in front of him, as if waiting for their reaction. "We won't take any chances. Cap, you're to leave some men here to keep an eye on things, until it's certain these critters have got their bellies full and are ready to settle down and behave themselves. OK?"

Cap Nordhoff was using his neck cloth just then, mopping dust and sweat from beard-stubbled jowls. His hand went still, and for a moment Hewlitt thought he was going to argue. But when the rancher said more emphatically — "OK?" — his foreman decided to let the matter go with nothing more than a shrug. "You're the boss," he said in a sullen tone, and York Ballard looked again at the homesteaders.

"Well?" he wanted to know. "Does that satisfy?"

Vance Hewlitt shared a look with Ferguson before he nodded. He would have gone on to say — "And I appreciate you listening to us." — but he wasn't given the chance.

York Ballard was already lifting the reins and turning his horse. He rode away from there without another word, as though impatient to get on to other, and more important, matters. By this time, Hewlitt told himself he should be learning what to expect from the owner of the Bar-Y.

A muttered oath from Cap Nordhoff drew his attention to the foreman. Nordhoff looked angry, his mouth hard beneath the black mustache. A tug at the silver *peso* settled the neck cloth into place again about his throat. Piling both hands on the glittering pommel of his *charro* saddle, he glared balefully at Hewlitt as he said: "Now that you've gone and laid extra work on us, the two of you can get back to your plowing. But I can tell you this . . . if Ballard would only listen to *me,* instead of to that stuck-up little bitch . . . the valley would have been rid of you sodbusters long before now." And he added a warning: "It could happen yet!"

When Vance Hewlitt merely returned the look, coldly and without comment, he saw the tough foreman's face darken. Red Riling stirred in his saddle. He suggested: "Cap, I can keep an eye on this other one, if you feel like finishing the thing you didn't get to that day on the town road."

"It's entirely up to him," Hewlitt asserted flatly.

Returning the challenge was an impulsive decision, made almost without thinking. But he was ready enough to step down from his saddle, when for some reason Cap Nordhoff appeared to hesitate. And now Len Ferguson chose to break the tension, saying: "We all got more important things we could be doing."

Hewlitt's stare still held on the big foreman, as he awaited an answer. For some reason it didn't come. He was all at once reminded of mean dogs he had seen, on occasion, that would back off once a smaller dog decided to stand its ground. After a moment he shrugged and turned away, telling Len Ferguson: "Let's go, then." And after that it was too late for Ballard's foreman to renew the challenge.

As they headed home, Vance Hewlitt commented: "Well, in spite of Nordhoff that could have gone worse. I was glad to have York Ballard tell us, on his own, that he still means to do business. Never hearing from him, for all we knew, he could have changed his mind. He's not exactly an easy man to deal with."

He got no answer to that. Ferguson had been casting looks behind him, as they rode, and now he pulled up and hipped about in his battered saddle. His friend saw that he was studying the sky over toward the west, where the sun was just sliding from sight behind a dark edge of cloud. With its going, the breath of wind against their faces seemed to strengthen and turn cooler. Len Ferguson suggested suddenly: "You reckon we might be in for a change of weather?"

"The country could use some rain," Hewlitt said.

"But we sure as the devil wouldn't want

anything like a thunderstorm."

"You're thinking about those steers of Ballard's?"

His friend reminded him: "I've heard old cowboys say that, on the trail drives, a little thunder and a few bolts of lightning was all it took, sometimes, to set them off . . . and once they started running, it was no telling when they would quit."

"I see what you're getting at," Hewlitt finished it for him. "If a storm should blow up behind that bunch and send them in our direction, yours would be the first place hit . . . but then they could go ahead and take all the rest of us, one after the other, straight down the line. Is that what you mean?"

"With no sign of a fence anywhere, what would stop them?"

Hewlitt had no answer for that. Instead, he lifted his head, keening the occasional stir of air that came toward them from the west. "So far, the clouds over there don't look like they're moving very fast . . . and I haven't caught any hint of rain."

"You've always had a good nose for weather," his friend conceded. "I guess we'll just have to keep our fingers crossed."

As they left the sights and sounds of the stackyard, Hewlitt suggested: "Too late to do anything tonight . . . but, come morning, it might be an idea if we looked for some jack-pine to cut, and put up some kind of barricade along your boundary line . . . just to play safe."

"If it isn't too late by then," the other commented.

Dusk was beginning as they approached the Ferguson cabin, its windows showing cheery squares of light. "Why not have supper with us?" his friend suggested. "Whatever Mattie's got cooking would probably be better than anything you're apt to stir up yourself." Hewlitt couldn't argue with that; he was glad to accept the invitation. They left their horses under saddle at the feed trough. Mattie was smiling in the doorway, to welcome them in.

Vance Hewlitt always felt that this cabin bore the imprint of the people who lived here. Len Ferguson, a solid, big-framed man whose world revolved about his wife and son, had built plainly but intending that the house should last. Mattie's loving attentions had made it a home. By contrast Vance Hewlitt's was a lonely place, with no other presence than his own, and no woman's hand to cheer the bleak interior with flowered curtains at the windows, or a woman's voice to lighten the silence.

By the time the men had washed up, and Hewlitt had lingered for an envious moment beside the sleeping baby's crib, food was already on the table.

He noticed that Len told his wife nothing about the problem at the stackyard, and he took his cue from that and found other things to talk about. Ferguson himself fell silent toward the end of the meal. Once he rose abruptly and carried his cup of coffee to the door, to stand there looking into the night. When he tossed out the dregs and returned, his wife looked at him with an expression that made Hewlitt wonder if she didn't know her man too well to fail to sense that Len was troubled.

With the meal finished, Vance Hewlitt thanked Mattie again for having him, and left. He was standing beside his horse, studying the night, when Len came out to join him. It was dark by now, moonless as yet, with only the brilliant mesh of stars overhead. "I notice the wind's fallen some, and it's moved more to the south," Hewlitt pointed out. "From that, I'd say it's safe for us to quit worrying about a storm any time tonight."

"I'd sure like to believe that." Even so, Len sounded considerably reassured.

Out of the dark expanse of bottomland, west from where they stood, a single spot of light dimmed and brightened — almost like a distant star fallen to earth. That would be fire belonging to the night watch on Ballard's cattle, to boil coffee and give light to drink it by. Vance Hewlitt said: "I hope they take their job seriously. I've just been wondering if it would be a good idea to mount a guard at your boundary line, ready to turn back any of those steers that happen to get too close? I'd be glad to stand a shift, and I reckon the others would, too."

But Len Ferguson rejected that idea flatly. "Nothing doing! I won't ask any man to protect my property for me. We all of us have our problems . . . this happens to be one of mine."

He was so adamant that there seemed nothing to do but let the matter drop. After a few final words Hewlitt swung into the saddle. As he rode away, he was conscious of his friend's standing alone there, watching him until the night swallowed him up.

Vance Hewlitt didn't go directly home. He wanted to discuss the situation with Guy Adcock, an older man whose opinions he respected. A widower, Adcock held down his claim with the help of a sixteen-year-old son. He sat thoughtfully, working up a cloud of pipe smoke, as he listened now to this latest problem.

"I'd be a little uneasy myself, in Len's place," he admitted. "I guess you don't necessarily need thunder and lightning to unsettle a bunch of beef and send them off . . . sometimes nothing more, maybe, than an unexpected noise, or a strong whiff of cat or bear. On the other hand, these critters of Ballard's aren't out in the middle of nowhere, on a trail drive where everything is strange. The valley is their home turf, and I'd think that might make a difference. But, who's to say?"

Hewlitt had to agree. "I offered to take turns helping Len watch his boundary line, but he wouldn't hear of letting me."

"He's a proud man." Frowning, Adcock considered the stem of his pipe. "We'll just have to hope York Ballard's men do their job. Tomorrow, I'm all for your idea of trying to rig something stout enough to keep Ballard's cattle where they belong." They both decided, for now, they must leave it at that.

On returning to his own place, something prompted Hewlitt to leave the mare under saddle a while longer. Despite the heat of the day just ended, tonight threatened to turn chilly. With a lamp lit, he occupied himself with shaking down the ashes in the stove he used for both heating and cooking, and laid the makings of a small fire, keeping his hands busy while his thoughts worked over that scene at the stackyard. He was reaching for a match when he paused, catching a first rumble of sound that suddenly stopped the breath in his throat.

All at once he knew he had been listening for this! He was quickly on his feet and making for the door. As he wrenched it open, the sound seemed almost to leap at him, the initial rumble suddenly welling. Hewlitt paused long enough to blow out the lamp and, as an afterthought, grope for the revolver lying on a shelf beside the door. He shoved the gun behind his belt, not knowing clearly what he meant to do with it, then he was outside and making for his horse. Catching up the reins, he threw himself into saddle, and a kick of his heel sent the startled mare floundering into a run.

A moon, near the full, had lifted above the eastern ridges to send a silver probe deep into the throat of the valley. Hewlitt peered grimly ahead, dry of mouth as he drove his mount, recklessly, to meet the thing he knew was approaching. The old workhorse did not have many such bursts of raw energy in her, and, when he pulled to an abrupt stop, her lungs were working hard against her ribs. But she had brought the trouble into view.

On hardpan, the drumming of hoofs would have thrown back waves of echoes from the valley's timbered walls; fields like these, that had been plowed and sown and irrigated, absorbed much of the sound. But, whatever had caused a stampede, on a night as calm as this one, it had already crossed the Ferguson claim and, with no apparent slackening, was coming straight toward him. And now, at last, moonlight made it visible — a shapeless, surging mass that showed an occasional glint of tossing horns, and made the ground shake as it thundered nearer.

Vance Hewlitt had halted just clear of danger, and, almost without thinking, he brought up the gun. There would be five bullets, for all the good they would do him. He waited until the leaders were almost even with him, before opening fire.

It was little more than a gesture. A few of the near leaders reacted to the streaking burst of flame, almost in their faces. They might have tried to halt or turn aside, except for the pressure of the stampede that caught them up and sent them on. With his final cartridge quickly spent, Hewlitt could do nothing then but lower the empty gun and feel the mare trembling under him.

In a matter of minutes the tide of beef was past.

Hewlitt released pent-up breath. He knew that Guy Adcock and the others to the east of him would be learning soon enough what was coming. With an empty gun and a spent horse under him, there was no way he could be of any help or even give them warning — probably nothing anyone could do, but wait for this thing to run its course. He stayed where he was, letting the panicked mare have time to settle.

Only daylight would show the full extent of damage done by the stampeding herd. Just now, his first concern was to find out how his friends, the Fergusons, had made out. When at length he spoke to the mare, it was to send her, at her own pace, in the direction of the claim that adjoined his own.

Lamplight glowed in the cabin windows. He called out as he approached, and at once Mattie threw open the door and hurried out, the baby clutched in her arms. Lamplight revealed the anxiety in her face. Pulling up, he said: "Is everyone all right here?"

Her voice shook as she answered. "It's Len . . . I don't know where he is! All through dinner I could see he was worked up, but I didn't know why. Finally he told me there was something he needed to check up on. He took his horse and rode away . . . and it couldn't have been more than a few minutes when. . . ." Her stammering voice broke off.

"Do you know which way he went?" Hewlitt was not surprised when she indicated the direction of the boundary line, to the west. "Try not to worry. I'll find him for you." And he reined away, hoping he had sounded more confident than he felt.

There'd be little enough a barricade could do now, he thought grimly. Even by moonlight he began to make out the devastation around him, as the exhausted horse picked a way over the hoof-torn wreckage of what had been plowed ground under a spreading cover of new vegetation. He went quartering across the ruined fields, uncertain how to go about this search for something he hoped not to find.

All too soon he saw a horse standing motionless, its head hanging, and as he came nearer made out the empty saddle on its back. He saw how the animal jerked up its head in terror; he spoke quietly and managed to catch the bridle. The horse moved a little, and he made out the dark streak across a shoulder, and felt warm blood where a sharp horn must have raked it.

The old mare snorted at the scent of blood, and Vance Hewlitt spoke sharply to it as he dismounted, holding both sets of reins. His knees were already unsteady, for by now he had seen the man who lay on the dark ground, one leg canted at an odd angle from the boot trapped in a saddle stirrup.

Len Ferguson had never been much of a horseman. With a stampede coming at him, it was easy to imagine his making a scramble to get out of the way, only to end by being thrown and dragged. Kneeling beside him, Hewlitt tried to assess the damage from trampling hoofs.

His friend still clung to consciousness. "Vance?" he murmured hoarsely. "Is that you?"

"Don't try to move," Hewlitt said. "Until I can find out how bad you've been hurt."

The other didn't seem to hear. As Hewlitt moved to try and free him from the stirrup, Len Ferguson clutched blindly at his arm. "Vance, I got to tell you! Those steers . . . it wasn't no accident. Gunfire started them off! You hear what I'm saying? There was. . . ."

It was all he managed to get out, before he went limp.

III

The sun rose gloriously, slanting its rays along the trough of the valley, turning Boulder Creek to liquid gold where it tumbled its way through the length of it. But this new day also revealed the full extent of ruin that had been brought to the valley homesteaders.

Warming sunlight found everyone gathered at the Ferguson place. Even the children seemed subdued, quieted by the somber manner of their elders who were virtually in a state of shock. And in the cabin he had built for his family, Len Ferguson lay on the bed with a threadbare quilt drawn over his face.

He had managed to hang on for most of

an hour, long enough to give a more coherent account of the gunshots last night — three of them, he'd said, and deliberately spaced, before the thunder of hoofs made any more shooting unnecessary. The faces of his hearers had turned bleak as they listened to his faltering voice, then the voice was silenced forever. Mattie had broken under the blow. Now she sat huddled in a corner, the baby in her arms, with some of the women trying to comfort her while others busied themselves preparing a meal for everyone.

Most of the men formed a grim conclave in front of the cabin, with Guy Adcock's teenage boy, Barney, for the first time finding himself included in grown-up deliberations. So far, they seemed to have got nowhere. The same words were being repeated, over and over again, in tones edged with helpless anger and despair.

Suddenly someone remarked, "Rider coming. . . ."

From the direction of the shallow creek crossing, the figures of horse and rider had become visible. They watched them take shape, coming steadily nearer across Len Ferguson's havoc-stricken fields. It was some time before one of the group could say: "Hell! It's the Ballard girl!"

"What's *she* want?" another exclaimed. "Come here to gloat?"

Connie Ballard rode into a dead silence. As she drew rein, looking from one person to another, her face held a pallor despite the rosy flush of morning. Her voice was not entirely steady as she said: "Will someone please tell me what happened here?"

A man answered harshly: "What happened was, the lot of us got put out of business last night!"

"If that's what you were sent here to find out," a second added, "you can tell York Ballard the job couldn't have been better done!"

He might almost have struck her. She stared at him as though not able to speak.

Now Guy Adcock entered a protest: "There isn't any call for such talk! We have no reason to think the girl knew anything about this."

"And why not?"

Heads turned. Hollow-eyed and haggard, Mattie Ferguson stood in the doorway, with hair fallen uncombed about her shoulders and deep lines in her face that had not been there a few hours ago. "Who can trust any Ballard?" she demanded hoarsely. "She was here one day, making a fuss over my baby . . . letting on that she wanted to be friends. But, it was only for show. She never bothered to come back . . . now, with my husband lying dead, all I want is to see her off this place! Make her go away and leave us alone!"

Mattie's voice broke on that, and she stood weeping, face twisted in anguish, until one of the women came from the house and put an arm around her, to lead her gently back inside.

Vance Hewlitt had been at the woodpile behind the cabin, venting some of his own pent-up emotions in clean and vigorous labor. When he rounded the corner of the house with an armload of kindling for Mattie's stove, he was brought to a halt at sight of Connie on her palomino, listening, while Len's widow poured out her bitterness. She remained speechless and unmoving, although her cheeks showed the sting of the words that were being thrown at her. But when the outburst ended and Mattie had vanished, a sudden jerk at the reins spun the palomino in his tracks. Head held high, and without another word or glance for anyone, Connie Ballard gave her pony the heel of her boot and sent him leaping into motion, to return by the same route they had come.

Belatedly Hewlitt jarred loose, dumping the armload of kindling as he started for his own horse. The sorrel mare was still recuperating from its hard work of yesterday. This was her mate from the wagon team — a cold-jawed gelding with a bone-shaking gait that required a firm hand on the reins. He piled onto it now, ignoring a question somebody shouted. Within minutes the Ferguson cabin and the men gathered there were left behind.

If Connie knew she was being followed, she didn't allow herself to give a sign of it, or try to alter her pace — she had been hurt, and a firm dignity was probably all the defense that was left to her. Hewlitt gained slowly, despite his sorry mount's lumbering gait. The girl on the palomino was almost ready to take the creekbed's stony crossing, before he was near enough to make himself heard: "Connie! Miss Ballard! Please let me talk to you!"

He thought at first she didn't hear, or pretended not to, but at the last moment she drew up and half turned her mount. Hewlitt reined in. The blue eyes beneath the flat-topped riding hat held no promise as the girl asked stonily: "What do you want from me?"

He spoke earnestly, not at all sure if he

could get through to her past the hurt and anger. "I had to ask you to try, if you can, to understand those people back there. Especially Mattie Ferguson . . . these past few hours have been the very worst of her life. Her sun rose and set in Len . . . the things she said to you came out of terrible pain. But in due time she'll remember them, and she'll be anxious to apologize."

She reminded him in the same cold voice: "*You* accused me, once, of coming here to spy for my father."

"I know . . . and I've hated myself for it, every day since. Right now is *my* turn for apologies, and I'm glad to have the chance. Only, please don't give up on us entirely. Not yet!"

All at once he saw her defenses melt, and suddenly her eyes swam with tears. "Everything's horrible!" she gasped. "I come for a ride, at sunrise . . . and I find *this!*" She gestured toward the ruined fields they had crossed. "Do you people really believe it could have been done on purpose?"

He proceeded to tell her, in a few words, what the dying Len Ferguson had reported as to the beginning of the stampede. "I suppose it might be possible to imagine hearing a pistol shot," Hewlitt said. "But . . . three of them, one after the other?"

He waited, giving time for the question to sink in. Connie's glance was lowered to her hands, tight upon the reins. The wide brim of the riding hat concealed her face. When she spoke, it was to say in a muffled voice: "I only know that . . . that my father. . . ." The rest was indistinct, and ended in silence.

Vance Hewlitt realized she was crying and all at once knew it could do no good to go on punishing her like this. He drew a breath. "All right," he told her quietly. "I honestly understand how you feel. I wish there was something more I could say, but I can't think what it would be. So, I won't trouble you any further."

She still did not look at him, but he gravely touched finger to hat brim as he brought the gelding around for his return to the Ferguson cabin. He left her there with the burbling music of the creek rising from the rocky ford just beyond.

But he had ridden scarcely a quarter of a mile when the sound of a cantering horse turned his head, to discover the girl on the palomino was coming after him. He had pulled the old gelding in and for some moments had been studying the trampled ground in front of him. He shifted position in the saddle and waited for Connie to come to a halt beside him.

She seemed to have regained her composure. She said: "It looked to me as though you might have found something."

"As a matter of fact, I think I have." And he pointed to a horseshoe print amidst the confusion of cattle tracks that lay across their route, and pointing in the same direction — east. "If I thought it would do any good, I'd be inclined to hunt for more." He shook his head. "But, I know my limitations: I'm only a farmer . . . I've never had much experience at reading sign."

"Well, I *have*," Connie told him. "When I was hardly big enough to sit the saddle in front of him, my father used to take me with him out on the range. He taught me all kinds of things, wonderful things I've never forgotten!" And, passing Hewlitt the reins to hold for her, she swung lightly down.

He stayed where he was, not wanting to interfere, as she studied the print closely. After a moment Connie apparently decided to make a search, following in the wake of the stampeded herd. Vance Hewlitt sat and watched, with growing respect, her concentration and care in choosing her steps, so as not to destroy the very thing she was looking for.

It began to look as if she'd told the simple truth: York Ballard must have given this daughter of his good training.

Presently she halted, to stand motionless while Hewlitt wondered what thoughts were going through her mind. She seemed to straighten her shoulders, then. She looked around for him, and beckoned.

Vance Hewlitt had already dismounted. He led both their mounts as he went to join her. Connie's manner was direct, now, and business-like. "There's plenty of tracks," she told him, although he could see nothing at all but confusion. "Whoever left them here, must have a good cutting horse under him. You can see how he kept him working, back and forth, lunging at the stragglers . . . forcing them to close up. . . ."

He stared at her. "Then, you're saying . . . ?"

She nodded, reluctant but too honest to deny the facts. "I'm afraid you and your friends are right. These steers were being driven . . . hard. And it would have taken more than one rider to do it and still hold them all together."

"I see. So, now we know." Vance Hewlitt spoke the words slowly, frowning as he gazed off in the wake of the vanished cattle. "It's strange that none of us, last night, caught so much as a glimpse of them. They must have pulled back, as soon as the herd was running good enough that they figured nothing could stop it. . . ."

Connie had become very quiet. With face averted, she turned suddenly to her pony.

Vance Hewlitt quickly followed. He held the stirrup as she mounted, and afterward stood trying to find words to say. In the end, he could only tell her: "I'm sorry about this, Connie. I'm truly sorry!"

Her troubled gaze studied him, and after a moment she nodded. "Yes, I really believe you are," she answered in a leaden voice. "But, if you people still claim that my father . . . that he deliberately. . . ."

"You haven't heard *me* say that," Hewlitt quietly reminded her, and let her think about it as he went to mount his own horse.

His toe was in the stirrup when a puzzling glimmer of brightness caught his eye, amid the general desolation about him. As Hewlitt was trying to center on it, the old workhorse suddenly decided to stage one of his protests against being made to wear a saddle. Tossing his head, moving his feet around, he threw his owner briefly off balance. As usually happened though, once Hewlitt had freed himself from the stirrup, a few words and a strong hand settled matters quickly enough. The old horse subsided, and a moment later Vance Hewlitt was in the saddle with the reins lifted, ready to ride.

Only then he remembered the glint of reflected light that had puzzled him. He almost decided to waste no more time, but curiosity won out and brought him down to have a look. Scanning the ground, he quickly spotted the thing, whatever it was. He was reaching to pick it up before he recognized it.

Hewlitt caught his breath, let it out in a low whistle. He walked over to Connie, who had been watching his odd behavior and showed her what he had found. "You've seen this before?"

She nodded, frowning. "Of course," she said. "But, what on earth?"

"I think," Hewlitt told her bleakly, "we're going to have to have a talk with York Ballard."

They found the rancher and his foreman at breakfast in the otherwise deserted cook shack. Cap Nordhoff put down his coffee cup as Connie and Hewlitt walked in. The Bar-Y owner gave a quick frown at sight of his daughter and this homesteader together. He told the latter, in his growling voice: "If this is a social call, it's pretty damned early for one."

Hewlitt suggested: "Could be your foreman will have an idea why I'm here. Or, did he happen to say anything about the stampede?"

"What stampede? What are you talking about?"

Ballard shot an inquiring look at Nordhoff.

The big man only shrugged as he grunted: "No point asking *me*."

"Dad, it's true." Connie was unable to hold back any longer. "That herd you were holding to ship . . . something set them running last night. Drove them right across the ground where the homesteaders have been putting in so much time and work. This morning I was out riding, early, and I saw the damage. Everything's in ruins!"

The rancher frowned, absorbing this and her evident concern. To his foreman he said: "You *did* set a guard? Like I told you?"

"Well, sure," the man answered gruffly.

"But I pulled 'em off, come nightfall. Those critters had settled, gave no sign of turning restless."

Vance Hewlitt commented: "Is this how he carries out your orders, Ballard?"

"I generally let my foreman use his best judgment," the rancher replied curtly. "Where are those cattle now?"

Hewlitt shrugged. "If they've stopped running, I imagine they're scattered somewhere outside the east end of the valley."

Ballard swore under his breath. "It'll be the devil's own job to round them up again!"

"But, Dad! You haven't heard the worst." Connie insisted. "A man is dead . . . and there's good reason to think the thing was started on purpose."

"Who says so?" Dishes rattled as Cap Nordhoff slammed both fists upon the trestle table. "Name him! I'll tell him to his face, he's a liar!"

"I'm afraid you won't be able to," Hewlitt answered him coldly. "Len Ferguson was the man that got dragged and killed. But he lived long enough to tell us he heard the gunshots that spooked those animals and got them going."

"Hogwash!"

"Is that all you've got to say? Then, how

about this?" Hewlitt brought it from his pocket and dropped it in front of the foreman. The metallic ring of the silver *peso* striking the table top was only partly muffled by a blue neck cloth, which still had one corner threaded through the hole drilled in the coin to anchor it. "Yours, isn't it, Nordhoff? Connie and I found it, just a little while ago. You dropped it while you were out pushing those steers across our land . . . making sure they didn't stop running!"

Hewlitt noticed how, at sight of the neckpiece, the big man started an involuntary motion toward his throat before he could check himself and jerk the hand away. Quickly recovering, Nordhoff resorted to denial: "Hell, I been wondering what happened to that thing. I lost it a couple days ago." He eyes took on a crafty look. "Maybe somebody found it . . . and this is how they mean to use it, to make trouble for me."

"Two days ago?" Hewlitt shook his head. "That's no good, Nordhoff. You were still wearing it late yesterday, when Ferguson and I ran into you at the stackyard. I remember . . . you were using it to mop your face with, while we talked. *You* were there, Ballard." Hewlitt turned to him. "You must have noticed."

But the rancher impatiently shook his head. "Why would I be expected to remember something like that? I've got more important things on my mind."

And seeing the implacable set of his features, Hewlitt realized suddenly that it was true: Ballard simply did not remember — what should have been evidence, implicating his foreman, meant nothing to him at all.

But the challenge had brought Cap Nordhoff to his feet. He stood glowering across the littered table at the man who accused him. He told his boss: "You don't remember because this whole thing's a lie. People like these wouldn't be above stampeding your cattle themselves, if they thought, by doing it, they'd finagle more out of you than those stinkin' claims of theirs will ever be worth. And if some jackass fell off his horse and broke his neck doing it . . . hell, what's that to us? York, I been telling you all along no good would ever come of it, letting them in your valley."

The moment hung fire. Ballard was still seated, scowling, head sunk forward like a man deep in thought. He drew a breath now and straightened, and, when he spoke, it was in a wooden voice, almost without emotion: "I'm beginning to see I made a bad mistake. I'd been told nesters were a quarrelsome lot, ready to blame their failures on the weather, or the railroads, or the cattlemen . . . on anything except themselves. I tried to tell myself the old days were gone, and in the end there'd probably be no choice but to try and get along with them. I thought if they just got it through their heads I wouldn't stand for any foolishness, maybe things would work out. But I was wrong. The long and the short of it is this valley is cattle country . . . there never was a place in it for the likes of sodbusters. It's just as plain as that."

Vance Hewlitt's hands, hanging at his sides, were clenched. "Are you saying that you intend to be rid of us?"

In the same toneless voice, the man answered him: "I didn't raise a hand to keep you from coming here . . . I won't do anything to stop you leaving."

Hearing this, Cap Nordhoff slapped his palms together and said in crowing triumph: "Boss, if they need any encouragement . . . I'll be more than glad to see they get it."

A cry of protest was stung from Connie Ballard — "Dad, this isn't *right!*" — but her words fell on deaf ears.

Vance Hewlitt, for one, had heard enough. He had been shown the futility of argument, and even of physical evidence like that lying on the table. Jaw clamped hard to hold back more angry and futile language, he was already putting his back to that scene. The solid *clomp* of a sodbuster's work shoes was the only sound as he strode to the door, and into a dazzle of morning sunlight.

IV

The men who gathered in Vance Hewlitt's cabin listened somberly to his report of the encounter at Bar-Y. Finished, he looked over their faces, and before anyone could speak he added: "I'd like to say one thing more, just so none of you will have to . . . I take the blame for this. I persuaded you all to let me offer Ballard a deal. I really believed, if he accepted one, he would stand by it. I'm still convinced he had no part in what happened last night. But he sure didn't lose any time cutting loose from us once the damage was done."

"By his own, handpicked crew of

toughs," Tobe Lykins pointed out. Lykins was something of a loner in this group, one of the few who had no family and scarcely any real friends. A bitter-eyed, quarrelsome fellow, he seldom had anything positive to say. "I never trusted Ballard for a second . . . and I ain't the one let himself get in thick with that girl of his."

Hewlitt felt warmth sting his cheeks, but he didn't rise to the bait. His tone was quiet as he answered: "I'll tell you this. Connie Ballard feels as bad about this whole thing as any of us. You can believe that or not, but it's true."

Lykins hunched his shoulders in a shrug, as his glance slid away from Hewlitt's. Guy Adcock spoke up then, and attention turned to him.

"There's no good in arguing about the past. We have a situation, and it's up to us to decide now what we do about it. So, let me ask you . . . do we give up? Tuck our tails and run? Personally, I don't see how we can. We have too much at stake, and through no fault of ours . . . we did nothing but act in good faith, and according to the agreement York Ballard had with us."

Somebody asked: "You got something else to suggest?"

"Yes!" Adcock spoke with firm commitment. "I think we have to call York Ballard's hand, without wasting any more time. I suggest we call on him, in a body, to make it clear we aren't leaving . . . and that we aren't to be bluffed into letting him out of his part of the bargain. Because, if he imagines otherwise, who else is there but us to set him straight?"

A few heads were beginning to nod; there were murmurs of approval. In the end only one or two hung back, still doubtful. It was Tobe Lykins who asked uneasily: "Do we take a vote on this?"

"We don't need one," Adcock answered him. "Time's still wasting. Any of you who agrees with me, be at my place in half an hour . . . with guns loaded, and saddled to ride. *That* can be your vote." And he left them to think it over.

Vance Hewlitt was among the first to gather at Adcock's claim when the half hour was up. He had dug up a holster and belt for the revolver; fully loaded, the weapon now rested on his right hip. Adcock was pleased but considerably astonished to see him. "Then, you're riding with us?"

"Did you think I wouldn't? I had my

240

turn," Hewlitt pointed out. "The rest of you backed me to the hilt when I suggested offering Ballard a deal. That idea didn't work out . . . now, whatever comes of this one, I figure I'm obligated to do my bit by helping in any way I can."

"You sound a little dubious."

"It's true enough. I imagine you are, yourself . . . at least, a little."

The other had to nod, admitting it. "But we've got to stand on what's right. The way I see it, that has to include full compensation for our losses, so we can make a second try. You think of anything else?"

"It's your show," Hewlitt told him. "I'd say you're doing fine." He added thoughtfully: "And I've been figuring, the odds against us could be worse. After all, we won't be facing Ballard's entire crew at Bar-Y. Connie tells me the older hands, who have stayed on out of loyalty to the brand, have no use at all for their new foreman, and anyway they're mostly in the high country right now with the main herd. In numbers, we're about even with Nordhoff and his bunch of toughs. I won't say how close we come to being a match for them. . . ."

By now the rest of the homesteaders had assembled — eight of them by tally, none of them too familiar to the saddle or to the odd collection of weapons they brought with them. Among the others, Hewlitt spotted Adcock's sixteen-year-old, looking a little pale but excited and proud to be one of them.

Somebody said: "We're shy a man . . . Tobe Lykins. Wouldn't you know?"

"Don't be too hard on him," Guy Adcock said. "You can't force a man to be a hero. Besides, it may turn out he's the only one among us that isn't completely crazy." He looked around at his company, whose ill-assorted mounts appeared to share the uneasiness of their riders. "Are we all ready?" He lifted an arm. "Then, let's go!"

With Adcock and Hewlitt in the lead, they rode out silently, nobody in a mood for talk now, each trying not to think too far ahead. They went purposefully, not pushing their horses. In due time they splashed across the creek's shallow ford, and there fell into the main valley road, turning west. The day had turned out beautiful — not too warm, a few fleecy clouds just cresting the hills that shaped the green trough of this valley and sent back the echoes of their passage

It hardly seemed the kind of day to be

facing a showdown.

When at length they reached the turn-off to Bar-Y headquarters, and the lane with its tall line of poplars leading arrow-straight from the entrance under its high gateway, some common impulse made them all draw rein. Into the murmur of swaying trees, Guy Adcock said a little uncertainly: "I wonder how we should go about this?"

"Just ride straight in," Hewlitt suggested. "Like we have business that gives us a right to be here."

"You're right," the other agreed, adding: "I've been thinking maybe you could do the talking for us? You've had more dealings with Ballard than anyone else."

"However you want it . . ." He broke off. Suddenly alert, Hewlitt found himself straightening in the saddle to peer ahead down the avenue of trees.

A rider had burst into sight at the end of it to come straight toward them at a drumming gallop through the pattern of light and leaf shadow. With exclamation Vance Hewlitt gave his horse a kick and sent it forward.

Connie Ballard was hatless, bright hair streaming as she peered behind her. When she turned and saw him coming to intercept her, she appeared almost not to recognize him, but, as they came together, she reined the palomino to a halt. Her face was ashen, her eyes dark with emotion.

"Connie," he said. "What's wrong?"

She clutched at the arm he reached to steady her. "Everything!" she cried. "It's Dad and Cap Nordhoff . . . they just had a terrible row. I'd finally got Dad to listen to me about last night. Nordhoff was drinking, and, when Dad called him in and demanded to be told, flat out, if that stampede was his doing, the man just laughed and admitted it. Then Dad told him he was fired . . . and Cap shot him!"

Hewlitt stared. "Dead?"

She shook her head frantically. "I don't *know!* I saw him fall, but I couldn't go to him because Cap started for *me,* and I was sure he meant to kill me, too . . . he hates me enough. But I'd left my pony saddled, and somehow I managed to get away. The last thing I heard was Cap yelling at his men that he wanted me stopped. . . ." She twisted about for another look, clearly expecting to see them coming at her heels.

Hewlitt had already drawn his gun. "Where is your father?"

"In his office . . . at the back of the house."

Vance Hewlitt turned to Adcock, who had been listening to this. "Quick! Get her out of sight . . . maybe in that clump of trees on the other side of the road." Without waiting for an answer, he kicked his old horse into a lumbering run straight down the lane of poplars, knowing that, whatever else happened, harm must somehow be kept from Connie Ballard.

As he broke out of the lane into the ranch yard, he looked first for Nordhoff but didn't see him. Activity and swirling dust in the circular holding corral told him a pursuit was starting. One man was hastily piling gear onto his horse. Another, already mounted, was at the corral gate, leaning to slip the rawhide loop that would allow it to swing open. Vance Hewlitt made directly for him, pistol leveled as he shouted: "Leave it closed! Get down off that saddle!"

The man's head jerked up. He was starting for a holster when Hewlitt pulled rein, just short of colliding with the gate, and reached an arm across it. His gun barrel clipped the man's skull. The blow knocked the hat from his head and sent him tumbling into the corral's dust at the feet of his own frightened mount.

Thrown off balance, Hewlitt had to grab

the saddle horn and right himself — just in time to meet a spurt of flame that split the dust film inside the corral. He almost thought he felt the bullet streak past his ear as he glimpsed the first man, turned now from his saddling to take a shot at him. But somewhere close to Hewlitt, another gun answered it. The man in the corral doubled over and went down hard, as the horses penned inside started going crazy.

Hewlitt turned hastily, found Guy Adcock sitting saddle nearby with a gun smoking in his hand — he looked a little stunned, knowing his bullet had actually hit a man and possibly killed him. Vance Hewlitt knew exactly how he felt, but at least those two in the corral no longer posed a threat to Connie Ballard.

Adcock guessed the question he wanted to ask and assured him briefly: "She went into hiding, like you said. I sent my boy Barney along with her . . . told him to use the gun I gave him, if they ran into any trouble. And I really believe the kid would do it."

The rest of the homesteaders were erupting into the yard, alert for danger. One spotted a man emerging from the barn, headed for the corral, carrying a bridle, and with a saddle on his shoulder. Before that one knew what was happening, a farmer on a crow-bait workhorse was looming over him, a pistol was pointed at his head as he was given the order to drop the saddle and, if he had a gun, to get rid of that, too.

Someone else made a quick check of the barn, and, when Vance rode over to find out if he'd seen anyone inside, he gave a negative answer. Indicating the prisoner, Hewlitt ordered: "Put this one out of action. You can use his own saddle rope. Tie him to one of those corral posts . . . just make sure he can't get loose."

Adcock was beside him, frowning. "This only makes three. Where are the rest?"

"There, maybe." Hewlitt indicated a low, shake-roofed building that had the look of a bunkhouse. Just at that moment its door was flung open, and someone came lunging outside. He was only partly dressed, the way he might have been when a sound of shouting brought him out of his bunk. *Sleeping in, this morning?* Hewlitt had time to think. *Maybe he was up late — running cattle!*

A glance around seemed to tell the man all he needed to know. He had brought a gun, and, when he saw Hewlitt starting to rein toward him, he leaped back inside, managing to fling a shot past the edge of the door before he jerked it shut.

At once a confusion of yelling voices broke out inside the building. A bullet through an open window split the air between Hewlitt and Adcock, but they were already pulling back from their exposed position.

"I guess we've found the rest of them," Hewlitt said quickly. "There should be three or four, at the most. Try and see if you and the others can pin them down in there . . . send somebody around back, to make sure they don't get out *that* way. I've got to find York Ballard."

"Alone?"

The other man wanted to protest, but Hewlitt didn't have time to listen. He turned his horse and, as he gave it a boot, could hear Guy Adcock already shouting orders.

Now the white-painted, two-story ranch house loomed just ahead, the pound of his horse's hoofs echoing back at him from its high, blank wall. Connie had said her father's office would be somewhere toward the rear, perhaps in a lower-roofed addition he could see back there. He started to swerve toward it. But at that moment a windowpane, almost directly in front of him, burst to splinters under the blow of a gun barrel. The old horse flung up his head in terror, just as muzzle-flame and ballooning smoke filled the shattered opening. A bullet meant for his rider took the horse instead and dropped him dead in his tracks.

Hewlitt never knew how he escaped being pinned underneath. Somehow he fell free, sprawling and even managing to hold onto his gun. From the ground he had presence of mind to drive a shot toward the window, and thought he saw someone there move hastily out of danger. It gave him a moment to scramble to his feet and try to make the building's rear corner, before another bullet could come hunting for him.

He reached over and pulled up, aware of the pounding of his heart — this business of shooting and being shot at was still a new one for Vance Hewlitt. There were no windows here, but two plank steps led up to a rear entrance where a screen door showed a shadowy interior. Hewlitt headed for that, mounting the steps with one stride. Cautiously, gun in hand, he drew the door wide enough for him to slip through, letting it ease shut against a heel.

The stillness of a narrow hallway confronted him. From outside, there now came only an occasional, wide-spaced gunshot that suggested the fight at the bunkhouse could have become a stand-off, both sides possibly wary of using up their supplies of ammunition. Here, where he stood, two closed doors faced each other with nothing to indicate which one would be York Ballard's office.

He did know that his horse had been shot from under him by somebody in that room to his right. When the knob turned suddenly under an unseen hand, he was ready — shoulders against the wall to make a smaller target, six-shooter leveled. The door sprang violently open, and Red Riling came bursting through. Hewlitt had thought it would be Cap Nordhoff, but he was not taken by surprise. Riling caught sight of him, and two shots sounded at almost the same instant, the mingled reports ear-punishing in that narrow space. Still unhurt and on his feet, Hewlitt watched the red-headed man stagger back against the door frame, then rebound to a limp sprawl on the uncarpeted boards of the hallway.

Although he had never shot anyone before, Vance Hewlitt felt Red Riling was probably dead. There wasn't time to make certain, so, hastily stepping around him, Hewlitt went for a look into that room. With the first glance he saw the window Riling had knocked out in order to take the shot that killed his horse. Mostly, however, there were things he wasn't expecting to find: piles of crates and barrels, shelves filled with canned supplies, similar odds and ends. No, this had to be a storeroom of some kind, not York Ballard's office.

Too late, he took warning. He hadn't heard that other door open, just behind him, but when the voice spoke, he recognized it well enough.

"All right, plow boy! How about letting me see you lose that gun you're holding. . . ."

V

The knowledge of defeat settled in Hewlitt like a leaden weight. Cap Nordhoff's words held the smug assurance of a leveled weapon. Plainly there was no choice but to let his revolver go, to thud on the floor at his feet.

"That's fine," the voice behind him said.

"Do you want to turn around and face me . . . or take it in the back?"

Slowly, both hands lifted and empty, Hewlitt came about so that the two stood confronted, with Red Riling's body between them. Nordhoff's six-shooter held steady. A metal cashbox was clamped under one arm. Looking past him into the office, Hewlitt could see a large safe, its door standing open. It had been ransacked, a scatter of papers and record books littering the floor in front of it. With cold contempt he said: "Robbing a dead man, Nordhoff?"

The heavy cheeks colored at the taunt. "It ain't what I planned," the foreman answered harshly. "Nothing like. This was a great set-up while it lasted . . . damned if I can see why it had to end. I had the old fool wrapped around my little finger . . . but, thanks to you and that little bitch. . . ." Hatred for Vance Hewlitt and Connie Ballard twisted the mouth beneath his black mustache. "The time has come to move on. Looks like I get to settle things with *you*, at least." The revolver in his hand lifted.

But the gunshot that broke the stillness did not come from it. Braced to take a bullet, Vance Hewlitt saw the other's mouth go slack, his eyes widen. Cap Nordhoff put out a hand as if reaching for something to steady him. The cashbox slipped from under his arm, springing open and spilling out a shower of coins and greenbacks. Then the big man's knees buckled, and he fell.

Hewlitt had presence of mind to turn and scoop up his own gun, where he had been forced to drop it. Moving cautiously forward, he saw one last spasm of breath lift Nordhoff's thick chest before the man lay still. The toe of a shoe edged the foreman's weapon clear of the limp fingers that had held it. Sliding his own gun into the holster, Hewlitt stepped past him and entered the room.

Besides the rifled safe, it contained a roll-top desk and chair near the window, a gun cabinet, a couch with a bright Navajo blanket thrown over it, and the mounted head of a bighorn on the wall above. On the floor by the desk, York Ballard lay, propped on an elbow. The bottom drawer of the desk had been hauled part way open, a shell belt and holster hung over its side. Ballard's fist, supported by the edge of the drawer, held a revolver that had acrid smoke leaking from its muzzle. As Hewlitt reached him, the rancher raised his head and with an effort managed to ask: "Did I get the son-of-a-bitch?"

"You damn' well did," Hewlitt assured him. "And with just one bullet. . . ."

"Good!" But the effort had taken its toll. The smoking gun slipped from Ballard's fingers. As his body went limp, Hewlitt caught him and managed to ease him into a better position.

What Nordhoff apparently had believed to be a mortal wound had only barely missed it. When Vance Hewlitt got the rancher's shirt open, he found far less blood than he expected to. From what little he could claim to know about gunshot wounds, this one appeared to have made a clean hole — he hoped — without damaging a rib.

Before he was able to learn more, he heard voices and a trample of footsteps approaching through the hallway. That brought him quickly to his feet, a hand on his holstered gun while he tried to calculate how many bullets it still held. Already the voices were just outside the door. He heard a man exclaiming: "My God, it's Riling . . . dead! And, look here! Isn't this . . . ?"

Then Connie Ballard appeared in the doorway. Hewlitt quickly let his hand fall away from his holster. The girl's face was white. She gave scarcely a glance to the lifeless body of Cap Nordhoff as she anxiously scanned the room, searching for her father. Now she saw him, and Hewlitt drew back to make way as she hurried to drop to her knees beside York Ballard.

"I think he's got a good chance," Hewlitt said. "There's a strong pulse, and not too awfully much blood. . . ."

Two more people burst into the room to join them. One was young Barney Adcock, the other a grizzled, sun-bronzed cowman named Pearsall — one of the original crew at Bar-Y, a veteran hand that Hewlitt had come to know to some extent and respected. It was to this man that Connie said: "Jim, we need the doctor! Do you suppose we have anyone who could ride to town in a hurry?"

Barney Adcock spoke up at once. "*I'll* do that, Miss Connie. Just leave it to me . . . I'll be proud to go fetch him for you." The smile and the nod she gave him were clearly the only thanks he needed. Being appointed her bodyguard must have been a supreme moment in the boy's young life. Barney was plainly smitten, eager for a chance to be of further service.

As he hustled away on his mission, Jim

Pearsall voiced a question that was eating at him. "Riling and Nordhoff . . . both dead! This your doing, Hewlitt?"

"I got Riling," the latter admitted, "with a very lucky shot, I might add. But your boss did for Cap Nordhoff. The man had gone through the safe and was making off with all the money he found there. All I can say is that Cap Nordhoff was careless not to make sure his boss was really dead."

Still on her knees, one of her father's hands in both of hers, Connie asked anxiously: "Do you suppose we could move him onto the couch? He looks so uncomfortable."

Pearsall rubbed his jaw, looked at Hewlitt. "Maybe, if we're careful. . . ."

The two did it between them. As they got him settled, with a pillow for his head and the Navajo blanket spread gently over him, Ballard uttered a groan and his eyes opened. He seemed to be confused and puzzled to find Pearsall hovering over him. "What the hell are *you* doing here?"

"Don't you remember?" the veteran 'puncher said. "You sent up word that your shipping herd had skedaddled during the night . . . I was to bring some of the boys, and go after them. Instead, we get here to find Miss Connie hiding for her life. And you shot, and Nordhoff and Riling both dead . . . and the rest of their crew being pinned down in the bunkhouse by homesteaders with guns! Damned if I knew what to make of any of it."

York Ballard appeared to absorb all this. He drew a long breath, and in a firmer voice made a pronouncement: "Jim, from this minute you're the foreman here. Your first assignment is to go and tell Nordhoff's friends the new order of things here at Bar-Y. Give them fifteen minutes to pack up their belongings, if they have any, and get the hell off this ranch. Will you do that for me?"

Pearsall's sun-darkened face split in a wide grin. "Boss, you'll never give me an order I'll enjoy half as much."

Turning to go about it, he caught Hewlitt's eye. "Can I bother you to lend me a hand for a couple of minutes?" When Vance Hewlitt nodded and followed him from the room, it turned out that Pearsall wanted to do something with Nordhoff and Riling, for the time being — "No reason why Miss Connie should have to be looking at them."

Hewlitt agreed, and together they moved the bodies across the hall, into the storeroom. A glance from the smashed-out window there showed them that the home-steaders, joined now by the 'punchers Pearsall had brought down with him, appeared to have the ranch yard under firm control. Hewlitt told the new foreman: "If you need any help getting Nordhoff's bunch saddled up and off the property, I'm sure my friends will be glad to lend a hand. All you have to do is speak to Guy Adcock. You can tell him that I'll be out there with them, directly."

It bothered him to think of all that money left lying around, some with Cap Nordhoff's blood on it. While Jim Pearsall set off about his business, Hewlitt used a few minutes to collect it. As he placed the cashbox and its contents on the desk, he told Connie: "I guess there's no limit to what that fellow Nordhoff was capable of." He added: "How's your father seem to be doing?"

She had moved the desk chair nearer to the couch, where she could keep a close watch. She appeared to have got over her recent ordeal; she managed a smile as she answered: "I think he's asleep."

But, he wasn't. A pair of fierce blue eyes seemed almost to skewer Vance Hewlitt as the rancher's rumbling voice suddenly demanded: "What happens now, Hewlitt?

Are you people still willing to deal with me . . . even if I *was* a fool that thought being tough could keep his world from changing?"

Hewlitt told him: "We're willing . . . but Cap Nordhoff hasn't left us much to deal with."

The keen eyes studied him. "Would there be time yet, this season, to get another crop into the ground? I mean, if you had the seed?"

"Plenty of time . . . if we had the seed."

"Then take the money out of that box on the desk. While you're at it, take enough to put your fields under wire . . . we can't risk something like last night happening again. What the hell," he added, as he saw Hewlitt's expression. "You people might as well have whatever you need. Cap Nordhoff came damn' near walking off with all of it."

Vance Hewlitt found his tongue. "This will really be good news for everyone . . . though, personally, I'd want to figure out just what our costs will be, and get your OK before we spend a dime of your money."

"Well, by God! You're a fair man, Hewlitt!" the rancher exclaimed. "I ain't known too many."

"I kept trying to tell you," Connie reminded him. "But there's another thing we mustn't forget . . . Missus Ferguson. Her husband was killed last night. And, she has a baby. . . ."

"You keep me posted on that." Ballard looked again at Vance Hewlitt. "So, do we have a deal?"

"It appears we do." He glanced over at the girl then, and her face was beaming, happy at the way things were working out between her strong-willed father and this man who had already begun to hold a place of great importance in her life.

And then Hewlitt, almost in disbelief, found himself staring at the hand York Ballard extended to him. He remembered another day when this proud man had turned away after reaching an agreement without the normal courtesy of a hand-shake. Now, in spite of his pain, the grip the rancher offered was firm. Vance Hewlitt returned it willingly.

Black Dunstan's Skull

The short-short story, of 2,000 words or less, could sometimes amount to little more than an anecdote topped off with an O. Henry trick ending — but, not in the pulps. There, however brief, it was expected to be a full-bodied *story*, with a real climax and all the ingredients, including at least a dollop of what we preferred to think of as "action," but which nowadays is called simply "violence." The short short had its attractions. For the author, it could be knocked off quickly, in one sitting — I turned this one out on December 6, 1946, during the week I spent trying to see how many words I could produce by working an eight-hour shift. (First, I finished a story for *Ranch Romances*, then I wrote this, and immediately afterward started a novelette for *.44 Western*.) What's more, you could usually count on a quick sale; in particular, the editors of *Fifteen Western Tales* and *10 Story Western* (where I sold this one) found short shorts useful in rounding out a full tally on the contents page, so that the magazine could live up to its name, or, they could create a bonus —

"Extra Story This Month!" — and at very little cost . . . I was paid all of $25 for "Black Dunstan's Skull." Incidentally, the editor titled it "Black Dunstan's Skullduggery." You'll notice I cropped that a bit.

I

A stranger in Clem Littlejohn's trail-side saloon was bound to notice the skull. Back to back with its own reflection in the bar mirror, it had sat there now for almost fifteen years. Turning yellow with time, its sightless eye sockets gaped across the polished mahogany at Littlejohn's customers.

It made a somber drinking companion, and no doubt business suffered because of it. Many a trail-dusty traveler might have stayed long enough to get drunk, had not that grisly decoration scared him away after the second or third shot of Clem's whisky. But Clem — graying now, getting soft and a little slow in his movements — never would consent to remove it.

There was a single customer in the place. Not many riders tonight on the trail that dipped out of the cedar-crested hills north of Clem's and wound across moon-bright flats toward the distant river. Clem Littlejohn had put out most of the lamps in the big, shadowy room to save expenses. Only one burned dimly behind the bar, laying its yellow wash over the pyramided bottles and glasses — and over the grinning, sightless skull.

The customer, a thin, sharp-faced man maybe ten years younger than Littlejohn, toyed with his drink. He broke a long silence suddenly to mutter: "Reckon there's a story to that thing, huh?"

Clem Littlejohn's soft, fat body did not stir. "Reckon there is. Maybe you remember, a long time ago, hearing about an outlaw they called Black Dunstan? He was killed up in the hills north of here."

Sharp-face's eyes narrowed, his face going thin and cautious. "Sure, I remember. Is that . . . him?"

"Some ghoul dug him up after he was buried, came by peddling his skull for ten dollars." Clem's mouth hardened a little with disgust, even now, recalling. "I bought it, and kept it here ever since. Why? Because Black Dunstan was my friend. I talked to him the night before he died."

"Yeah?"

"Just fifteen years ago, and a few months. He headed through the valley, a posse maybe a couple hours behind. Him and another owlhooter named Kyle Barter. Dunstan left his pal in the trees and come up to the place on foot. I hadn't any customers. He knocked on that side door, right over there. . . ." Clem Littlejohn pointed into the shadows gathered at the far end of the big room.

" 'Clem,' Dunstan said, 'I risked stopping long enough to say good bye. They're on my tail . . . and this time I know somebody's gonna get me.'

"I laughed at him, I remember. I said . . . 'That's nonsense. They'll never catch up with you, Black!' But he told me . . . 'You can't fool a Scotchman, Clem. I got the second sight. I'll be dead by morning.'

"And he rode off into the night, tall, and dark . . . as fine a man as ever forked leather and laid a trail to throw the John Laws. And by next noon the word drifted back out of the hills. Black Dunstan was dead, his saddle pard captured. Dunstan had called it straight."

There was silence, and the grinning skull of Dunstan sat there before the bar mirror looking sightlessly at them. The man across from Clem Littlejohn took his drink in a gulp, as though he suddenly felt cold and needed something to warm him. But as he set the glass down his careful glance met Clem's, and the stranger said slowly, hesitantly: "That night . . . he didn't maybe leave something with you? Something he wanted you to keep for him?"

Littlejohn's frown darkened. "How would you know about it?"

"You tell me what he gave you," Sharp-face suggested. "Then I'll tell you how I know."

Eyes fastened on the man, Clem reached under the bar and brought up a six-gun. "Are you a lawman?"

"No."

For a long moment Clem held the gun leveled, unwavering. "All right," he said then, and laid it on the bar. The stranger straightened slowly, relaxing. At sight of the weapon he had dropped back a pace, one hand starting for the holster at his hip. Without a word now he lifted his hands, empty, and put them on the edge of the mahogany.

Clem turned away, moved heavily to the skull, and picked it up. An old envelope was beneath it. He took this and replaced the skull. Coming back to the bar, Clem reached stubby fingers into the envelope and brought out a fold of yellow paper that had a jagged edge, as though it had been torn across. He did not unfold it. He looked at Sharp-face. "Well?"

Without a word, the stranger drew a cracked leather wallet from his pocket, produced another piece of paper. It, too, had a jagged edge. It looked as though the two pieces of paper would fit together.

Clem Litttlejohn said: "You're Kyle Barter?"

"That's right. I got out of prison a month ago. All the time I've kept this, waiting. Before he died, of that lawman's bullet, Dunstan slipped it to me. He told me . . . 'Littlejohn has the other half. It's a map. Put the halves together and they'll tell you where my cache is located. There's fifty thousand hidden . . . and you two are my only friends. I want you to share it.' "

"The money must still be where Dunstan hid it," Clem said quietly. "It was never found." Slowly he opened the brittle folds, laid the paper flat upon the bar.

The room seemed to hold its breath around them. The skull of Dunstan looked on, grinning, while Kyle Barter unfolded his half of the map, placed it next to Clem's. The torn edges touched, fit. Clem Littlejohn grunted.

"There's the river." He pointed with a thick forefinger. "That's Round Butte. The cross-hatching must be the lava flow at its base. The loot, then, is buried somewhere among those boulders." Clem shook his head, ponderously. "Don't that beat hell! I could have guessed from your half of the map alone. But mine had nothing I could identify."

Kyle Barter's eyes were touched with a glow of greed. "Fifty thousand dollars. Split two ways. . . ."

"No," said Clem bluntly. "It's stolen money. It goes to the state."

"What?" Their glances clashed, held. "Damn it, Littlejohn! What's the difference after fifteen years? Maybe you don't need *your* share, but I have to have a stake. I'm just out of stony lonesome, don't you understand? And Dunstan meant. . . ."

He made a quick move as though to snatch the halves of the map, but Clem's big, soft palm came down smartly, covering them. "How do I know you're really Barter? I never saw the man. He waited in the trees that night Black Dunstan came up to say good bye. You could have stolen this, for all I know. You could be making up a story, and never even knew Dunstan."

Sharp-face scowled. Then he spoke fast: "Look. I can at least prove I knew Black Dunstan, and knew him well. He wore his black hair shoulder-length, didn't he? But not many knew it was in order to hide the mark of a bullet that once tore off half an ear and then raked a furrow across his scalp . . . just missed killing him. Take a look at the skull. There ought to be a groove in the bone where the slug hit."

Slowly Clem Littlejohn nodded. "Yes, I guess you must be Kyle Barter." He added: "I had to be absolutely sure . . . before I killed you."

The stranger gaped into the muzzle of the six-gun, all at once in Littlejohn's big hand.

"I've waited fifteen years for this," Clem told him. "With Dunstan's poor skull sitting there for bait, knowing someday you'd come along and ask these questions. You see I talked to the sheriff who headed that posse. He told me his men never got close enough to trade lead with Dunstan. They found him shot from behind and close up . . . so close the muzzle fire burnt his clothing.

"And that night, just before he left me, Dunstan had said . . . 'I don't trust the guy I'm ridin' with. That's why I'm tearing this map in two. He can't get my money without coming to you with the other half. And if he does that . . . you'll know I'm dead and he murdered me to get it.' "

A snarl burst from Barter as he moved with amazing quickness. His left hand lashed forward, gripped the muzzle of Clem Littlejohn's gun, jerked with a force that hauled Clem half across the counter. At the same moment Barter's right streaked down, came up fisting the gun from his own hip holster. It winked lamplight, arcing down.

Both feet off the floor, wind cut off by the pressure of the mahogany's edge against his fat middle, Clem kicked out desperately. One heel caught the edge of a shelf behind the bar with just enough leverage to send him forward. Bottles and glasses smashed as his heavy body slid across the slick wood. Then both men went down, Clem on top.

As they struck, the gun jerked in Clem's fingers with a muffled roar.

Sobbing for breath, Clem Littlejohn climbed shakily to his feet, one hand clutching the bar's edge for support, the smoking gun dragging down his other arm. At his feet, Kyle Barter stared sightlessly.

Clem turned to the shelf behind the bar, where in a litter of broken glass those other eyes, mere empty sockets in a yellowed grinning skull, stared unwinkingly.

"There it is, Dunstan," said Clem, his words sounding odd against the silence following that single shot. "After fifteen years. I thought it would never come. And when it did, I was almost a fraction too slow. Time . . . it gets a man!"

Born to the Brand

People often ask: "Where do story ideas come from?" The answer? From almost anywhere — only, I could never afford to wait around for them. Usually I would try to think of an opening — perhaps no more than a mental image, but interesting enough to attract attention while I deftly planted a few questions to lure my reader on to the second page. The original germ that grew into this next story: A rider, under heavy pressure of some kind, gets down to water his horse and himself and finds something extremely unpleasant in the creek, just upstream from where he is drinking. On top of everything else, this discovery is just more than he can handle, and he tosses his cookies. . . . The idea sounded sort of poignant. Now for the questions: Just who is this hero of mine? Where did he come from, and what's his problem? Is the dead man someone he knows or a stranger? — and how was he killed? And so on. By the time I'd come up with some answers I liked, I was already into the story. In the story is another seventeen-year-old as in "The Taming of Johnny Peters," although he's not at all like Johnny Peters. I liked to use them once in a while, when I found the right story — youngsters that age are so damned vulnerable! Incidentally, I couldn't think of a good title so I'm keeping the one the editor supplied. "Born to the Brand" has a kind of a ring to it — even if I'm not absolutely sure what it means in connection with this particular story.

I

He let the horses drink first.

Still in saddle, the kid pulled off his shapeless big hat. The sweatband left a white mark across his forehead. Wearily he sleeved away sweat that had worked down in trickles across the fuzz of his thin cheeks, running salt and sour into his mouth. He ran bony fingers through damp, tangled hair, dragged the hat on again.

Bud Jenkins had been on the go since early morning, working southward into what he counted as enemy territory. He forked the lineback dun mare that had been his dad's. What few possessions he'd managed to salvage were lashed with an inexpert diamond hitch on the back of the crow-bait roan that Bud himself had always ridden before today.

It was bleak range he traveled — a range already touched by the frost of fall but with late summer's burning sun on it now. Smothering heat haze blanketed sage clump and juniper. The snow caps to westward, and smaller hills closer in the north, shimmered behind curtains of heated air.

Swinging to earth with a weary aching of muscles, Bud moved a few yards above the drinking horses and threw himself prone at the edge of the stream. The water was good, cool. He drank recklessly, swelling his empty stomach.

He came to his knees, wiping his mouth on shirt sleeve, and stayed like that a moment, resting — a tall, bony figure of a lad, with almost the beanpole growth of a man and a tired, old look in red-rimmed eyes. He wore a much-repaired shirt and Levi's that his dad had handed down to him; a worn six-shooter was stuck behind his waistband. Extra shells for it were in his pocket, along with his pocketknife and a dirty handkerchief.

The horses had finished drinking and were cropping at the tough bunch grass.

Bud turned his head, ran a glance upstream. He froze.

Close enough to touch with outstretched arm, the dead man lay on his back with sightless eyes staring at the sky, mouth open, barrel chest bloody from the bullet wound that had finished him. His body and legs were on the bank, but the head and one arm had slipped backward into the water and floated there only inches from where Bud had been drinking, the tawny yellow hair spread out fanwise around the dead and bloodless face.

It was too much, added to all the rest he had lived through. The kid turned away, deathly sick. He curled up on his side in the sand and lay there retching.

After a long time, it seemed, he pushed to his feet, weak and shaky. He stood over the body, nerving himself to look at it more carefully. No one he had ever seen before, and not many hours dead. Studying the grisly corpse, it occurred to him it might prove useful to him, help with the thing he was trying to do.

Bud went for the crow-bait roan. It was a temperamental beast, but by tying his neck cloth over its eyes, he managed to get the bronc' over near the dead man and snub its reins to a tough sage clump. It was a harder job to lift the body, unaided, sling it across the top of the pack, and lash it into place there. Some of the blood came off on Bud's shirt and hands. White of face, he washed them in the stream and then, with his shirt wrung out and drying on his back, Bud Jenkins was again in saddle and heading south once more, the roan with its added burden following at the lead rope.

The freakishly hot sun crossed the zenith, tipped down toward the high snowcaps to westward. The character of the land was changing, turning richer and greener with more water in the bottoms as Bud worked farther down the shelving valley floor. He began to see cattle grazing, bearing a spur brand for the most part. And farther ahead were the scattered buildings of ranches, and something that looked like a town.

Along toward afternoon, Jenkins trailed his packhorse into the yard of a small, two-man spread. Its ramshackle house and barn and corrals bore a general air of clutter and untidiness. The pair fixing a broken wagon axle straightened from their work and watched Bud approaching. They looked like father and son, although the younger was a black-browed hulk of a character, and the other smaller, slighter, but straight as a ramrod and with a fanatic sort of fierceness in the eyes that peered out above his white and tangled beard. Both men had the unkempt appearance of their home.

Bud could feel the silent weight of their eyes on him, stiffened himself against it. When he was near enough for them to catch sight of the bloody burden lashed to the roan's back, their suspicion and hostility flared up openly. The older man whirled suddenly, ran to a chopping block, and snatched up the double-snouted shotgun that leaned against it. He came back with the weapon rock-steady in his gnarled fingers.

He shouted at Bud, in a high-pitched voice that had a tone of ferocity in it: "Stop where you are, you son o' Satan! I'm opposed to killin' . . . but you try pullin' a gun and I'll let both hammers drop on you!"

Bud Jenkins let no hint of fear shadow his hard young features. He halted the lineback dun, heard the stamp of the roan's hoofs behind him. He kept his hands well clear of the old six-gun in his holster. "What's the matter, grampa?" he grunted. "Am I that scary?"

The oldster ignored his words. He told

his son: "Ahab, git around there and see whose corpse he's totin'. Could happen it's somebody we know."

"If it is," Bud told him, "you're one up on me, mister."

He watched Ahab closely out of the tail of his eye as the black-headed giant moved around him toward the pack horse. The kid wasn't trusting this pair. Maybe they were less interested in the corpse than they were in the kid's belongings, and in whatever they might find worth helping themselves to. Bud was about to snap a warning to Ahab to be careful what he got into back there, when a grunt from the latter forestalled him.

"Stoll?" Ahab said. "Pop, it's Wally Stoll."

"By the eternal!" A look of sheer astonishment distorted the face of the old man, and the shotgun wavered a little. "Who are you anyway, kid? And what's between you and the Spur iron?"

"I already told you," Bud said, "that I don't know this jigger. And I didn't kill him, either. This here's the exact way I found him."

"Yeah?" The oldster showed plainly he wasn't prepared to believe all he heard. But he shrugged, added: "Well, the Lord savvies the ways of the wicked, and the Lord sends his avengin' lightning. Wally Stoll had his needin's, and he got 'em. Amen!"

Bud grunted impatiently. "Do your Bible quoting after I'm gone, old man. I ain't got time to listen. I'm looking for the county seat."

"You'll find yourself a seat in eternal hellfire, younker, talkin' disrespectful of Holy Writ!"

"OK, OK!" The kid waved him aside, turned, and jabbed a thumb at the big, black-headed man who was listening with an unreadable look on his face. He had not offered a word after identifying the corpse of Wally Stoll. "You, Ahab!" rapped Bud Jenkins, "don't you quote nothin' at me. Just tell me if I'm headin' right to find me some law. Ought to be a sheriff's office somewheres here about."

Ahab shot a nervous look at his father. He was some years older than the beardless kid in the saddle. And he was a head bigger and pounds heavier, but he chose to take no exception to this youngster's impudence. Instead, he replied sullenly: "It's nine miles to Shumate, same direction you was going. You can see the town from any of the hills around here. Sam Warren's sheriff."

Bud nodded a curt thanks. He picked up the reins boldly, ignoring the oldster and his double-barreled shotgun. "I'll be headin' that way, then. I want to see your sheriff . . . on this and some other business."

Neither father nor son made any move to stop him. Bud rode out through the heat and stillness, hit a dusty ribbon of wagon road leading away from the ranch buildings, and let it take him up a shallow rise in the rolling land. The county seat, Shumate, lay like a black splotch in the shimmering distance. Bud kicked the dun with spurless heels, sent it off down the yonder slope with the hoofs of both bronc's lifting dry and tawny dust.

He glanced behind him once and spotted a pair of riders trailing him slowly, keeping a careful distance of brown road between them. Bud's eyes narrowed as he saw a flash of dirty white beard in the slanting sunlight.

"Grampa," he muttered, "and Ahab! Why are they so curious about this jigger?"

He squared around in the saddle again, a dark look about him. The kid was a stranger, on a tough mission, and now it looked to him like he was riding into a set-up.

He thought belligerently: *They just better hadn't crowd me, that's all. Ain't nobody on this range too proddy for me to handle.*

Two hours later, Bud found himself closeted with Sheriff Sam Warren in the latter's clapboard office, sweating from the stifling heat of the room and from his own uneasiness. He didn't like it. He sat stiffly on the edge of his chair, giving curt replies to the sheriff's questions.

Sam Warren was a large, broad-faced man, with pleasant features and a good deal of patience. But finally even he lost his temper, and he slapped his pencil down hard. "Now, listen here, kid! You better get down off your high horse and talk civil. This is official business, you savvy?"

Bud tucked his chin down against his chest. "I never killed 'im," he grunted.

"Nobody yet says you did!" With a visible effort the sheriff got control of his temper. "Look. If you don't like me for some reason, that's too bad and I'm sorry. But this report has to be filled out. You found Wally Stoll's body, and you got to tell me everything you know about it. So, loosen up and quit giving me trouble."

The questions went on, and the kid's brief answers. A battered clock on the desk chattered out the time to the hot, still room. It marked, for Bud Jenkins, a very bad half hour.

A couple of other men were there, listening. One, a gangling, chinless creature with a gun-hand look about him, was Warren's chief deputy, Lew Prentiss. The other was Nate Carmody, partner of the dead Wally Stoll and now sole surviving owner of their Spur iron. It was natural that he would be present, and Bud gathered from things he heard that Spur was the biggest outfit in the region. He remembered the number of cattle he had seen on the range, carrying that brand.

The sheriff laid his paper down finally, and swiveled about to face the room. "Well," he said, "that seems to be it. Wally Stoll was killed by a bullet from the front . . . probably sometime this morning, according to the doc. Party or parties unknown. That's all we know, and all we're likely to."

Nate Carmody took the statement in silence. He rubbed the ball of one thumb across a cheek bone, and he looked like a man with a bad taste in his mouth. "Wally's pockets was searched, Sam? You didn't find any cash on him?"

"Twenty bucks and some change."

Carmody waved that away impatiently. "I don't mean chicken feed. You see, Wally Stoll rodded a short drive north to the rail-head at Dixon last week. We already had a buyer, so it was just a matter of collecting. I figure he was on his way back with the money when somebody met him."

"Murder *and* robbery!" Warren's face was serious. "The money's gone, all right, so that's the way it is." The sheriff heaved to his feet, crossed the room to Bud Jenkins's chair. "Well, kid, even if we didn't hit if off so good, I appreciate your help. I'll have to ask you, though, to stick around town a while. . . ."

"Now just a minute!" Bud was off the chair. "Don't soft-soap me, tin badge! Am I under arrest, or ain't I?"

"I don't reckon you killed Wally Stoll, if that's what you mean, because then where would be the sense of your bringing his body in and letting yourself in for all these questions? At least that's how I look at it." He smiled, put a hand on Bud's shoulder. "No, kid, it's just that you're our only wit-ness, and. . . ."

At the touch of the lawman's fingers the kid stepped back so quickly that the chair behind him went over with a crash. "Don't touch me!"

Warren's face went brick red, but he dropped the hand. "What's the matter with you, anyhow?" He got no answer. All the friendliness was gone from the sheriff's eyes as he said coldly: "A pretty tough youngster, ain't you?"

"I'm tough as hell!" Bud's young-old face twisted into a strange and bitter mask.

The sheriff shrugged, turned sharply on his heel, and strode again to the desk. Over his shoulder he flung back: "Then you can get out of this office. But remember what I said . . . you ain't to skip town!"

Alone on the sidewalk, Bud still felt the constriction to his breathing. A weakness ran through his body suddenly. It passed, leaving him limp and cold despite the day's sultry heat.

He started to move away. Behind him the office door opened again, and there were brisk footsteps. A voice called his name. Bud turned as Nate Carmody came up with him. "And what do *you* want?" the kid demanded suspiciously.

His manner seemed to have no effect on the big man. The rancher said easily: "I want to help you, Bud. That is," he explained quickly, warding off a scornful word from the kid, "if you're going to have to stay around Shumate for a while, as the sheriff says, you'll likely be needing a job. Maybe I could use you at my ranch."

"You?" Bud repeated, still suspicious.

The rancher grinned. "Sure. I like 'em salty, youngster. The way you stood up to old Sam was really comical. He didn't know for sure what hit him."

"Well, don't you go laughing at me, mister," the kid retorted.

"Sure . . . sure." Carmody quickly sobered. "I wasn't making fun, Jenkins. What about the job? Want it?"

He started to say no. But then he thought of the few odds and ends of loose change in his pocket, and he thought of the jaded bronc's that needed a good feed of oats, and of his own empty belly. And he thought of the grim job that had brought him down here, out of the north, to Shumate.

"All right," he grunted. "Only I don't want charity. I work for a man's wages, and I do a man's job."

"Exactly." Carmody sounded highly pleased. "Let's have a drink on that. And I want you to meet a few of the boys."

The big barroom of the Silver Dollar was almost deserted at this hour of late afternoon. A few Spur riders who had come into town with their boss were having a round or two before heading back, and a potent silence rode these men — the death of Wally Stoll was a somber shadow on them all.

Bud acknowledged the introductions briefly. A hard bunch, he labeled them, and close-mouthed. Bud figured he was pretty tough himself, and the fewer questions asked about him and his affairs the better he liked it. The fact that Carmody, who hired such riders, figured him man enough to make one of that crew was a matter of secret pleasure to the kid.

Nate Carmody motioned to the barkeep, got a bottle and glasses set out. But when he started to pour drinks all around, one of the men slapped his glass aside with a cut from one hard palm. "Count me out," the rider grunted, an ugly scowl on his face. "I ain't drinkin' with this punk."

All their heads jerked up. Bud straightened, pushing his own glass away. He had gone cold inside, but there was also a sense of relief, knowing that he might get out of having to down the liquor with all these grown men looking on to watch him struggle with it.

"So, what's the matter with you, Dirk?" Carmody said.

"It's plain enough, ain't it? Wally Stoll

and I were cousins. I ain't drinkin' with the little rat that ambushed him and took money off his corpse."

"That's a lie!" Bud started for his accuser. He never got to Dirk, because Carmody shoved in between them, pushed Bud back with one meaty shoulder as he faced the older man.

"Quit it, you fool," the Spur boss told Dirk. "The kid didn't kill Wally. If the story he tells satisfied Sheriff Sam Warren, *you* got no kick coming . . . so take it easy. Bud Jenkins is workin' for Spur . . . and you're drinkin' with him."

Dirk didn't look convinced. He was in sour humor as he backed down and turned again to the bar, but he let Carmody fill his glass, and he stood there holding it and glowering at the amber liquor.

"Don't pay no attention to Dirk Tabb," Carmody told Bud as he headed the furious youngster back to his own drink, standing on the bar. "One of these days he'll open that big mouth of his once too often."

Plainly Carmody was not standing for a row between members of his crew. By sheer force of his presence he had damped down the flames of mutual anger. Now to finish the matter, he closed his big hand on one of the filled glasses, hefted it. "Bottoms up, men," he grunted, and it was not an invitation, but an order.

Bud got the liquor down and held it, although the effort to keep from gagging it back brought tears smarting in his eyes. No one seemed to notice his trouble, however. With a swagger of newfound confidence, Bud followed after the others, when Carmody slapped money on the bar and told his men it was time to shove off.

II

They rolled their spurs along the scarred boardwalk — a hard, tight-knit group of men, arrogant in the power and importance of the outfit they rode for. Bud noticed a certain hostility in other men they chanced to meet in the town. He remembered the old man and his son Ahab, and the bitter words the father had had for Wally Stoll and Spur. Adding things up, he began to suspect that this spread was not too well loved by its neighbors. Which was OK with *him*, he figured savagely.

Better to have power than be too damned popular and easy-going. Like

287

Bud's dad. Fred Jenkins had had his share of friends, but what good did they do him when the crisis came? The thought of that could still make the kid sick and bitter inside when he dwelt on it.

Suddenly Dirk Tabb, up front, sang out: "Hey, look . . . the Beechers! What do you suppose they're doin' in town?"

Nate Carmody showed surprise. He said grimly: "That Bible-spouting Tom Beecher ain't givin' me any trouble . . . I can promise you that."

It was Ahab, of course, and his white-bearded father. The rat-tailed nags that had brought them into town were tied to a gnawed hitch rail in front of the sheriff's office, and the two stood near them, waiting as the group from Spur approached.

"They know about the killing," Bud told Carmody. "They trailed me into town."

His new boss only grunted.

"Good news for this range today!" old Tom Beecher yelled out defiantly, eyes blazing at the men bearing down on him. "Praise heaven, there's one less of your hell-spawn breed to plague honest, God-fearin' men!"

Carmody hauled up in front of him. For a long moment he said nothing, but when he did speak, his voice sounded ice-hard and held under rigid control. "You try a man's patience, sometimes."

"Not to mention your greed," Tom Beecher retorted. "With only my boy and me to look after 'em, easy enough to see what a temptation our beef herd must be for the likes of you. Hardly any wonder at all that you cain't keep your hands off!"

"You old fool!" the other exclaimed. "Why would Spur have any interest in the scrubs you Beechers run on that starve-out ranch?"

"You wouldn't mind havin' the *land*," the old man shot back at him. "Even though the good Lord knows you got more now than you know what to do with. But I know what it is you're *really* after . . . them springs of ours, that never went dry even when the whole range gaunted out durin' the big drought three years ago. You'd like nothing better than to help us go broke, and let you walk in and take them. Deny it if you can!"

There was a restless stir among the riders at Carmody's back. Waiting to see how his new boss would respond to such a charge, Bud was surprised to see the Spur owner appeared to have swallowed his anger. His voice, when he spoke again, held a note of cold amusement.

"I almost take you serious sometimes, Tom, listenin' to your talk about this outfit. But then you talk a little more, and I see you're just an old feist' dog without no teeth left, and the noise you make don't mean a damn' thing. You ain't even a good nuisance."

"By all the saints!" Old Tom's glare was a blaze of wrath; his two skinny hands rose, shaking, clenched into helpless claw-like fists. "You spawn o' Satan! You'll say nuisance when the avengin' lightnin' strikes!"

Carmody made a face impatiently. "Don't start preachin' at me, you old scalawag."

A door slammed, and Sam Warren came pegging toward them from his office. The sheriff wore an angry look as he cut in upon that scene. "What's going on here?" he demanded. "You baiting old Tom again, Nate?"

Other townsmen had gathered, drawn by the shrill insistence of the oldster's voice.

Carmody indicated Tom with the shove of one broad-nailed thumb. "This old goat is trying to give Spur a bad name. You've heard him often enough. If I didn't reckon he was harmless, I'd bring him into court for libel."

The look Warren gave Carmody was

slow and searching, and Bud had a feeling he was about to make a sharp answer to the Spur boss. But he shrugged and turned instead to Tom Beecher. His voice, although kindly, showed more than a trace of impatience.

"You do yourself no good shouting on street corners, Tom. If you've got a case, come to me with it. After all," he added, smiling a little, "the law has its own avenging lightning, and it strikes hard sometimes. But for now, why don't you and Ahab go back to your place . . . or at least stay away from Nate until he and his boys leave town?"

"We're pullin' out *pronto*," Carmody assured the lawman. And at that the whiskered oldster lifted his upper lip in a sneer.

"Scared!" Tom Beecher asserted triumphantly. "Scared of an old man and a half-wit younker . . . and the power of the Lord's truth!" Before Carmody could argue that with him, Beecher had whipped around, and he strode out to his waiting bronc'. "Hit saddle, Ahab!" he ordered, his voice ringing the length of the street. "We'll leave this place of Sodom and Gomorrah to the wicked. Someday the town and the range'll get the cleanin' the godly are prayin' for!"

The group of Spur riders watched them go in silence. Sheriff Warren, next to Carmody, had his thumbs shoved into shell belt.

The onlookers had started to break up and drift away, not talking much. Dirk Tabb began to swear under his breath, but a word from his boss silenced him. Carmody said with a shrug: "I got more to think of than that old lunatic's ravings."

It was getting pretty close to sunset. The heat of the long day was breaking before a west breeze. Carmody nodded to the sheriff, moved on toward the livery where the Spur bronc's had been left while the crew was in town. Bud started to follow when the voice of the sheriff halted him.

"You ridin' with Spur now?"

Bud nodded curtly, not softening any to the sheriff's friendly interest. But he waited while Warren looked at him, frowning and seemingly having trouble with what he wanted to say.

"You don't like any part of me, do you, Jenkins?" the sheriff finally said bluntly. "I'm sorry. I'm sorry, too, that I flew off the handle there in my office a while ago. I'd like us to be friends."

"Yeah?" Bud put a sneer into the words for he had reasons for hating this man.

"Whatta we got to be friendly over?"

The sheriff shook his head. "Sometimes I wonder, the attitude you take. But I just can't think that's natural. I got an idea you're in trouble, kid, or something has hurt you right bad. And I'd like to help. . . ."

"I told Mister Carmody that I ain't no charity case," Bud retorted. "He gave me a job. I'm drawing straight wages. Nobody's wiping' my nose for me."

Unperturbed, the sheriff went on: "I bet it's a long time since you had a real home-cooked meal . . . roast and gravy and potatoes, and hot, buttered biscuits. And, pie? Why, you never sunk a tooth in the kind of pie Missus Warren bakes . . . sweet and juicy, with just enough cinnamon . . . and flaky brown crust that melts away when you go to bite into it. I'd be mighty pleased to have you home for supper this evening, if you'll come. Kind of like you to meet my family. . . ."

Bud swallowed hard, his empty stomach growling at the word-picture. But he kept control of himself and was all set to rap out a scornful refusal when Carmody interrupted. The Spur owner had missed Bud and was coming back for him, and irritation showed in his heavy features.

"What's holdin' you up?"

The sheriff lifted an eyebrow as he looked at the rancher. "I was asking him to supper, Nate. Couldn't think of any reason why you would mind."

Carmody hesitated, as though he had started one answer and then checked himself. Bud sensed suddenly that there was something wrong between these two, something that did not show on the surface, and it puzzled him. He was sure that when Carmody finally answered, it was not the reply he wanted to give.

"Why, sure. That's right decent of you, Sam."

Bud's jaw set. "Now, wait a minute," he began stoutly. "I never said I wanted to go. . . ."

"I happen to remember," Carmody went on, cutting him off, "I got some business to attend to in town this evening. You go ahead with the sheriff, kid, and I'll stop by for you on my way to the ranch."

Warren smiled.

When they were alone, he told Bud Jenkins: "Those two bronc's of yours look pretty well used up . . . why not leave them in the stable tonight? I'll lend you a mount, and later in the week you can bring it back to me and get your own critters."

The other nodded.

"I'll pick you up at the livery, then. Got to drive around to the doc's house for my little girl . . . she's spent the day visitin' with some friends in town."

Bud was standing in the big door of the barn, feeling the first chill of evening and listening to the hanging sign creak in the rising wind, when the wagon and team came for him. Sam Warren was not alone. He made the introductions briefly. "Judy," he said, "this is the young gent I was telling you about. Well, hurry up, Bud . . . hop in! I'm gettin' hungry."

Bud swung to the high seat, awkward and nervous. He hadn't figured on sharing it with a half-grown young woman, and it seemed pretty crowded with her jammed in between him and her father. He edged as close as he could to the metal guard rail at his end of the seat, but big Sam, apparently unaware of the lack of room, filled his place solidly and spread his elbows wide as he slapped lines at the team, shoving his daughter right over on top of the kid.

If Bud was embarrassed, Judy was not. She chatted brightly as they rode along — a friendly girl with a sweet face and pleasant manner. Bud figured her a couple of years younger than himself, which would make her just exactly fifteen.

The sheriff's place was a mile or so northeast of town. It was almost dark when they came into the yard. Soft lamplight from the windows spread yellow squares upon the ground.

Mrs. Warren seemed pleased to have company for supper. Bud liked her. He thought, watching her, that this motherly woman with her cheery smile gave a pretty good idea what Judy Warren would be like thirty or forty years from now. And then he turned a little bitter, thinking what a long time that was, and wondering what would become of him in the empty years ahead.

The Warrens sensed his mood, and they tried to cheer him up as the four sat at the table with good food steaming in front of them. But Bud wouldn't talk much through the meal, and even a mammoth chunk of Mrs. Warren's apple pie did little good.

At last Mrs. Warren put down her fork, exchanged a look with her husband. The sheriff had already found a moment alone with her to tell her something of Bud's story; he nodded to her now encouragingly. She cleared her throat and said brightly: "Have another piece, Bud?"

He shook his head. He said gruffly —
"Naw!" — then, feeling Judy's eyes on him,
changed his refusal to a more polite: "No,
ma'am." He wondered afterward why he
had bothered to do that.

Mrs. Warren persisted, determined apparently to drag him out. "What's the
matter, didn't you like it? Most folks say I
make pretty good pies."

"Oh, yeah," he agreed hastily. "Yeah. It's
swell!"

"But then, I suppose you'd like your
mother's better."

The kid swallowed. He couldn't even remember his mother. He said nothing.

Mrs. Warren sighed, her shoulders
lifting, and gave Sam a despairing glance.
The talk languished. Then Judy stepped in,
trying to make her voice sound very gay.

"Gee! I wish I was a boy, so I could
saddle up and strike out and ride any old
place I felt like. You must have seen lots of
country, Bud . . . met ever so many
people. . . ."

Bud sat bolt upright. "What is this, anyway?" he demanded harshly. "Sheriff, is
that why you brought me here . . . so your
womenfolk could help pump me? Why the
hell can't you leave me alone?"

They were all on their feet suddenly —
Mrs. Warren and her daughter stunned,
Bud Jenkins shaking with fury. Sheriff
Warren said sharply: "Now, just a minute,
young man! You can't talk like that to
Missus Warren. . . ."

The woman put up a hand, wearily.
"Don't, Sam," she begged. "The boy's all
upset. We've got to be kind to him."

Bud retorted: "Don't waste your kind-
ness on me! I don't need it."

A gasp broke from Judy. "Why, I think
you are the . . . the rudest, most. . . ."

"That's enough, Judy!" her mother cut
her off.

And then the tension broke as a voice
from the night called in to them: "Hello
the house!"

Sam Warren said: "It's Nate Carmody."
He strode to the door, threw it open. "All
right, Nate," he answered. "The kid'll be
right with you." He turned back to Bud,
leaving the door open on the outer darkness. "Here's your boss, come for you," he
went on, voice tight with suppressed anger.
"You'll find a black gelding in the corral
. . . you can take that, and a saddle and
bridle from the back room."

"Toby?" Judy's exclamation was sharp.
"That's *my* horse. He can't have Toby. . . ."

Her father silenced her with a gesture. "I'll see that he brings him back. Good night, Jenkins," he added with curt finality.

Bud had lost his anger suddenly. Hat in hand, he stopped at the door, looked back at the three people standing in the friendly, lamp-lit room. He wanted to say something to them, but he found all at once that his lower jaw had begun to tremble, and instead of trying to speak he turned again quickly and bolted from the house.

Mrs. Warren turned on her husband. "Oh, Sam!" she exclaimed. "That poor boy! He . . . he's all twisted up inside. He needs our help."

The sheriff shrugged away some of his own irritation. "I dunno why I bother," he growled. "The kid hates me for some reason, that's plain."

"*Hates* you?"

"Yes, though I'm sure I never saw him before this afternoon. And now he's gone and lined up with Nate Carmody . . . a land-grabbing, cattle-rustling crook who'll go behind bars someday if I can ever prove a case against him. I only hope . . . if that day ever comes . . . I won't have to pick up Bud Jenkins in the same net."

III

The night was soundless, except for the noise of their bronc's and the song of the wind above them. Judy Warren's little black was a sure-gaited animal, but Bud had had to let the stirrups out before he could mount the regulation, single-cinch saddle.

Bud, still miserable over that scene in the sheriff's house, had little enough to say. And big Nate Carmody, forking a heavy bay stallion beside him, let ten minutes go by in silence. Finally, however, he began to query the kid about his time with the Warren family.

"Good feed?"

"I guess so."

Nate, catching his tone, cast a quizzical look at Bud. He ventured carelessly: "Suppose they asked you a bunch of personal questions. They're a nosy lot."

Bud groaned. "They sure are!" he agreed savagely, because that made him feel better for being rude to them.

"Uh . . . they say anything about you workin' for me?"

"No," Bud answered, after thinking it over. "I don't remember anything about that."

Carmody seemed satisfied to drop the matter, and presently they came down a dry slope and the home buildings of Spur lay around them.

It was a big outfit, all right, to judge from the size and numbers of its corrals, barns, and sheds. As best he could see, Bud thought that everything looked pretty well cared for and in good working order.

Lights shone in main house, bunkhouse, eat shack. There were male sounds of activity in the bunkhouse, and, when they went past, it a man came to the open door and looked out, and Bud recognized the lean shape of Dirk Tabb. He watched in silence as his boss and the new hand rode in.

At the barn Carmody swung down, tossed the reins to Bud. "Take care of my horse, Jenkins," he ordered. "Tack room's up front. And throw in some oats for him."

"Yes, sir."

Bud left Toby saddled while he stripped Carmody's bay, rubbed the animal down with clean straw, and shoved it into a stall. He got hay and grain into the manger; then, as the bronc' went to work on that, he gathered up saddle and blanket and bridle and lugged them down the long aisle of the barn.

It was dark in the partitioned tack room.

Bud dropped his burden while he got a lantern going that he found there on a nail, and then carefully he hung up saddle and bridle, smoothed out the sweaty blanket. When he turned away, he was surprised to see Carmody in the doorway.

He had Dirk Tabb with him, as well as another rider named El Nugent. The three had moved in soundlessly, and the way they stood they had the door blocked. Bud stopped, puzzled, looking at them.

"All right, kid," Carmody came toward him, a disarming smile on his broad face. The other two followed him in. Dirk Tabb closed the tack room door. "Just wanted to talk to you a minute." Suddenly Nate's big hand lashed out, flipped the six-shooter from Bud's waistband.

Bud gave a squawk, made a grab for the weapon as Nate dragged it free. But it was too late, and then he was staring, cold with sudden fear, at the change that flashed across Carmody's dark features.

"Now, then," Carmody said, his voice deadly. "Talk, and talk fast! Where's the money?"

Bud stared, not understanding. "Money? What do you mean . . . ?"

"Oh, come on!" Anger and distaste were in the big man's eyes. "Do you think I'm as blind as all that, kid? I know well enough that you killed Wally Stoll . . . that you took the herd money off the body. It beats me why you'd drag him into town. Playin' some deep game of your own, most likely . . . but not deep enough to fool *me,* even if you have got Sam Warren buffaloed. But tell me where you ditched the cash, and maybe I'll go easy on you."

The kid, still unable to grasp the sudden change in Carmody, could not speak for a moment. He looked at Dirk Tabb. He stammered: "I've told nothin' but the truth. I never killed your partner. And I never saw no money."

"Listen here, kid. Don't think I'm bluffing. If I tell people you quit your job tonight and took off over the next hill, who'll think different? You got no friends, and you know it. So . . . quit stalling, if you know what's good for you."

Bud could only shake his head doggedly. "I got nothing more to tell."

"All right, Dirk," Carmody said quietly. "He's all yours."

He stepped aside, and Dirk Tabb moved in, lean body crouched, a look of pleasure across his swarthy face. Bud backed away a step, bringing up his fists in a tentative gesture of self-defense; Dirk batted his arms away and smashed a rock-hard fist into Bud's face.

He went clear down as the blow landed, his head hitting the straw-littered floor. Stunned, he tried to push to his feet, but Dirk was on him, and a heavy boot slammed into Bud's chest, stretching him out again. Then Dirk's fingers were fastened in his collar, hauling him up bodily. And the man's other fist took him again, square in the face, and drove him back to double up over the edge of a makeshift wooden table.

"Ready to change your story?" Nate Carmody's voice seemed to come from a long, long distance.

Clutching the table, blood streaming from battered nose, Bud Jenkins shook his head feebly. It was all he had the strength to do. And then Dirk Tabb came in on him again.

Nate Carmody and the other Spur rider watched calmly as Tabb worked, his eyes showing a fierce joy in inflicting pain. He punished the kid slowly along the wall of the tiny room. For long moments the only sounds were the scuffling of feet, the slam of fists bruising, hurting. And the labored breathing of the kid's tortured lungs.

At last even Nate Carmody seemed to

get a stomachful of that. He ordered suddenly: "Hold it, Dirk! Let's see what he says now."

Dirk Tabb stopped his pummeling fists, stepped back, breathing a little from the exertion. And Bud Jenkins, knees buckling, fell forward against him and clutched at Dirk's sinewy frame, leaned against him, trembling and faint with pain. His face was a bloody wreck, eyes swelling shut and blinded by blood from a cut across his forehead.

The third Spur man, El Nugent, seemed to grow a little sick looking at him. He suggested in a shaky voice: "Maybe the kid was telling the truth, boss. Maybe he don't know. . . ."

Carmody swore, spat into the litter on the floor. "We *will* kill him at this rate," he growled. "But I still say he's lying."

Bud Jenkins heard their words dimly. Kneeling there, bony hands grasping Dirk Tabb, battered head laid against the man's hard thigh, he was fighting a terrific battle to keep hold of the weakening thread of consciousness. There was no one who could save him now — no one but himself. Even through blinding pain, his reason could tell him that much. He had to hold out, had to. . . .

His wild thoughts stumbled, and then hope flashed through him, and with it new strength filled brain and body. The fumbling fingers of his left hand, clutching at Dirk Tabb's waist, had found smooth, hard leather. Tabb's holster — a holster with a gun in it! The kid's breathing faltered; his laboring heart seemed almost to stop.

The three were standing over him, watching, talking about him as though he were far away. He moved, and he moved fast. With the last of his hoarded strength he came stumbling up to his feet, left hand closing on Dirk's six-gun and jerking it out of leather before Dirk could stop him. At the same time he pushed Dirk backward, saw him topple against Carmody, heard the surprised yells of all three men.

Bud pulled trigger, left-handed. There was a wild scramble as the gun's blast thundered in the little room, and he made a frantic lunge for the door. It gave before the drive of a bony shoulder, and he was in the big main room of the barn. He slipped on straw underfoot and came up with legs pumping. Fear gave him speed.

He was halfway down the long aisle when the first gun lashed out behind him. The bullet flew wide into the upper shadows of the barn, the noise of the shot setting horses to stomping. Bud knew, with horrible certainty, that the slug had been meant to kill him. And there were the other Spur hands, already, no doubt, on their way from the bunk-house. . . .

Then he saw Toby — Judy Warren's black gelding. He had forgotten, until that moment, that Toby still wore saddle and bridle. Nothing ever filled the kid with greater thankfulness than sight of the bronc' standing patiently inside the big front door of the barn. He might make it.

He fumbled for stirrup, got his boot set in it, and swung up. Nate Carmody and the other two were close at his heels. Bud, looking back, saw them running up the length of the barn, and he saw the bloom of gun flame in their hands. The shots thundered in the big room, but they were wild.

Bud had switched Dirk Tabb's gun to his right hand, and he answered their fire, the bucking of the weapon against his bony wrist kicking it well off the mark. Then he was square in the saddle and pounding the black with spurless heels, and Toby, frightened and eager to go, burst out of the barn's doorway with a clatter of steel-shod hoofs.

Outside was a confusion of shadows and

lamplight, of running feet and men shouting. Bud pointed the bronc' toward the open space between barn and corrals and clung grimly, giving Toby his head. The black lined out, twisting and dodging the minor obstructions of the ranch yard.

"Stop him! *Stop him!*" It was Carmody's voice. At once guns opened up, and the night became a mass of red, lancing flame. Still, he hung on, and the buildings and the guns fell away into darkness behind him.

The ground lifted, a black tangle of brush and deep grass underfoot. Toby took the slope at a steady run. They topped the crest, and then they were on higher land. The night wind blew strongly here, fanning the high stars to flickering, twinkling brightness.

Bud revived some under the wind's cold touch, but his body seemed an aching mass of bone-deep bruises. He urged the horse on. This was a barren slice of ground, merging in rougher country ahead. The pound of Toby's hoofs over this hard earth made a jarring rhythm, battering at the kid's hurt body. He wondered how much of it he could stand.

In a shadowed clump of juniper he hauled rein suddenly. He couldn't go on.

He slid out of saddle, welcoming the solid feel of the ground. And he saw the black silhouettes of Spur riders as they poured up over the rim of the slope behind.

Bud shoved back into the tree's shadow, got a palm over Toby's muzzle, and stood that way, leaning his shaky strength against the hard flank of the horse. His own breathing seemed horribly loud to him and the thunder of his heartbeat. The knot of horsemen swelled nearer, seemingly headed straight toward him, but then, as Bud waited, heart in mouth, they swept past and were bound for the broken ground beyond, and he heard their voices. The noise of their rush faded rapidly.

Relief flooded through the kid. When they were safely gone, he brought Toby out of the trees, fumbled for the stirrup, and painfully hauled himself up. He hung on and pushed the bronc' ahead at an angle that took him away from Spur and away from the direction Carmody's crew had taken.

Unmeasured time passed. Bud was alone with the night, and the cold wind, and the pain of his tortured body. He lost all sense of direction, of his whereabouts. Every plodding step the bronc' took was a piston blow rocketing up into him, and soon that was the only thing in his awareness.

Then conscious thought slipped away, and he knew nothing more at all.

IV

Sheriff Sam Warren, alone in his office with the chatter of the clock stirring the room's silence, sat looking glumly at the morning mail without energy or interest enough to open it. It was a gray, heavy morning — very different from yesterday's heat. The wind last night had brought at last a break in the freakish weather, and now low clouds weighted down the heavens, and scraps of paper blew and swirled in the dust of the cold street outside.

Sam picked up an envelope, turned it over, laid it down again. Damn it! Why did that ornery kid keep interfering with his thoughts? He was a lawman, not a sentimental idiot to waste time and pity on a tough little devil like that. He had seen Bud's type often enough before, he told himself: hard-boiled hellions gone bad before they even got their full growth and headed for no good end.

He had thought for a while that Bud was

different — that something in the kid's background had put him on the defensive, given him his hard hatred of lawmen and all they stood for. He'd thought sympathy and the right treatment might draw the lad out and break down the barrier he had built between himself and society. But the only good that had done, he remembered grimly, was to expose Sam's own wife and daughter to the kid's surly insolence. His face went bleak as he recalled the scene last night.

Forget it, Sam, he told himself. *You've done all you could.*

With that he went savagely to work, ripping open envelopes with one broad thumbnail, plowing through the dull official letters as though his job depended on getting this done as fast as possible.

He had just tossed aside the last sheet when his deputy, Lew Prentiss, shoved open the door, letting in a blast of chill air. "Visitors, Sam," he announced briefly.

Sam looked around, surprised at the sight of Tom Beecher and his son Ahab. The sheriff wheeled his swivel chair, tilted back, eyed the lean pair as they trooped in. Prentiss followed them in, closing the door softly.

"Well?" grunted Warren. He added half

humorously: "I told you, Tom, if you ever had a case against Carmody to come to me with it. I didn't expect you so soon."

"It ain't about Carmody we've come, Sheriff," the old man announced loudly. "It's Wally Stoll."

"Stoll?" The sheriff sat forward suddenly in his chair.

The beard stirred as old Tom nodded. He turned on his son fiercely. "Tell him, Ahab . . . just like you told me."

Ahab Beecher looked at Tom, dropped his glance, and scowled at the floor, so low that Sam could barely hear him when he said: "I killed him."

"You?" Warren choked out the word.

Tom gave his son a poke with one bony hand. "Tell it . . . you hear me? Tell it all. May the Lord's lightnin' strike you dead if you give him a word that ain't true!"

Ahab, under his father's relentless prodding, blurted it all in a wild rush as though it were something he had held in too long and now wanted to get rid of.

"I didn't aim to! I ain't ever wanted trouble with that fellow, but *he* was the one couldn't seem to leave it alone. Always carryin' on every chance he got . . . about me being ugly and simple in the head . . ."

The sheriff nodded. "I've heard him."

Tom Beecher told his son curtly: "Get on with it, boy!"

Ahab dragged in a breath. "Well, yesterday mornin' I was out huntin' strays on our north range. I'd stopped at a crick to water my hoss when here come Stoll, heading south, like he was on his way back from Dixon . . . I heard he'd been up there with a bunch of beef to sell. He was riding alone, none of the crew with him.

"I stood waiting for my hoss to finish his drink, sort of hopin' Wally Stoll would decide to go on by, this time, but as he come closer I seen he'd been doing some drinkin' himself. The whisky was in his hand, and, when he pulled up, he drained off the last of it and chucked the empty bottle away. His face was all red, and he had a mean look to him."

Warren said: "So what happened?"

"So he started in on me as usual. I tried to pretend I didn't hear . . . thought if he couldn't get a rise out of me, maybe he'd give it up and ride on. But he kept at it, and the things he was saying got worse. And suddenly I heard his gun slide out of the holster. I looked around, and it was pointed straight at my head!

"Wally Stoll pulled back the hammer, and he said . . . 'I've had all I can stand of that ugly face of yours!' I figured for once he really meant it, and I was a dead man for sure. I yelled . . . 'No! Don't!' . . . and I don't know how, but somehow I managed to get my own gun from behind my waist belt and . . . and I pulled the trigger." His voice broke off.

The sheriff prompted him: "And . . . ?"

"He just looked surprised, at first. Then he sort of doubled over and slid sideways off the saddle. The gun dropped out of his hand . . . he never fired or nothin'. . . ." All at once the fellow was shaking uncontrollably. "I still don't understand. Maybe he was only pesterin' . . . but I honest to God *thought* he intended to shoot me."

The two older men shared a look. Sam Warren demanded: "So then, what did you do, Ahab? Just leave him there?"

"I couldn't right off believe he was dead . . . I'd never in my life dropped *anything* with my first shot. I grabbed him, and I dragged him over to the crick and started throwin' water on him, but it didn't do any good. Meantime, his bronc' had spooked and took off. And . . . and then I seen the blood, and I *really* got scared."

"He just left him there," old Tom finished sourly. "And he never told me a thing, not even when that strange kid come totin' Stoll's carcass into our yard. Kept on acting innocent, he did. But today I found Stoll's wallet in his coat pocket, and at last I got the truth out of him . . . I hope I put the fear of the Lord into the lyin' whelp, for good! And now here I am turning him over to you, Sam, to let the law see that he gets whatever he has comin'."

"The wallet," Sam Warren said. "You bring it with you?"

Tom dug the shapeless, sweat-blackened leather object from his pocket and tossed it on the desk. The sheriff looked inside, made a quick estimate of the sizable amount it held. "This will be the beef money from the cattle he sold at Dixon." Motioning to his deputy, who had been standing by watching all this in silence, Sam Warren said: "I want you to come over here and count this money, Lew . . . real careful. We'll watch."

Deputy Prentiss hauled a chair to the desk and set about the chore, his eyes made solemn by the denominations of the bills as he stacked them up.

Into the stillness Tom Beecher spoke in heavy tones: " 'Thou shalt not steal. . . .' And, to rob a corpse . . . !"

Ahab stammered in protest: "I only took it because I thought you might figure some of it was rightfully ours, for the beef you're always saying Spur has stole from us. But when I got home, I was just too scared to open my mouth."

"Scared!" the old man echoed scornfully.

"I'm always scared of you," Ahab muttered.

"Not scared near enough, it looks like. He's all yours, Sam," Tom told the sheriff in the same unyielding tone. "I wash my hands of him. Let the law give him what he has coming."

"I'll hang, I reckon." Ahab's voice shook with bottomless despair. "And I'll be headin' straight for hell. . . ."

Sam Warren took his time about answering. Having consulted with his deputy, he wrote some figures on a piece of paper and dropped the wallet into a drawer of the desk. Shoving the drawer shut, he turned again to his visitors.

"It appears that the money's probably all there. I do appreciate you bringing it in, and helping to clear this matter up. If I should need anything more from either of you, I reckon I can find you easy enough."

They stared at him. Tom said: "Ain't you gonna put him in jail?"

"Nope." The sheriff stood up, marking

an end to the scene, and the Beechers got to their feet more slowly. "Tom, I'm turning the boy over to you for now. When the judge comes around on circuit, there'll likely be a hearing . . . but that won't happen for another month, or nearly, and meanwhile you'll be needing him at home. Just give me your pledge that Ahab will be available for a summons."

He thought old Tom looked almost a little disappointed, but he got a curt nod of agreement. "Good," the sheriff said. He added quietly: "I'd suggest you try not to be too hard on the boy. Drunk or sober, Wally Stoll should've known that, if you threaten to shoot somebody, you'd better go ahead and do it. Besides, Ahab has been going through a bad time . . . I see no point in making it worse. I'm no expert on the Bible, Tom, but don't I remember something in there about 'the quality of mercy'?" Seeing the old man's blank and baffled look, he shrugged. "I dunno. Maybe it's some place else I heard that. . . ."

An hour later, big Nate Carmody shoved open the door and a chill gust of wind, freighted with street dust, followed him into the office. "What's this that your man,

Prentiss, has been telling me?" he wanted to know.

In answer, Sam Warren put aside the newspaper he was reading, brought out Wally Stoll's wallet, and tossed it on the desk. He watched Carmody walk over, pick it up, and thumb through its contents.

The rancher looked at him and demanded: "What about Ahab Beecher? I understand you didn't even lock him up."

"That's right. County funds won't pay the cost of having him on my hands for the next three weeks. Besides, those cells back there ain't fit to be occupied at this time of year, with the weather starting to turn. Ahab has been released into his father's custody, pending a court order."

Carmody, standing before the desk, gave the lawman a heavy scowl. "That ain't good enough. He shouldn't be running around loose. Everyone knows the lunkhead is half crazy . . . and now he's admitted murdering my partner."

"He's admitted killing him in self-protection. The law makes that distinction, if you don't. And this has to be a matter for the court to decide. Not me . . . and certainly not you!"

For a long moment their stares clashed above the littered desktop. In the end it was the rancher who broke gaze. As he turned to leave, Sam Warren thought he heard the words — "We'll see." — uttered half beneath his breath. The door slammed behind him.

The sheriff was left scowling, fingers drumming the desktop as he listened to the wind at work, scouring the street outside.

V

They were burning the shack again — the flames shooting skyward, sparks streaming eerily toward the stars. The guns were going. Their racket, and the yelling of men and pound of hoofs, boiled in a nightmare of sound that seemed to engulf the kid as he watched and listened. He wanted to help. He strained and struggled to rise, but something held him back. Something pushed him back and down, restraining his frenzied efforts.

His dad! Bud saw the silhouette against swirling flames, recognized it. He saw the gun in his father's hand buck and blaze, answering those other weapons. But there were too many — too many. And Bud couldn't get there to help. . . .

★ ★ ★

A bright streak of sunlight from the window lay across the bed. Bud's eyes, with the horror of the nightmare still in them, gazed feebly about the pleasant room; he wondered where he was and how he had got there. His features felt stiff and sore, his eyes so swollen he could barely open them. And there was a sharp pain in his body. In a rush then, he remembered Carmody and the scene in the tack room. And the night. And men riding after him with guns. . . .

Quick footsteps tapping in the hall swung his head toward the door in sharp alarm. The trapped feeling faded slowly when the door opened and Mrs. Warren entered.

"You must have had a bad dream . . . I heard you cry out. You poor boy. It's no wonder."

She drew up a straight chair, sat down near the bed. "Someone almost killed you, Bud." An edge of anger touched her voice. "Who was it? Carmody?"

He wouldn't answer her question. "I suppose this is Sheriff Warren's house?"

She nodded. "Toby came in this morning with an empty saddle and broken reins. We felt sure something had happened to you. Sam had already left for town, so Judy took a horse and backtracked, and she found you out on the range, unconscious."

Bud's mouth twisted. "Kind of a sorry mess, ain't I?"

"Someone gave you a terrible beating. Your whole face is battered and swollen, and I'm afraid that cut over your left eye may need stitches. But, after all, you're a young, healthy person. I know you'll get over this, if there isn't some inward hurt that we don't know about."

"I'm all right," he said gruffly.

"Are you sure you don't want to tell us what happened?" she asked anxiously.

"It's nobody else's affair."

When he made the least attempt to move, he was aware of weakness and pain, but he was determined he could stay here no longer. He started to throw back the covers, and at once the woman's hand was on his shoulder. "Don't do that," she pleaded. "Son, you need rest."

"I've rested. I'm getting out of here."

"No, you're not."

And for all his effort, the gentle pressure of her fingers held him where he was. After a moment he gave it up. He put a hand to his face, found the bandages that covered it. All at once he was shaking, his resolution struggling against tears that fought to be released.

Mrs. Warren said: "There's something burning in you. You've been lying here, twisting and turning. Talking, too . . . about your father, about some terrible thing you're carrying bottled up inside."

And with that, Bud dropped back upon the pillow, taut with misery as the last of his hard-built defenses crumbled and the tears came at last, burning tight-shut, swollen eyelids.

"It will do you good to tell somebody," the woman said quietly, unrelenting. "Just to let it all out. . . ."

And it came — slowly at first, then more surely as his voice filled the quiet of the room, and he lived it all over again.

"There were just the three of us . . . Dad, and me, and Uncle Harry. . . ." No sound now but the kid's voice in the quiet room — speaking slowly at first, then calming as the words started to flow and the past to live again. "My ma died long before I can remember. We had a little spread in the Milk River country, back in Montana . . . I grew up there. And then, last winter, came the big freeze-out. It finished us. Dad had a little money, but he'd loaned it to his friends, and they couldn't pay him back. We had nothing left.

"Come spring, we packed and headed south . . . Dad said he'd never spend another year in Montana. He was getting kind of old, I guess, and the snows had licked him. And Uncle Harry said there was better chances for us in warmer country."

Bud had forgotten Mrs. Warren, forgotten everything but the events that he was reliving, and the ugly climax to which they led. The woman, sitting by the bed with her eyes upon his tired, pinched face, heard a step at the doorway. It was Judy. Her mother quickly motioned to her to be silent, and the boy went on unaware of her presence.

"We drifted over a couple of states looking for jobs, but nobody'd hire a pair of stove-up relics and a kid who didn't look like he could do a day's work. Our money give out . . . our clothes begun gettin' ragged . . . these same clothes I got on now . . . and we came to miss a few meals. Dad and Uncle Harry turned kind of bitter.

"We reached Dixon, and I had an idea they were plannin' something. They left me just outside town, and I waited, wonderin' what they were up to. And then, after an hour or so, they come out again

. . . at a gallop. Uncle Harry had a bullet in him. They told me later they'd tried to crack the bank, but, of course, they was only amateurs and they didn't get away with a dime.

"Still, the law was after them. A posse trailed us into the hills between here and Dixon, and we managed to lose them. But Uncle Harry was about done for, and we figured we must be in another county by then, and we decided not to run any longer.

"We found an old abandoned cabin on a flat under a spur of the hills with a stream runnin' through it. Dad said we were stoppin' there . . . might even start us a new spread, if it looked like we had shook the law off our heels. But Uncle Harry kept gettin' worse. And there was traffic through that place. One morning a herd of cattle went through, headin' north, and Dad had me duck into the timber to hide . . . I hadn't been involved in that bank stick-up, and he didn't want me getting into trouble because of it. The men with the herd stopped and chinned with Dad a few minutes, and they saw Uncle Harry, and then they drove on through toward Dixon.

"Two days later . . ." — Bud choked, had

to swallow before he could go on —
"Uncle Harry died. We'd done our best for
him, but it wasn't good enough. So we
give 'im a Christian burial, and then. . . ."
He stopped.

Mrs. Warren looked at him. "Go on,
Bud," she urged.

"I . . . can't. You wouldn't want to hear
the rest, Missus Warren."

"What happened to your father?" she
persisted.

A shudder of remembered horror seized
the kid. "Ain't you guessed?" he shouted.
"Don't you know what I'm leadin' to? It
was three nights ago that Sam Warren fired
that shack . . . and killed my dad in cold
blood!"

She straightened quickly. The girl in the
doorway went suddenly white. Mrs.
Warren said crisply: "You don't know what
you're saying."

"Oh, don't I?" His lips curled, the old
bitterness and hardness returning to his
face and his voice now. "I was hid in the
trees above the shack . . . we'd seen the
riders coming by moonlight, and Dad
wanted me out of the way again. They was
a whole crew of them . . . at least a dozen.
And the man in the lead yelled . . . 'This is
the law speakin' . . . don't put up a fight!'

But Dad tried it, single-handed . . . and they burnt the shack down around him and filled him with lead. I seen it all!" His face twisted; his voice shook with agony. "If I'd had a gun, I'd have gone in there, all right, and wiped 'em out . . . the damned, filthy pack of. . . ."

"Bud!" Mrs. Warren's voice cracked sharply, cutting across his frenzied rush of words. "Don't say it. Because it isn't true . . . it's *not* true, I tell you . . . that my husband had anything to do with what happened that night."

He laughed harshly. "Try and tell me that. They said it was the law, didn't they? They come out of the south, didn't they? And Sam Warren is the law south of Dixon. Why do you think I took my Dad's gun and his horse and rode down this way after buryin' him with my own hands? I didn't know who I was lookin' for, but I meant to kill him when I found him. And I ain't given up on that yet. . . ."

"I'm telling you the truth," the woman insisted, her voice still quiet and very calm. "Sam Warren was at home three nights ago, and so was Lew Prentiss . . . his deputy. Whoever it was committed that horrible deed, they had nothing to do with the law. They only said so to cover themselves. Won't you believe me?"

Bud Jenkins looked squarely into her eyes for a long moment, and then suddenly all the hostility ran out of him and he rolled over in the bed, cradled his head on a thin, bent arm, and sobs wrung his tortured body. "Sure," he groaned. "I got to believe you. You're good and fine. . . ."

In that moment the tough kid, who had ridden into Shumate with a bold scowl on his face and a dead man lashed to his packhorse, was gone and forgotten. In his place was a tired and broken-hearted youngster, hurt and beaten. Mrs. Warren looked at his trembling shoulders and bent, tousled head with a look of infinite compassion in her kindly face. The scene tore an exclamation of pity from Judy.

At once Bud raised up, humiliation flooding him as he saw Judy.

Mrs. Warren was saying: "If we could only learn who it was attacked your father . . . and why? And how they knew he was someone who had reason to fear the law. You're sure they couldn't have come from the north . . . from Dixon, perhaps?"

He shook his head doggedly. "They come out of the south, I tell you, and they rode away south again when they'd finished their chore. From where I was hidin',

I couldn't see none of 'em well enough to know 'em again. Though I did hear a name. . . ."

"A name?"

"One I ain't likely to forget." His tone was grim. "It belongs to the man who threw the fire bomb and drove my pa outside where the whole bunch of them could shoot him down. So far, I ain't heard the name again, but I sure been keeping my ears open. Because, when the rest were yelling this fellow on, I heard what one of them called him. It sounded to me like Yuma. . . ."

A gasp broke from the girl. At the same moment Mrs. Warren came to her feet abruptly. Seeing her daughter about to speak, she shook her head in warning, and, as she headed for the door, she said firmly: "Come along, Judy. You've got to ride to town at once and get your father."

With that she was gone, but, when the girl started to follow, Bud halted her with a word. "Judy?" She hesitated, then slowly turned back. Her face was pale with some emotion.

"What are you folks holdin' from me? Do you know this man Yuma?"

"No . . . no." But she spoke too hurriedly, and one hand went to her throat.

"Oh, yeah, you do." All at once he was out of bed, fully clothed except for his boots. Striding toward her, he seized her wrist. "Tell me!" he gritted fiercely.

She began to cry convulsively. "Please! Why do you want to get yourself killed?"

"Who is it?" Some fury made him tighten his grip, the eyes in his bandaged face almost glaring.

Judy seemed to crumple, brown curls falling forward over her lowered face. "Oh, Bud," she sobbed pitifully, and then: "It's Dirk Tabb. My father told me," she went on, still not looking at him. "The man's supposed to have served some time, once . . . in the prison. And now and then the crew tease him about it, calling him the Yuma Kid. . . ."

Sight of the angry mark of his fingers where he had gripped her arm brought him back to his senses. "I'm sorry, Judy!" he exclaimed. "I never meant to hurt you!"

But she was already running blindly from him down the dark hallway.

VI

For a long moment Bud looked after her, then he swung the bedroom door quietly shut, saw a key in the lock, and turned it. His boots were on the floor by the bed, and he got into them, plucked his battered hat from the knob of a chair back. Someone had left Dirk Tabb's six-gun lying on the dresser; he took that with him as he went to the window and raised it, letting a blast of chill air into the room.

Fortunately it was on the ground floor. Just as he dropped one leg across the sill, a hand fell on the doorknob and rattled it, and the next moment Mrs. Warren's voice cried out his name in sudden alarm. Bud's jaw tightened. He went over the low sill, hearing the woman's fist pounding the door as he took the short drop to the ground.

He misjudged the distance and landed with a jar that nearly shook all the strength out of him. But he steadied himself against the wall of the house and then was off at a run for the corral.

A bronc' was there, already saddled. Not Toby, but a dappled mare that Judy must have ridden that morning to backtrack the black gelding when he came lagging in with broken reins and empty saddle. Bud counted this a very lucky break — he wouldn't have had the strength or the time, now, to rope a bronc' and juggle a heavy tree onto its back.

As it was he barely managed to jerk the mare loose from snubbing post and swing astride before the screen door at the house slammed and Judy came running down the steps. She called out to him, and then stood helplessly as Bud swung onto the mare and kicked her into a gallop. He refused to answer or to look at Judy.

Spur looked deserted when, at last, he pulled in at the head of the slope above it, and made a quick survey of the buildings. He wondered at this, thinking at first glance there was no one at all around the home ranch. But then he saw smoke penciling from the cook shack chimney and a wagon and team standing in front of the door.

Bud eased down the slope and into the yard warily, walking the mare and with one hand curled around the butt of Dirk Tabb's gun. As he neared the wagon, a man came pegging out the door of the cook shack with his arms full of clothing and other gear. He was an oldster, with weathered features that showed he must have been a cowboy in his day. He had a wooden leg. He dumped his armload in the back of the wagon and looked glumly at the strange figure of the shirtless kid with his bandaged face and body. And he eyed the gun in Bud's waistband.

"Don't waste lead perforatin' me, Jenkins," he snapped. "I'm only the cook . . . and, anyway, I'm leaving."

Bud hauled up, looked at the other, puzzled. "You know me, do you, Pop?" the kid said. "I didn't see you around here last night."

"Maybe not, but I could guess your name, lookin' at the shape you're in. I heard what Dirk Tabb done to you . . . it's why I'm quittin'." The old cook put his one foot on the hub, swung his peg leg up to the seat of the wagon. He took the reins.

He turned on the kid suddenly, fiercely, as though Bud had been arguing with him and he had to justify himself. "They's a limit to everything, see? Even for an old pot-wranglin' relic like me. I've seen a lot of stuff go on around this outfit, but I had a good job and I didn't know where I'd find another as good, and I figured I could keep my mouth shut. But last night. . . ."

He grimaced, shook his head. "Spur is turning into a nest of mad dogs. I got to get out, or I'll never be able to hold up my head again."

Something about him gave Bud an idea that here was a man he could talk to — one who could give him information he needed. He said swiftly: "Dirk Tabb . . . ain't he the one they call Yuma?"

"That firebug?" The oldster gave a snort. "Yeah, he scares the hell out of me. He's crazier'n both the Beechers put together."

With lips that felt suddenly dry, Bud said carefully: "Pop, think for a minute. Would you know where Tabb might have been three nights ago? Tell me anything you can."

There was no hesitation. "Why, Wally Stoll took a herd up that way to market, and found this guy and his wounded pal in a shack near the trail, and acting suspicious when he tried to talk to them. It wasn't good for Spur for them to be there, because a lot of the beef Carmody ships don't always belong to him and anyone watching the drives go through might catch on and make plenty trouble.

"So when Wally Stoll got into Dixon and heard descriptions of the pair that had held up their bank, he guessed it was the same two guys. But the Dixon sheriff wasn't interested, because the bank had dropped its charges against them . . . they bein' obviously a couple of amateurs and not havin' got anything, anyway. So Wally gets him a smart idea and sends a rider burnin' leather, all the way back here to Nate Carmody, to tell him about the guys in the cabin. And Nate sent Tabb with a bunch of gunnies, and they cleared the place out."

Bud's face was tight and stiff under the bandages, his young-old eyes hard with grim anger. He whirled on the old cook. "And all the time you knew about Spur . . . and yet you kept your mouth shut?"

The cook shrugged. "I allus been loyal to the outfit I worked for," he grunted doggedly, "ever since the days I wrangled a brandin' iron instead of a stove poker. Still, a man's stomach can hold only so much, and mine's plumb full!"

He slapped the horses with the reins smartly, and the wagon started to roll out of the yard. Bud stared after the rig. Just before the wagon disappeared around the side of the big house, the oldster hipped around suddenly and called back: "If you were looking for Carmody or the Yuma Kid, they'll be makin' a call on the

Beechers just about now. That crazy loon Ahab done told the sheriff today it was him killed Wally Stoll . . . and it's handed Carmody the excuse he'd been waitin' for, to go after those two and get rid of both of them. . . ."

The old man was out of sight before he finished speaking, and his voice was swallowed up in the racket of the wagon, but Bud had heard enough. He jerked reins, kicked his heels into the belly of the dappled mare, and got her stretched out in a fast gallop. The sharp wind hit him hard, but he pushed straight into it, the weakness and ache of a battered body nearly forgotten now as he headed across the rolling bunch grass flats. He cut as direct a line as he could, not bothering about trails or the contours of the land. As minutes crept by, he felt the tension grow tighter — maybe his goal was farther than he imagined, or he had his directions all wrong. And just what did he think he was going to do, once he got there? Likely it was already too late, for any chance to give a warning.

But warning the Beechers was only a part of this. . . .

Of a sudden, the breath clogged in his throat as the wind brought him a rattle of gunfire somewhere ahead. Heart pounding, he crossed a rise and saw the scatter of timber marking the spring at the Beecher place. Moments later he pulled up and was tumbling out of the saddle. With trembling fingers, he managed to anchor the reins securely to a pine branch before he set off at a run through the trees.

He had already checked the loads in Dirk Tabb's pistol and knew it contained three unfired shells of a different caliber from the cartridges he had in his pocket. *Only three bullets!* He tried not to think about it.

Now the trees thinned, bringing into sight the hard-scrabble ranch and the bright glint of water from its spring, just as gunfire ended as abruptly as it had started. Bud halted in the shadow of a narrow-boled pine at the very edge of the clearing. He leaned a palm against the rough bark to steady himself, breathing shallowly and weak in the knees, and heard Nate Carmody's voice above the returning stillness.

"You, there in the house! You hear me, old man? That was a sample to show we mean business. You're cornered, and you know it . . . if you got any sense, you'll send that killer out to us!"

Bud thought he had the attackers

spotted now — a half dozen or so, they had left their horses somewhere and taken cover wherever they could find it in the area facing the ramshackle ranch house. The raw wind, under a low cloud ceiling, scoured the clearing and whipped away the smoke from the shack's stovepipe chimney.

Old Tom's reply came clearly through the gap of a broken windowpane, knocked out in the shooting: "You devils are only wasting your time! Sam Warren has given the boy into my custody, till he sends orders to bring him in on court day."

The Spur boss retorted: "It's nothing to me if the sheriff is fool enough to think you'd actually do it!"

"He has my word!" To old Tom, that was evidently enough. He went on in the same stubborn tone. "But you're set on having things your own way. So be it, then! I got a double load of roofin' nails in this ol' Greener . . . if you're that anxious to join your dead partner . . . come right ahead!"

Total silence met his invitation. Bud had an idea that mention of Tom's shotgun had been enough to turn careful even this bunch of hardcases.

Nate Carmody and one of his riders were ensconced behind the wagon the

Beechers had been working on yesterday when Bud had ridden in with a dead man in tow. Carmody's voice held an edge of frustration as he responded to Beecher's challenge: "Old man, what's become of your religion? All the talk I've heard from you, claiming to be against the very idea of killing . . . I guess that didn't mean anything."

For a moment that got no answer. Bud had a sudden mental picture of the old man — on his knees perhaps, the tangled white beard spread across his chest, the sharp eyes closed in a fierce, inward search for guidance. . . .

"I done got the sign!" Old Tom's cry came, suddenly vibrant with fanatic triumph. "The Book says . . . 'I give you power to tread on serpents and scorpions.' So . . . come right ahead, you sons of Satan! I'm of a mind to do some treadin'!"

There were still no takers, but someone from Spur must have thought he saw a target and sent a bullet in through the window. It was answered, not by the shotgun but by a revolver, probably in the hand of young Ahab, and on the instant a savage barrage unleashed itself against the flimsy cabin.

This time the shooting seemed to go on

and on, without any sign of a let-up. The last windowpane went out. A wild bullet took down the stovepipe chimney in a cascade of soot. Watching unobserved, Bud Jenkins stood dry-mouthed and hardly aware of the pistol in his own tight grip as he listened to the guns banging. So far they seemed to be having little effect, beyond filling the yard with a fog of smoke and the stench of burnt powder. *But sooner or later,* he told himself.

And, in fact, someone from Spur must have grown careless about staying under cover. All at once a tremendous blast of muzzle flame and smoke erupted through the empty window frame. It was answered by agonized screams as two of the attackers were caught in the spreading charge from Tom Beecher's double-snouted Greener.

The barrage broke off completely, as if in shock, with one man fallen motionless and another writhing on the ground in pain. For a moment Bud Jenkins found himself wondering whether Spur's tough crew had met its match. Tom Beecher might be a frail old man, but he had an uncommon and stubborn ferocity that looked, just now, as though it had Nate Carmody stopped cold.

But a new voice said loudly: "The rest of you keep your heads down. I guarantee *this* will fetch 'em out of there!" And here came Dirk Tabb, striding into action.

The bottle he held was full of something that looked like kerosene, with a twist of burning rag stuffed into it for a fuse. If Tom Beecher was aware, the old man would likely be struggling frantically right now, trying to get his shotgun reloaded. He would never do it in time.

So, as Tabb positioned himself, arm drawn back to make the throw, Bud Jenkins shot him — with his own pistol!

Through a burst of muzzle smoke, Bud watched the Yuma Kid stagger and go down, as his last fire bomb spilled from his fingers to splinter harmlessly against a rock. Knowing he had apparently killed a man hardly seemed to matter to Bud at that moment — only the fact that he'd done something to help, a little, in squaring matters for his pa.

And even this had barely time to register. At the corner of a shed yonder, El Nugent was gesticulating wildly and yelling: "Hey . . . it's that Jenkins kid! What the hell? I thought he was *dead!*" Suddenly Bud realized that he had moved clear into the open, intent on taking his shot. There he stood, in front of them all, and for that moment the Beechers were completely forgotten.

Nate Carmody, crouched behind the wagon, showed a look of pure hatred as the barrel of his gun came around. There was no way a bullet could miss. With some wild hope of throwing the man off his aim, Bud spent one of his two remaining bullets even as he was spinning to make a frantic lunge for cover.

He knew he was lost when a boot slipped on loose rubble, and he felt himself start to go down. At that moment Carmody's gun, behind him, went off. Something struck the meaty part of his left leg. He had put out both hands to try and catch himself and succeeded only in having Dirk Tabb's pistol jarred out of his grasp. The kid landed heavily, face down in dust and pine duff.

Bud knew he must have been hit by a bullet and wondered vaguely when he would begin to feel it. All his senses seemed dull and confused, detached from the predicament in which he found himself. But then something broke through to help clear his head for him — the sound of approaching footsteps. He didn't need to be told who was coming toward him — Nate Carmody would want to know for sure his bullet had done its job. The last thing he needed was a witness, left alive to testify what had happened today at the Beecher place.

Suddenly the kid was beginning to feel that bullet. Oh, *yes!* It throbbed to the pulse of his heartbeat, inexorably swelling until it was suddenly worse than anything he could ever have imagined. He clenched his jaw against crying out; his eyes squeezed tight as he lay waiting for a second gunshot that would, mercifully, finish him off.

For some reason, it didn't come. Instead, he was vaguely aware of something new — a growing confusion of sounds, of a good many horses, and of men's voices shouting. Unable to understand why he was still alive, Bud Jenkins stirred himself to try and make out what was going on.

The Beechers' ranch yard seemed to have filled with men and horses in a swirl of dust raised by milling hoofs. Bud thought he glimpsed the lanky deputy, Lew Prentiss. It was only when he saw Sam Warren himself, revolver in hand, that he realized he must be looking at some kind of posse.

The sheriff was giving orders for the men from Spur to throw down their weapons. Plainly they had been taken by surprise; they gaped at the guns that covered them, and those who were still able slowly raised their arms. Next moment the door of the shack burst open, and Tom Beecher came tumbling out, brandishing his shotgun and with Ahab in his wake. "The good Lord be praised!" old Tom's gleeful shout carried above the other racket. "He sent you to us just in time, Sheriff! This spawn of the devil was planning to burn us out and kill us both. We heard 'em say it!"

"I believe you." Sam Warren was sizing up the wreckage — Dirk Tabb's body, and the other two who had been badly injured by a blast from the old man's shotgun. The sheriff's voice was bleak as he told his prisoners: "I hope you all know that you'll be going to jail for the judge to deal with whenever he gets here. And damned if I care much if you freeze, waiting for him in that cellblock . . . I'd say you got it coming." Even as he spoke, a chill blast of wind out of the cloud ceiling struck the ranch yard, whipping at coats and hat brims and giving point to his words.

Sam Warren peered around him. "But, I don't see your chief. Where the hell is Nate Carmody?"

Bud Jenkins twisted about for a hasty look. Carmody hadn't moved since he saw him last, not far distant from him but now with his whole attention on that scene in the ranch yard. And something seemed to yell a warning at the kid, even before he saw the man's arm lift and the gun in his hand settle in deliberate aim on the sheriff's back. Suddenly frantic, Bud searched for the weapon with the single bullet in it that he'd lost as he fell. When he failed to see it, he resorted to his one remaining option — cupping a hand to his mouth, he yelled as loudly as he could: "Sheriff! *Behind you!*"

Sam Warren's head jerked about. He was turning in the saddle just as Carmody's gun spoke. The shot missed. And not giving the Spur owner a second chance, the lawman fired a single bullet that dropped him in his tracks. As the echoes played out, he gave his horse a prod with the heel of his boot. Grim of face, he rode over for a closer look at this man who had just tried to murder him.

Apparently satisfied with the effect of his shot, Warren shoved the gun into its holster. He had located the place where Bud Jenkins lay wounded, and now he reined his horse over there to sit for a moment, looking down at the kid. "You singing out like that," he said bluntly, "is the only reason I ain't dead. And, I don't understand . . . I thought you hated my innards!"

Bud found his voice. "Maybe I did, once. But I've since found out, it's Nate Carmody's innards I was supposed to hate."

"Hmm." The lawman gave his head a puzzled shake. "Looks like you and I may have some things we need to clear up. . . ." He was coming down from the saddle, then, for a better look at the youngster's bruised and bandaged face, and the blood soaking into the material of his jeans. "A lot of things seem to have been happening to you, since I saw you last. Was this all Carmody's doing?"

The boy nodded. "I was figuring you might have heard something about it from Judy . . . I was there when her ma told her to head for town and fetch you."

"I never saw her. Probably left already, before she got there."

With a surprisingly gentle touch, the sheriff set to work probing the damage to the youngster's bullet-skewered leg. "To tell you the truth," he said, "I never had any use for Carmody, even studied the notion he might have killed that partner of his himself. But today, when I told him I'd learned it was Ahab Beecher's doings, there was something Nate Carmody let drop that started me worrying . . . afraid that he might intend coming over here and making real trouble. The idea gnawed at me so that, finally, I called some of the boys together, and we rode out, just in case. And a damned good thing that we did."

He gave Bud a reassuring touch on the shoulder as he came to his feet. "That hole don't look so bad. You stay real easy, you understand? Don't try to move. I'll have a couple of the boys take you into Tom's shack . . . I'll be able to do something there to stop the bleeding, until we get you to a doctor."

The kid nodded wordlessly. The sheriff had spotted a revolver lying in the pine duff. He picked it up, sniffed the fresh-burnt powder and checked the one unfired cartridge. He gave Bud a sharp look. "This belong to you?"

"It was the Yuma Kid's. I borrowed it . . . and I killed him with it."

Sam Warren blinked. "Whoa, now! Sounds like we *have* got some catching up to do."

As Warren shoved Dirk Tabb's gun behind his belt and turned to his horse, the
youngster added quickly: "Something
more I need to tell you. That dappled mare
of yours . . . I borrowed that, too. You'll
find her tied back in the trees somewhere."

He would have lifted a hand to point,
but the sheriff stopped him. "All right, all
right . . . I'll take care of the horse. One
thing at a time, OK?" But with the reins in
his hand, Sam Warren paused, frowning.
"How old did you tell me you were? Seventeen?" And as the kid nodded: "I expect
you've done some fast growing up in the
last few days. When the doctor's seen you,
I better take you home with me and make
sure you give that leg a decent chance to
mend. I guarantee you'll get well a whale
of a lot faster with Missus Warren fussing
over you."

As the lawman spurred away to finish his
business here, Bud Jenkins lay thinking he
hadn't noticed feeling particularly grown
up — more like a hurt kid, still shaken by
everything that had happened to him. And
yet, peering up into the pine branches and
trying to believe his leg didn't really hurt,
the youngster could almost begin to feel a
strange sort of peacefulness. Maybe the
sheriff was right, maybe it was best that he

just let go, while his leg mended, and turn everything over to Sam and Mrs. Warren — and Judy.

Let them spoil him a little. He suspected he'd be facing reality again, soon enough. . . .

About the Author

D(wight) B(ennett) Newton is the author of a number of notable Western novels. Born in Kansas City, Missouri, Newton went on to complete work for a Master's degree in history at the University of Missouri. From the time he first discovered Max Brand in Street and Smith's *Western Story Magazine*, he knew he wanted to be an author of Western fiction. He began contributing Western stories and novelettes to the Red Circle group of Western pulp magazines published by Newsstand in the late 1930s. During the Second World War, Newton served in the U.S. Army Engineers and fell in love with the central Oregon region when stationed there. He would later become a permanent resident of that state, and Oregon frequently serves as the locale for many of his finest novels. As a client of the August Lenniger Literary Agency, Newton found that every time he switched publishers he was given a different byline by his agent. This complicated his visibility. Yet in notable novels from *Range Boss*, the first original novel ever published in a modern paperback edition, through his impressive list of titles for the Double D series from Doubleday, *The Oregon Rifles*, *Crooked River Canyon*, and *Disaster Creek* among them, he produced a very special kind of Western story. What makes them so special is the combination of characters who seem real and about whom a reader comes to care a great deal and Newton's fundamental humanity, his realization early on (perhaps because of his study of history) that little that happened in the West was ever simple but rather made desperately complicated through the conjunction of numerous opposed forces working at cross purposes. Yet, through all of the turmoil on the frontier, a basic human decency did emerge. It was this which made the American frontier experience so profoundly unique and which produced many of the remarkable human beings to be found in the world of Newton's Western fiction.

Additional copyright information:

"Reach High, Top Hand!" first appeared in *Lariat Story Magazine* (7/47). Copyright © 1947 by Real Adventures Publishing Company, Inc. Copyright © renewed 1975 by D. B. Newton. Copyright © 1995 by D. B. Newton for restored material.

"The Taming of Johnny Peters" first appeared in *Ace-High Western Stories* (3/48). Copyright © 1948 by Popular Publications, Inc. Copyright © renewed 1976 by D. B. Newton. Copyright © 2001 by D. B. Newton for new material.

"Tinhorn Trouble" first appeared under the title "River Tinhorn's Blood-Bet" in *Ace-High Western Stories* (5/48). Copyright © 1948 by Popular Publications, Inc. Copyright © renewed 1976 by D. B. Newton. Copyright © 2001 by D. B. Newton for new material.

"Breakheart Valley" first appeared under the title "Gunslammers' Valley" in *Big-Book Western* (12/50). Copyright © 1950 by Popular Publications, Inc. Copyright © renewed 1978 by D. B. Newton. Copyright © 2001 by D. B. Newton for new material.

"Black Dunstan's Skull" first appeared under the title "Black Dunstan's Skullduggery" in *10 Story Western* (7/47). Copyright © 1947 by Popular Publications, Inc. Copyright © renewed 1975 by D. B. Newton. Copyright © 2001 by D. B. Newton for new material.

"Born to the Brand" first appeared in *Lariat Story Magazine* (9/46). Copyright © 1946 by Real Adventures Publishing Company, Inc. Copyright © renewed 1974 by D. B. Newton. Copyright © 2001 by D. B. Newton for new material.

The employees of Thorndike Press hope you have enjoyed this Large Print book. All our Large Print titles are designed for easy reading, and all our books are made to last. Other Thorndike Press Large Print books are available at your library, through selected bookstores, or directly from us.

For information about titles, please call:

(800) 223-1244

To share your comments, please write:

Publisher
Thorndike Press
295 Kennedy Memorial Drive
Waterville, ME   04901